Nadine cursed the day she'd met Hayden Garreth Monroe IV.

As raindrops drizzled from the sky, her mind wandered back to when she'd been young and naive and ripe for adventure, and Hayden had shoved his way into her world . . . and turned it upside down.

Falling in love with him had seemed so right at the time. Though born with a silver spoon stuck firmly between his lips, to her, Hayden had been more than just a rich boy. For a little while, anyway.

Until he'd shown his true colors.

Until he'd proved himself no different than his father.

Until he'd used money to buy off her affections.

Nadine bit her lower lip. She'd been such a fool. Such an innocent, adoring fool . . .

Dear Reader,

Welcome to Silhouette **Special Edition** . . . welcome to romance. Each month, Silhouette **Special Edition** publishes six novels with you in mind—stories of love and life, tales that you can identify with—as well as dream about.

And this wonderful month of May has many terrific stories for you. Myrna Temte presents her contribution to THAT SPECIAL WOMAN!—our new promotion that salutes women, and the wonderful men who win them. *The Forever Night* features characters you met in her COWBOY COUNTRY series—as well as a romance for sheriff Andy Johnson, whom many of you have written in about. Ginny Bradford gets her man in this gentle tale of love.

This month also brings *He's the Rich Boy* by Lisa Jackson. This is the concluding tale to her MAVERICKS series that features men that just won't be tamed! Don't miss this tale of love at misty Whitefire Lake!

Rounding out this special month are books from other favorite authors: Barbara Faith, Pat Warren, Kayla Daniels and Patricia McLinn—who is back with *Grady's Wedding* (you remember Grady—he was an usher in *Wedding Party*, #718. Now he has his own tale of love!).

I hope that you enjoy this book, and all the stories to come. Have a wonderful month!

Sincerely,

Tara Gavin
Senior Editor
Silhouette Books

LISA JACKSON

HE'S THE RICH BOY

Silhouette®

SPECIAL ▼ **EDITION**®

Published by Silhouette Books New York

America's Publisher of Contemporary Romance

SILHOUETTE BOOKS
300 East 42nd St., New York, N.Y. 10017

HE'S THE RICH BOY

Copyright © 1993 by Susan Crose

ISBN: 0-373-09811-1

First Silhouette Books printing May 1993

Printed in the U.S.A.

LISA JACKSON

was raised in Molalla, Oregon, and now lives with her husband, Mark, and her two sons in a suburb of Portland, Oregon. Lisa and her sister, Natalie Bishop, who is also a Silhouette author, live within earshot of each other.

The Legend of Whitefire Lake

It is said that when the God of the Sun creeps above the mountains and aims his flaming arrow to the sea, sparks and embers drop into the lake, causing the mists to rise like white fire on the water.

The man who drinks of this water before the mists are driven away by the sun will inherit much wealth and happiness and will be destined never to leave the hills surrounding the lake. But the man must sip the magic water and drink only until his thirst is quenched. For if he takes more of the sacred water than he needs, the God of the Sun will be angry and the man will be cursed. He will lose his wealth, and that which he loves most on earth will be stolen from him.

PROLOGUE

Whitefire Lake, California

The Present

Prologue

Nadine Warne rubbed the kinks from the back of her neck and considered taking a bubble bath to soothe her stiff joints. How long had it been since she'd allowed herself the luxury of an hour soaking in a tub of hot water?

Years.

She simply didn't have the time. With the tiring job of cleaning other people's houses, a smaller business on the side that she was trying to get off the ground while single-parenting two rambunctious preteen boys, there didn't seem to be a minute she could call her own.

"Such is life," she told herself pragmatically.

She carried her mops and pails and boxes of wax and cleansers into the house and stashed them inside the cupboard near the back door of her small cabin. The house wasn't much, but it was paid for and the land it rested on, on the south side of the lake, would be valuable someday. She was counting on it. This small plot of land was her investment for the future—her boys' education, and nothing, not heaven or hell, would take it from her. She'd been robbed of the education promised to her, and ever since then she'd vowed to herself that her children wouldn't have to make that particular sacrifice.

And she wouldn't be as foolish as her father and believe in a rich man's dream. She scowled and refused to think about the wealthy bastard who had swindled her father.

She'd put all her hopes and dreams into this little piece of real estate. Even though the prime properties were located on the north shore of Whitefire Lake, soon enough there would be no more land for wealthy people to build dream homes and they would have to search elsewhere; most likely on the south side.

Nadine was convinced that there would come a time when water-frontage upon Whitefire Lake would all be worth a pretty penny. At least she hoped so. That was why, when she and her ex-husband, Sam, had divorced, she'd fought like a terrier to keep this old cottage.

She smiled as she reheated a pot of coffee and glanced at the kitchen. Large enough for a table pushed against one wall, the cozy room boasted a few pine cabinets, a small expanse of wooden counter and one window surrounded by red gingham curtains that matched the three place mats stacked beneath the napkin holder and salt and pepper shakers on the table. Not much, but all she could afford.

In addition to the kitchen there was a living room, single bath, one bedroom, a large pantry converted into her sewing room and "office" and a loft with bunk beds for the boys. Not exactly the Ritz, but comfortable enough, and what John and Bobby lacked in creature comforts was surpassed by the fact that they lived practically in the wilderness, with the lake a bare twenty yards from the front porch. Frogs, deer, rabbits, squirrels, raccoons and birds were in abundance. Her children, whether they knew it or not, were far from deprived.

They should be returning soon, she thought, and glanced toward the road. Each day after school they rode their bikes to a neighbor's house where they stayed until Nadine arrived home. John was old enough to protest being "baby-sat,'' but both boys were too young to fend for themselves even for a few hours.

Pouring coffee into a mug, she wondered how things would have worked out if, as she'd hoped, Turner Brooks, a rancher she worked for, had shown her the least bit of interest. She'd been attracted to him for years, even fantasized that he would someday open his eyes and fall in love with her, but it hadn't happened. He'd found his own true love with Heather Leonetti, a beautiful girl from his past, and Nadine had surprised herself in letting go of her dream so easily. Maybe she hadn't really loved him after all. Maybe, after the pain of her divorce, Turner had seemed a safe haven—a no-nonsense cowboy who talked straight and didn't promise her the moon.

Unlike the other men in her life.

Sam, her husband, had been a dreamer who'd spent too many hours drinking to actually make any of his plans come together, and the other man—the one to whom she'd given her heart so many years ago—was a forbidden and bitter thought.

Hayden Garreth Monroe IV. Even his name sounded as if it had been hammered in silver. At one time Hayden had been the richest boy in town, with only the Fitzpatrick boys, his cousins, for rivals to the title. And she'd been silly enough, for a brief period, to think that he cared for her.

Stupid, stupid girl. Well, that was all a long time ago, thank God.

She heard gravel crunching on the drive and knew the boys and their bicycles had arrived. Hershel, the mutt they'd inherited when someone had dumped him as a half-grown pup, yipped excitedly at the back door. With the pounding of quick feet and a few insults hurled at each other, the boys scrambled into the house, Hershel jumping at their heels.

''Shoes!'' Nadine said automatically.

''Aw, Mom!'' John complained, his face an angry pout as he kicked off a pair of high-tops.

Bobby, her seven-year-old, did the same, black Converse sneakers flying against the wall as he shed the shoes and made a beeline in his stocking feet for the cookie jar.

"Hey, wait a minute!" John ordered, concerned lest he somehow not get as many cookies as his younger brother.

"You both wait a minute," Nadine interjected, grabbing John by his thin shoulders and hugging him. "The least you could do is say hello and tell me how your day went at school."

"Hello," Bobby said cheerily, snatching two peanut-butter cookies before the jar was wrested away from him by John. "I got a B on my spelling test."

"That's great."

"Yeah, well, I got a 'biff,'" John retorted with a touch of defiance as he snagged a couple of cookies for himself.

"A what?"

"He got put up against the wall at recess," Bobby eagerly explained. "By the duty."

"Why?"

"'Cause she said I said a bad word, but I didn't, Mom, honest. It was Katie Osgood. *She* said the *S* word."

"I think I've heard enough. But I don't want to hear that you've been saying *anything* that even brushes upon swearing. Got it?"

"Yeah, sure," John said sullenly, looking at the floor. "Uh, Mrs. Zalinski's gonna call you."

Nadine's lungs tightened at the mention of John's teacher. "Why?"

"'Cause she thinks I was cheating on a test, and I wasn't, Mom, really. Katie Osgood asked to use my pencil and I told her to buzz off and—"

"Stay away from Katie Osgood," Nadine cut in, and John, now that his admission was over, muttered something about Katie being a dweeb and followed Bobby into the living room. Hershel, eyes fixed on the cookies, bounded after the boys, his black-and-white tail wagging wildly.

The phone rang and Nadine sent up a silent prayer for her confrontation with the teacher. John was always having trouble in school. He, more than Bobby, had shown open defiance and anger since her divorce nearly two years before.

"Hello?" she answered as the theme music for the boys' favorite cartoon show filtered in from the living room.

"Mrs. Warne?" The voice was cool and male. *Principal Strand!* Nadine braced herself.

"Yes."

"This is William Bradworth of Smythe, Mills and Bradworth in San Francisco. I represent the estate of Hayden Garreth Monroe III...."

Nadine's heart nearly stopped beating and her stomach curled into a hard knot of disgust. Hayden Garreth Monroe III had been the catalyst who had started the steady decline of her family. She'd only met him once, years before, but the man was brutal—a cutthroat businessman who had stepped on anyone and anything to get what he wanted. Including her father. In Nadine's estimation, Monroe was a criminal. She felt little remorse that he was dead.

"What do you want, Mr. Bradworth?"

"Your name was given to me by Velma Swaggart. I'm looking for a professional to do some housekeeping." At this moment in time, Nadine would gladly have strangled her aunt Velma. Just the name Monroe should have been enough of a clue for Velma to come up with another maid service. "So I'm willing to pay you the going rate to clean the house at 1451 Lakeshore Drive," Bradworth continued, and Nadine held back a hot retort.

Instead she stretched the phone cord taut so that she could look through the window and across the lake. Far in the distance, on the north shore, surrounded by tall redwood and pine trees, the Monroe summer home sprawled upon an acre of prime lakefront property.

"The job would entail a thorough cleaning and I'd want a report on the repairs needed. If you could find someone in the area to fix up the place, I'd like their names—"

"I'll have to think about it, Mr. Bradworth," she said, deciding not to cut the man off too quickly, though she would have liked to have sent him and his offer packing. But right now, money was tight. Very tight. Aunt Velma knew that she was hungry and Velma had probably swallowed her own pride in giving out Nadine's name.

There was a deep pause on the other end of the line. Obviously Mr. Bradworth wasn't used to being put off. "I'll need an answer by tomorrow afternoon," he said curtly.

"You'll have one," Nadine replied, and silently cursed herself for looking a gift horse in the mouth. Who cared where the money came from? She needed cash to fix up her car, and Christmas was coming.... How would she afford to buy the boys the things they needed? But to take money from old man Monroe's estate? She shuddered as she hung up the phone.

Her eyes clouded as she walked out the back door and along the path that skirted the house and led down to the dock. A stiff, November wind had turned, causing white-caps to form on the lake's usually smooth surface. She remembered the old legend of the lake, conceived by local Native Americans but whispered by the first white settlers. The story had been passed down from one generation of white men to the next, and she wondered how much of the old myth was true.

Rubbing her arms, she stared across the graying water, unaffected as raindrops began to fall. The Monroe estate. Empty for nearly thirteen years. A splendid summer home, which Nadine had never had the privilege of visiting, but which had gained notoriety when it was discovered that Jackson Moore and Rachelle Tremont had spent the night in the house on the night that Roy Fitzpatrick was killed. Jackson had been the prime suspect as Roy's killer and Rachelle had been his alibi. She'd ruined her reputation by admitting that they'd been together all night long.

Few had gone back to the house since. Or so the gossip mill of Gold Creek maintained. Nadine had no way of knowing the truth.

She thought for a poignant moment about Hayden, the old man's son. Named for his father, born and raised with a silver spoon stuck firmly between his lips, Hayden Garreth Monroe IV had been more than a rich boy. At least to Nadine. If only for a little while. Until he'd shown his true colors. Until he'd proved himself no different than his father. Until he'd used money to buy off her affections.

Nadine bit her lower lip. She'd been such a fool. Such an innocent, adoring fool!

Her Reeboks creaked on the weathered boards of the dock and the wind blew her hair away from her face. Shivering, she rubbed her arms and stared across the lake to the wealthy homes that dotted the north beach of Lakeshore Drive.

To the west, the Fitzpatrick home was visible through the thicket of trees, and farther east, the roofline of the Monroe summer home peeked through the branches of pine and cedar.

"Damn it all," she whispered, still cursing the day she'd met Hayden.

Meeting him ... riding in his boat ... thinking she was falling in love with him had seemed so right at the time. Now she knew her infatuation with Hayden had been a mistake that would remain with her for the rest of her life. She could recall their short time together with a crystal-clear clarity that scared her.

As raindrops drizzled from the sky, she let her mind wander back to that time she'd told herself was forbidden: when she'd been young and naive and ripe for adventure, and Hayden Garreth Monroe IV had shoved his way into her world and turned it upside down....

BOOK ONE

Gold Creek, California

The Past

Chapter One

"You make sure you pick me up at quittin' time," Nadine's father said as his truck bounced through the gravel lot of Monroe Sawmill, where he worked. He parked in the shade of the barking shed, twisted his wrist and yanked the key from the ignition of his old Ford pickup. The engine shuddered and died, and he handed the key to his daughter.

"I won't be late," Nadine promised.

Her father winked at her. "That's my gal."

Nadine's fingers curled over the collar of her father's dog, Bonanza, who lunged for the door and whined as George Powell climbed out of the cab and walked toward the office where he'd punch in before taking his shift in one of the open sheds. "Hold on a minute," she told the anxious shepherd. "We'll be home soon."

Thinking of the Powells' rented house caused a hard knot to form in her stomach. Home hadn't been the haven it had once been and the chords of discontent in her parents' marriage had, in the past months, become louder. Sometimes Nadine felt as if she were stranded in the middle of a battlefield with nowhere to turn. Every time she opened her mouth to speak, it was as if she were stepping on a verbal and emotional mine field.

Squinting through the dusty windshield, she tried not to think of life back at the house by the river, concentrating instead on the activity in the yard of the mill. Trailer trucks rolled through huge, chain-link gates, bringing in load after load of branchless fir trees, and a gigantic crane moved the loads to the already monstrous piles in the yard. Still other cranes plucked some of the logs from the river, to stack them into piles to dry.

Men in hard hats shouted and gestured as to the placement of each load. One by one the logs were sorted, their bark peeled, and the naked wood squared off before it was finally sawed into rough-cut lumber, which was stacked according to grade and size. Her father had been a sawmill man all his life and had often told her of the process of taking a single tree from the forest and converting it into lumber, plywood, chip board, bark dust and, in some cases, paper. George Powell was proud of the fact that he came from a long line of sawmill men. His father had worked in this very mill as had his grandfather. As long as there had been Monroe Sawmill Company in Gold Creek, a Powell had been on the payroll.

From the corner of her eye, Nadine saw a car roll into the lot—a sleek navy blue convertible. So shiny that the finish looked wet as it glinted in the sunlight, the Mercedes was visibly out of place in an assemblage of old pickups and dusty cars. The sports car looked like a Thoroughbred sorted into a field of plow horses by mistake.

Nadine slid over to the driver's side of the truck and while petting Bonanza, studied the driver as he stretched out of the leather interior. He was tall, but young—probably not yet twenty—with thick coffee-colored hair that had been ruffled in the wind. His eyes were hidden behind mirrored sunglasses and he slung a leather jacket over his shoulder.

Nadine bit her lip. She didn't have to guess who he was. Hayden Garreth Monroe IV, son of the owner of the mill. She'd seen him years before when she was still a student in

Gold Creek Elementary. He'd lived here for a short time, the only son of rich parents. His first cousins were the Fitzpatricks who owned the logging company that supplied most of the trees for this milling operation.

"The Monroes and Fitzpatricks—thick as thieves," her mother had often said. Between the two families they owned just about everything in Gold Creek.

Nadine remembered Hayden as a twelve-year-old boy, not as an angry young man, but now he appeared furious. His strides were stiff and long, his jaw set, his mouth a thin line of determination. He glared straight ahead, not glancing left or right, and he took the two steps to the sawmill's office as if they were one. He stormed into the small company office and the door slammed shut behind him.

Nadine's breath felt hot and caught in her lungs. She pitied whoever was the object of his obvious wrath. Fury seemed to radiate off him like the heat rising off the ground.

Suddenly she wished she knew more about him, but her memories of the Monroes and their only son, "the prince" as her brother Ben had referred to him, were vague.

She was pretty sure that the Monroes had moved to San Francisco about the time Hayden was ready to start high school and they only returned in the summer, to live in their home on the lake. Though Hayden's father still owned this mill, he had several others, as well. He only traveled to Gold Creek a couple of days a week.

Her father had summed it up at dinner one night. "Some job Monroe has, eh?" There had been a mixture of awe and envy in George Powell's voice. "Garreth takes a company helicopter from his office building in the city, whirs over here, strolls into the office about nine o'clock, glances at the books, signs a few checks and is back in the city in time for his afternoon golf game. Rough life."

Nadine had never thought much about the Monroes. They, like the Fitzpatricks, were rich. The rest of the town wasn't. That's just the way things had always been and always would be as far as she could see.

Her fingers, clenched tightly around Bonanza's collar, slowly uncoiled. The dog licked her face, but she barely no-

ticed. She spied her father walking from the office to the
main gate of the work yard. He waved before entering one
of the sheds. Nadine rammed the pickup into reverse,
backed up, then shoved the gearshift into first. The truck
lunged forward and started to roll toward the road.

"Hey!" A male voice boomed through the opened
windows.

Glancing in the rearview mirror, she slammed on the
brakes. Her heart did a silly little flip when she saw Hayden, the prince himself, jogging to catch up with her—
probably to tell her that the tailgate of the truck had
dropped open again.

In a choking cloud of dust, he opened the door to the
passenger side of the Ford and Bonanza growled. "Can you
give me a ride into—?" His voice stopped abruptly and
Nadine realized he thought she was one of the mill workers. He obviously hadn't expected a girl behind the wheel of
the banged-up old pickup.

She glanced at the Mercedes. "Isn't that your car?"

His eyebrows knotted. "Look, I just need a lift. I'm
Hayden Monroe." He flipped up his sunglasses and extended a hand.

"Nadine Powell." Self-consciously she reached across
Bonanza and shook his hand. His fingers clasped her palm
in a strong grip that caused her heart to pound a little.

"Ben and Kevin's little sister," he said, releasing her
hand.

For some inexplicable reason, she didn't like to be
thought of as a kid. Not by this boy. "That's right."

"Are you going into town?"

She wasn't, but something inside her couldn't admit it
because she knew if she told him the truth he would slam the
door of the truck right then and there. She lifted a shoulder. "Uh . . . sure, climb in. I, uh, just have to stop by the
house—it's on the way—and tell my mom what I'm doing."

"If this is a problem—"

"No! Hop in," she said with a smile. She glanced guiltily through the grimy back window and silently prayed that
her father wasn't witnessing Hayden sliding into the cab. As

the door clicked shut, Bonanza growled again, but reluctantly gave up his seat, inching closer to her. Nadine let out the clutch. With a stomach-jolting lurch, they bounced out of the lot. She only hoped her mother would understand and let her drive Hayden to Gold Creek. These days, Mom wasn't very understanding.... Sometimes she wasn't even rational. And though Dad blamed his wife's moodiness on her "monthly curse" or the strain of raising three headstrong teenagers, Nadine knew differently. She'd overheard enough of her parents' arguments to realize that the problems in their family ran much deeper than her mother's menstrual cycle.

So how would Donna react to her only daughter's request? Nadine's hands felt suddenly sweaty. She could just drive Hayden into town, show up late at home and take the consequences, but she didn't want to risk any more trouble.

"I just have to drop off the dog at the house," she explained, casting him a glance.

"I'm not in a hurry." But the tension in his body claimed otherwise. From the first moment she'd seen him screech into the sawmill yard, he'd looked like a caged tiger ready to pounce. His muscles were coiled, his face strained. He snapped his sunglasses back over his eyes.

"Trouble with your car?" she asked.

"You could say that." He stared out the window, his lips compressed together as Nadine turned onto the main road into town.

"It's . . . it's a beautiful car."

He flashed her an unreadable look through his sunglasses. "I told my old man to sell it."

"But—it looked brand-new." The Mercedes didn't even have license plates yet.

"It is."

"I'd kill for a car like that," she said, trying to ease the tension that seemed to thicken between them.

His lips twitched a little. "Would you?" Quickly his head was turned and his attention was focused completely on her. Her hair. Her eyes. Her neck. Nothing seemed to escape his scrutiny and she was suddenly self-conscious of her faded cutoffs and hand-me-down blouse. Holding her chin proudly, she felt sweat collect along her backbone. Her pulse began to throb as he stared at her with an intensity that made her want to squirm.

"I—You know what I mean."

"Well, my old man didn't ask me to 'kill' for it, but close enough...." He rubbed the tight muscles in one of his shoulders.

"What do you mean?"

"You ever met The Third?"

"What?"

"Hayden Garreth Monroe 'The Third'."

She shook her head. "Not really. But I've seen him a couple of times. At company picnics."

"Oh, right." Nodding, he turned his gaze back to the dusty windshield. "I even went to a couple of those. A long time ago. Anyway, then you know that my father can be— well, let's just call him 'persuasive' for lack of a better word. Whatever The Third wants, he usually gets. One way or another."

"What's that got to do with your car?"

"It comes with a price—not in dollars and cents, but a price nonetheless, and I'm not willing to pay."

"Oh." She wanted to ask more, to find out what he was really thinking, but he fell into brooding silence again and she knew by the sudden censure in his expression that the subject was closed.

The pickup cruised by dry, stubble-filled fields of grass and wildflowers, and Nadine turned onto a county road that wound upward through the hills to the little house by the river. Never before had she been embarrassed of where she lived, but suddenly, with this rich boy in the pickup, she was self-conscious. It was bad enough that he'd had to share the tattered seat of a banged-up twenty-year-old truck with a smelly dog, after riding in the sleek leather interior of a new sports car, but now Hayden would see the sagging front porch, rusted gutters and weed-choked yard.

She pulled up to the carport and said, "I'll just be a minute. . . ." Then, remembering her manners, she added, "Would you like to come in and meet my mom?"

He hesitated, but his polite upbringing got the better of him. "Sure."

As Bonanza streaked across the dry grass, startling robins in the bushes, Nadine led Hayden up the steps to the back porch and through the screen door. "Mom?" she called, as they entered the kitchen.

A pan of apple crisp was cooling on the stove and the small room was filled with the scents of tart apples and cinnamon. Hayden took off his sunglasses, and Nadine was witness to intense blue eyes the shade of the sky just before dusk. Her heart nearly skipped a beat and her voice sounded a little weak and breathless when she pulled her gaze away and again called for her mother. "Are you home?"

"Be right down," Donna shouted from the top of the stairs. Quick footsteps sounded on the bare boards. "What took you so long? Ben's got the car and I've got groceries to buy and—" Donna, with a basket of laundry balanced on her hip, not a trace of her usual makeup and her hair tied back in a careless ponytail, rounded the corner and stopped short at the sight of her daughter and the boy.

Nadine said quickly, "I'll pick up whatever you need at the market. I have to go into town anyway. I promised Hayden." She motioned toward him. "This is—"

"Hayden Monroe?" her mother guessed, extending her free hand while still managing to hold on to the laundry. She forced a smile that seemed as plastic as the basket she was carrying.

"That's right." He shook her hand firmly.

"This is my mom, Donna Powell."

"Nice to meet you," he said, and her mother's lips tightened at the corners as she drew back her hand.

"You, too."

Nadine was mortified. Her mother was usually warm and happy to meet any of her friends, but despite her smile, Donna Powell exuded a frostiness she usually reserved for her husband.

"You should offer your friend something to drink," she said, her suddenly cold gaze moving to her daughter. "And, yes, you can get the groceries. The list is on the bulletin board and there's a twenty in my purse...." She glanced back at Hayden again, opened her mouth to say something, then changed her mind. "Don't be long, though. I need the eggs for the meat loaf." She set the laundry on the table and tucked an errant lock of hair behind her ear before walking crisply to the kitchen closet where she kept her handbag. From within the folds of her wallet, she pulled out some money and handed the bill to her daughter.

"I'll come right back!" Nadine was grateful to be leaving. She grabbed a couple of cans of Coke from the refrigerator, then snagged the grocery list as they headed outside. Hayden said goodbye to her mother and paused in the yard to scratch Bonanza behind the ears before he yanked open the passenger side of the pickup and settled into the seat.

Nadine was so nervous, she could barely start the engine. "You'll have to excuse my mom. Usually she's a lot friendlier...but, we, uh, surprised her and—"

"She was fine," he said. Again his blue eyes stared at her, and this time, without the sunglasses, they seemed to pierce right to her soul. She wondered what he thought of their tiny house by the river. Was he laughing at a cottage that must appear to him a symbol of abject poverty? He seemed comfortable enough in the truck, and yet she suspected he was used to riding in BMWs, Ferraris and limousines.

"Hold on to these," she said as she handed him the cans of soda, then backed the truck around, heading into town. She knew she should keep the question to herself, but she'd always been quick with her tongue. Her brother Ben had often accused her of talking before she thought.

"What did you mean about a price you weren't willing to pay—for the Mercedes?"

He flipped open both cans of cola and handed one to her. His gaze was fastened to the view through the windshield—dry, windswept fields. Propping an elbow on the open window, he said, "My father wants to buy my freedom."

"How?"

His lips twisted into a cold smile and he slipped his sunglasses back onto the bridge of his nose. "Many ways," he said before taking a long swallow of his drink. Nadine waited, but Hayden didn't elaborate, didn't explain his cryptic remark as he gazed through the windshield. She noticed his fingers drumming on his knee impatiently. It was as if she didn't exist. She was just providing transportation. She could as well have been a gray-haired man of eighty for all he cared. Disgusted at the thought, she juggled her can of soda, steering wheel and gearshift, driving along the familiar roads of the town where she'd grown up.

"Where do you want me to take you?" she asked as they reached the dip in the road spanned by the railroad trestle. They were in the outskirts of Gold Creek now, and houses, all seeming to have been built from the same three or four floor plans in the late forties, lined the main road.

"Where?" he repeated, as if lost in thought. "How about Anchorage?"

"Alaska?"

"Or Mexico City."

She laughed, thinking he was making a joke, but he didn't even smile. "Don't have that much gas," she quipped.

"I'd buy it." He said the words as if he meant every one of them. But he wasn't serious—he couldn't be. He rubbed a hand across the pickup's old dash with the rattling heater. "How far do you think this truck would get us?"

"Us?" she said, trying to sound casual.

"Mmm."

"Maybe as far as San Jose. Monterey, if we were lucky," she said nervously. He was joking, wasn't he? He had to be.

"Not far enough."

He glanced at her, and through the mirrored glasses, their gazes locked for a second, before he snaked a hand out, grabbed the wheel and helped her stay on the road. "I guess if we wanted to go any farther, we should have just taken the damned Mercedes!"

She grabbed the wheel more tightly in her shaking hands. He was talking like a crazy man, but she was thrilled. She found his rebellious streak fascinating, his irreverence endearing.

Flopping back against the seat, he shoved his dark hair off his face. They drove past the park and hit a red light.

The truck idled, and Nadine slid a glance at her passenger. "Since we don't have the Mercedes and since the truck won't make it past the city limits, I guess you're going to have to tell me where you want to go."

"Where I want to go," he repeated, shaking his head. "Just drop me off at the bus station."

"The bus station?" She almost laughed. The boy who'd given up the keys to a Mercedes was going to buy a ticket on a Greyhound?

"It'll get me where I have to go."

The light turned green and she turned left. "And where's that?"

"Everywhere and nowhere." He fell into dark silence again. The bus station loomed ahead and she pulled into the lot, letting the old truck idle. Hayden finished his Coke, left the empty can on the seat and grabbed his jacket. Digging into the pocket, he pulled out his wallet. "I want to pay you for your trouble—"

"It was no trouble," she said quickly.

"But for your gas and time and—"

"I just gave you a lift. No big deal." She glanced up at his eyes, but saw only her own reflection in his mirrored lenses.

"I want to." He pulled out a ten and started to hand it to her. "Buy yourself something."

"Buy myself something?" she repeated, burning with sudden humiliation. All at once she was aware again of her faded cutoff jeans and gingham shirt and hand-me-down sneakers.

"Yeah. Something nice."

He *pitied* her! The bill was thrust under her nose, but she ignored it. "I can't be bought, either," she said, shoving the truck into gear. "This was a favor. Nothing more."

"But I'd like for you—"

"*I'd* like for you to get out. Now."

He hesitated, apparently surprised by her change in attitude.

"If you're sure—"

"I'm positive."

Scowling, he jammed the bill back into the wallet. "I guess I owe you one." Lines creased his forehead. "I don't like being in debt to anyone."

"Don't worry about it! You don't owe me anything," she assured him, her temper starting to boil. For a minute, with all his talk about driving away from Gold Creek, she'd thought he'd shown an interest in her, but she'd been wrong. Humiliation burned up her cheeks. What a fool she'd been!

"Thanks for the ride." He opened the door and hopped to the dusty asphalt.

"No problem, Prince," she replied, then stepped on the gas before he had a chance to close the door. She didn't care. She had to get away from him. The old truck's tires squealed. Mortified, she reached over and yanked the door shut, then blinked back tears of frustration. What had she been thinking? That a boy like that—a rich boy—would be attracted to her?

"Idiot!" she told her reflection, and hated the tears shining in her eyes and the points of scarlet staining her cheeks. She took a corner too quickly and the truck skidded a little before the balding tires held. "Forget him," she advised herself but knew deep inside that Hayden Monroe wasn't the kind of boy who was easily forgotten.

Chapter Two

Nadine's mother was waiting in the kitchen. Running a stained cloth over the scarred cupboard doors, Donna glanced over her shoulder as Nadine opened the door. She straightened and wiped her hands as Nadine set the sack of groceries on the counter. The scent of furniture polish filled the room, making it hard to breathe.

"Running with a pretty rich crowd, aren't you?"

"I'm not running with any crowd." Nadine dug into the pocket of her cutoffs, found her mother's change and set four dollars and thirty-two cents beside the sack.

"So how'd Hayden Monroe end up in our truck?"

"I was just in the wrong place at the wrong time," Nadine admitted.

"I thought you took your father to the mill."

"I did." As she began to unpack the groceries, she gave her mother a sketchy explanation of how she'd met Hayden. Donna didn't say a word, just listened as she folded her dust rag and hung it inside the cupboard door under the sink.

"And he just left a brand-new Mercedes in the lot of the mill?" She twisted on the tap and washed her hands with liquid dish detergent.

"Yep."

Shaking the excess water from her fingers, she said, "You know, it's best not to mingle with the rich folks. Especially the Monroes."

"I thought the Fitzpatricks were the people to avoid."

"Them, too. They're all related, you know. Sylvia Monroe, Hayden's mother, is Thomas Fitzpatrick's sister. They've had money all their lives—and lots of it. They don't understand how the other half lives. And I'll bet dollars to doughnuts your friend Hayden is just the same."

Nadine thought of the ten-dollar bill Hayden had tried to hand her and her neck felt suddenly hot. But her mother probably didn't notice her embarrassment. Donna was already busy cracking eggs into a bowl of hamburger, bread and onions.

"Thick as thieves, if you ask me."

"You don't know him. He's not—" A swift glance from her mother cut her justification short and she quickly bit her tongue. What did she know about Hayden and why did she feel compelled to defend a boy who had mortified her? She remembered the look on his face as he'd tried to pay for her company. He was clearly surprised that she wouldn't take the money. Her mother was right. All Hayden had ever learned was that anyone who did him a favor expected money in return. People were commodities and could be bought...if the price was right. "He's not like that," she said lamely.

"What he's 'not' is our kind. There have been rumors about him, Nadine, and though I don't believe every piece of gossip I hear in this town, I do know that where there's smoke there's fire."

"What kind of rumors?" Nadine demanded.

"Never mind—"

"You brought it up."

"Okay." Her mother wiped her hands on her apron and turned to face her daughter.

Nadine's heart began to thud and she wished she hadn't asked.

"Hayden Monroe, like his father before him, and his grandfather before him, has a reputation."

"A reputation?"

"With women," her mother said, cheeks flushing slightly as she forced her attention back to her bowl. "I've heard him linked with several girls...one in particular...."

"Who?" Nadine demanded, but her mother shook her head and added a pinch of salt to the meat. "Who?" Nadine repeated.

"I don't think I should spread gossip."

"Then don't accuse him of doing anything wrong!" Nadine said with more vehemence than she had intended.

For a moment there was silence—the same deafening silence that occurred whenever her mother and father were having one of their arguments. Donna's lips pinched as she greased a loaf pan and pressed her concoction into the bottom. "I thought you were going out with Sam."

Nadine wanted to know more about Hayden and his reputation, but she knew that once her mother decided a subject was closed, there was little to do to change her mind. She lifted a shoulder at the mention of Sam Warne. She and he had dated a few times. He was fun to hang out with, but she wasn't serious about him. "We might go over to Coleville and see a movie Friday night."

The ghost of a smile touched her mother's lips. She approved of Sam—a nice boy from a good family in town. His father was employed with Fitzpatrick Logging and his mother came into the library often where Donna worked a few afternoons a week. As far as Donna was concerned, Sam Warne had all the right criteria for a future son-in-law. Sam was good-looking. Sam was middle-class. Sam was only a year older than Nadine. Sam was safe. He probably would make a good husband; but Nadine wasn't planning to marry for a long while. She had high school to finish and college—if not a four-year school, at least a two-year junior college.

Though she couldn't get Hayden from her mind, Nadine held her tongue. Her curiosity was better left alone, she decided, as she spent the next few hours vacuuming the house and helping her mother weed the garden where strawberries, raspberries, beans and corn grew row by row.

An hour before her father's shift was over, Nadine took a quick shower and combed her red hair until it fell in lustrous waves to the middle of her back. She slipped into a sundress and glossed her lips, thinking she might see Hayden again. Her silly heart raced as she dashed to the pickup with Bonanza leaping behind her. Guiltily she left the dog behind. She couldn't take a chance that he would soil or wrinkle her clothes in his enthusiasm for a ride.

A few minutes before quitting time, Nadine turned the old truck into the lot of the mill. Other workers were arriving for the next shift and men in hard hats gathered near the gates, laughing, smoking or chewing tobacco as they talked and relaxed for a few minutes between shifts.

From the cab of the Ford, Nadine scanned every inch of the parking area, but discovered the sleek Mercedes was gone. Her heart took a nosedive. She looked again, hoping to see signs of the car or Hayden, but was disappointed. Her brows drew together and she felt suddenly foolish in her dress.

"Don't you look nice!" Her father opened the pickup's passenger door. Smelling of sawdust and sweat, he shook out his San Francisco Giants cap, squared it onto his head and climbed into the warm interior. "Goin' out?"

"Nope." She stepped on the throttle. "I just wanted to get cleaned up."

He smiled at her and she felt foolish. "I thought maybe you and Sam had decided to go somewhere."

"Not tonight," she replied, irritated at the mention of Sam. Yes, she dated him, but that was all. Everyone assumed they were going together—even her family.

"Boy, am I glad it's quittin' time," he said, rubbing the kinks from the back of his neck. "Hardly had time for lunch, today." He leaned against the back of the seat and closed his eyes as Nadine drove him home.

It wasn't until later, during dinner, that Hayden's name came up. The Powell family, minus Kevin who was working the swing shift at the mill, was seated around the small table. Over the scrape of forks against plates, the steady rumble of a local anchorman's voice filtered in from the living room. From his chair at the head of the table, George could glance at the television and despite his wife's constant arguments, he watched the news. "It's a man's right," he'd said on more than one occasion, "to know what's goin' on in the world after spending eight hours over that damned green chain."

Donna had always argued, but, in the end, had snapped her mouth shut and smoldered in silence through the evening meal while her husband had either not noticed or chosen to disregard his wife's simmering anger.

But this night, George hardly glanced at the television. "You shoulda seen the fireworks at the mill this afternoon," he told his wife and children. Smothering his plate of meat loaf and potatoes with gravy, he said, "I was just punchin' in when the boss's kid showed up." He took a bite and swallowed quickly. "That boy was madder'n a trapped grizzly, let me tell you. His face was red, his fists were clenched and he demanded to see his father. Dora, the secretary, was fit to be tied. Wouldn't let him in the office, but the old man heard the commotion and he came stormin' out into the reception area. Old Garreth takes one look at Hayden and the kid tosses a set of keys to his father, mutters some choice words not fit to repeat at this table, turns on his heel and marches out. Damn, but he was mad."

"What was it all about?" Ben asked, buttering a slice of bread and looking only mildly interested.

"I didn't stick around to find out. But the kid didn't want his car—a honey of a machine—Mercedes convertible, I think."

"Why not?" Ben asked, suddenly attentive.

"Hayden claimed he was old enough to see who he wanted, do what he wanted when he wanted, with whom he wanted—you know, that same old BS we hear around here. Anyway, the gist of it was that he wasn't going to let Garreth tell him what to do. Said he wasn't about to be . . . just how'd he put it?'' Her father thought for a minute and chewed slowly. "Something to the effect that he couldn't be bought and sold like one of Garreth's racehorses. Then he just flew out of there, leaving me and Dora with our mouths hangin' wide open and old Garreth so mad the veins were bulgin' big as night crawlers in his neck."

"Sounds like Hayden finally got smart," Ben observed as he reached for a platter of corn on the cob. "His old man's been pushing him around for years. It was probably time he stood up to him. Although I, personally, would *never* give up a car like that."

"Maybe you would if the price was too high," Nadine interjected.

"Hell, no! I'd sell the devil my soul just to drive a Mercedes."

"Ben!" Donna shot her son a warning glance before her knowing eyes landed on Nadine again. For a second Nadine thought her mother would tell the family about Hayden's visit, but she couldn't get a word in edgewise.

"I've never seen Garreth so furious," George said. "The old man looked like he was about to explode, and I hightailed it out to the yard and got to work. None of my business anyway, but it looks like Garreth's got his hands full with that one."

Donna shot her daughter a glance. "Nadine gave Hayden a ride into town."

Squirming in her chair, Nadine caught Ben's curious stare. "Is that right?" Ben asked.

Her father's eyes, too, were trained in her direction.

"What'd he say?" Ben wanted to know as he tried to swallow a smile.

"About the same thing that Dad overheard."

Ben snorted. "If you ask me, the whole fight isn't about a car, it's over Wynona Galveston."

"Galveston?" Donna picked up her water glass. "Dr. Galveston's daughter?"

"I think so," Ben replied. "Anyway, I heard something about it from his cousin Roy."

"I wouldn't trust anything Roy Fitzgerald said," Nadine cut in.

Shrugging, Ben said, "All I know is that Roy said Hayden's supposed to be gettin' engaged to her and she's the daughter of a famous heart surgeon or something. Roy was bragging about how rich she was."

"Well it seems Hayden isn't interested." George glanced to the television where the sports scores were being flashed across the screen. Conversation dropped as he listened to news of the Oakland A's and the San Francisco Giants, and Nadine was grateful that the subject of Hayden Monroe had been dropped. She picked up her plate and glass, intending to carry them both into the kitchen, when she caught a warning glance from her mother. *See what I mean,* her mother said silently by lifting her finely arched eyebrows. *Hayden Garreth Monroe IV is way out of your league.*

The next time she saw Hayden was at the lake on Sunday afternoon. Nadine and Ben had taken the small motorboat that Ben had bought doing odd jobs for neighbors to the public boat launch. They spent the afternoon swimming, waterskiing and sunbathing on the beach near the old bait-and-tackle shop on the south side of the lake.

Several kids from school joined them and sat on blankets spread on the rocky beach while drinking soda and listening to the radio.

To avoid a burn, Nadine tossed a white blouse over her one-piece suit and knotted the hem of the blouse under her breasts. She waited for her turn skiing and watched the boats cutting through the smooth water of the lake.

From the corner of her eye she saw Patty Osgood and her brother, Tim, arrive. Patty carried an old blanket and beach basket. A cooler swung from Tim's hand.

"I didn't think we'd make it!" Patty admitted as she plopped next to Nadine and began fiddling with the dial of the radio.

"I wonder how she escaped," Mary Beth Carter whispered into Nadine's ear. "I thought Reverend Osgood preached that 'Sunday is a day of rest.'"

"Maybe he thinks hanging out at the beach is resting," Nadine replied. Though she and Mary Beth were friends, they weren't all that close. Mary Beth had an ear for gossip and an eye for the social ladder at school. She was already trying to break into the clique with Laura Chandler, and as soon as she was accepted by Laura, a cheerleader, and Laura's crowd, Mary Beth would probably leave her other friends in her dust.

Patty found a soft rock station and, humming along to an Olivia Newton-John song, began to smooth suntan oil onto her skin. "Your brother here?" she asked innocently, and Nadine bristled inside. Lately she'd had the feeling that Patty was interested in Ben, and had been searching out Nadine's company just to get close to her brother.

Patty tucked her straight blond hair into a ponytail and took off her blouse to reveal a pink halter top that, Nadine was sure, would have given the Reverend Osgood the shock of his life.

"He's in the boat," Nadine said, though she suspected that Patty, already scanning the lake, knew precisely where Ben was.

Her pretty lips curved into a smile at the sight of Ben's little launch. "Umm. I wonder if he'd give me a ride."

"Probably." Nadine turned her attention to the water. The day was hot and sunlight glinted on the shifting surface of Whitefire Lake. Several rowboats drifted lazily, as fishermen tried to lure rainbow trout onto their lines. Other, more powerful motorboats, sliced through the water, dragging skiers and creating huge wakes that rippled toward the shore.

A candy-apple-red speedboat careened through the water at a furious pace. Nadine's breath caught in her throat. Hayden was at the helm. Her throat closed in upon itself and she tried to ignore the funny little catch in her heartbeat as she watched him.

Wrapping her arms around her knees and staring at the red boat as it streaked by in a blur, Mary Beth clucked her tongue. "So he's back this summer." Her eyes narrowed a fraction. "I thought he'd never show his face around here again."

"His family comes back every year," Nadine pointed out, wondering why, once again, she felt the need to defend him.

"I know. But after *last* summer, I thought he'd stay away." Mary Beth and Patty exchanged glances.

"Why?" Nadine asked, nudging a rock with her toe.

"Oh, you know. Because of Trish," Patty said with an air of nonchalance.

"Trish?"

"Trish London," Mary Beth hissed, as if saying a dirty word. "You remember. She left school last year."

"She moved to Portland to live with her sister," Nadine said, trying to decipher the silent code between the two girls. Trish London was a girl who was known to be fast and easy with the boys, a girl always on the edge of serious trouble, but Nadine had never heard Trish's name linked with Hayden's. In fact, she was certain that most of the rumors about Trish were gross exaggerations from boys who bragged about sexual deeds they'd only dreamed about. The rumor with Hayden was probably nothing more than malicious gossip.

"You mean you don't know why she left?" Patty asked innocently, though her eyes seemed to glimmer with spiteful glee.

Nadine's guts twisted and she wanted to hold her tongue, but she couldn't suppress her curiosity. "I never thought about it."

"She was pregnant!" Mary Beth said, lifting her chin a fraction. "She went to Portland to have the baby and give it up for adoption without anyone from around here knowing about it."

"But—"

"And the baby was Hayden Monroe's," Patty insisted, a cruel little smile playing upon her lips.

"How do you know?"

"Everybody knows! Hayden's father caught him with Trish in the boathouse last summer. Garreth was furious that his son was with a girl from the wrong side of the tracks and he shipped Hayden back to San Francisco so fast, he didn't even have time to say goodbye to her. Not that he probably wanted to. Anyway, a few weeks later, Trish moved to Portland. Very quick. Without a word to anyone. It doesn't take a genius to figure out what happened." One of Patty's blond eyebrows rose over the top of her sunglasses.

Nadine wasn't convinced. "Just because they were together doesn't mean that—"

Patty waved off her argument while glancing at her reflection in a hand mirror. Frowning slightly, she reached into her beach bag and dragged out a lipstick tube. "Of course it doesn't mean that he's the father. But Tim knows Hayden's cousins, Roy and Brian. The Fitzpatrick boys told Tim that old man Monroe put up a ton of money to keep Trish's family from talking."

"Roy and Brian Fitzpatrick aren't exactly paragons of virtue themselves," Nadine pointed out.

"Believe what you want to, Nadine. But the story's true," Mary Beth added with a self-righteous smile. "And it doesn't surprise me about Trish. She's following in her mother's footsteps and everyone in town knows about Eve London!"

Nadine's stomach turned over. Eve London had earned a reputation as the town whore. With three ex-husbands and several live-in lovers, she'd often been the talk of the town. Trish had grown up in her mother's murky shadow.

Patty touched the corner of her lips where she'd smeared a little lipstick. "But that's old news. I heard that Hayden's about to get engaged to some rich girl from San Francisco. I wonder what she would say if she found out about Trish."

"She'll never know," Mary Beth predicted.

Patty lifted a shoulder. "She's supposed to come and visit Hayden at the summer cabin. There's always the chance that she'll overhear some of the gossip." With a wicked little grin, she reached for the radio again and fiddled with the dial. "I wonder what she'd say if she found out Hayden was a daddy."

"You don't know that—"

"Oh, Nadine, grow up!" Mary Beth interjected. "What is it with you? Why won't you believe that Hayden Monroe made it with Trish?"

"Maybe Nadine's got a crush on the rich boy," Patty said as she found a country station. Settling back on her blanket, she turned her attention to Nadine. "Is that it?"

"I don't even know him."

"But you'd like to, I'll bet," Mary Beth said. "Not that I blame you. Sexy, handsome and rich. Yeah, I can see myself falling for a guy like him."

Nadine had heard enough. She didn't like the turn of the conversation and she didn't want to believe any of Patty and Mary Beth's gossip. The fact that her own mother had hinted about some sort of scandal revolving around Hayden just a few days before bothered her, but she'd lived in Gold Creek long enough to know that gossip swept like wildfire through the small town. Sometimes it was true, other times it was just people starting rumors to add a little spice to their own boring lives.

Slinging her towel around the back of her neck, she walked to the edge of the dock, plopped down and dangled her feet over the edge until her toes touched the water. The sun was hot, intense rays beating against her scalp, the bleached boards of the deck warm against her rear end. Squinting, she watched as Hayden drove his boat flat-out, the engine screaming, the prow slicing through the water.

Her heart did a funny little somersault as she focused on his dark hair blowing in the wind and his bare chest, lean and muscular. Was the story about Trish London true? Or just a figment of a small town's imagination? And what about his engagement to Wynona Galveston? Her stomach wrenched a little at the thought of Hayden getting married, but she chided herself for her silly fantasies. She'd given him a ride home. Period. As far as Hayden was concerned, she wasn't even alive.

Ben returned, anchored his boat and hoisted himself onto the dock. "You comin'?" he asked, dabbing his face with the corner of her towel. Nadine shook her head. "Fine. Have it your way." Over the sound of Kenny Rogers's gravelly voice, she heard Ben's retreating footsteps and the low laughter of Patty Osgood. Sliding a glance over her shoulder, Nadine thought she might be sick. Patty's coral lips were curved into a sweet smile and she was leaning on her elbows, coyly thrusting out her chest, which was tanned and slick with oil. Ben sat down beside her and could barely keep his eyes from the plunging neckline of the reverend's daughter's halter top and the heavy breasts confined therein.

Shuddering, Nadine turned her attention back to the lake and the sound of an approaching boat. Her heart nearly stopped when she spied Hayden edging his speedboat closer to the dock.

"I was pretty sure I recognized you," he said, once the boat was idling. He was wearing cutoff jeans that rode low on his hips, exposing a bronzed chest with a sprinkling of dark hair. Sunglasses covered his eyes again and the old cutoffs hid little of his anatomy.

Nadine's throat was suddenly dry as sand.

Throwing a line around one of the pilings, Hayden stepped out and plopped next to her on the edge of the dock. Water beaded in his dark hair and ran down his chest. Nadine's insides seemed to turn to jelly as she stared at him. "I figured I could pay you back for the other day."

Her temper inched upward at the thought of their last conversation. Why had she bothered defending him to her family and friends? He was just as bad as they'd all told her he was. "I thought you understood how I felt about your money."

A sexy grin stretched lazily across his jaw. "I wasn't talking about cash. How about a ride?" He cocked his head toward the boat.

"I don't think that would be a good idea," she said quickly, though a part of her yearned to take him up on his offer. Alone. With Hayden. Knifing through the water with the wind screaming through her hair. The thought was more than appealing, but she didn't trust him. Despite the fact that she'd fantasized about him daily, she still wasn't sure that being alone with him was the right thing to do.

"Look, I owe you—"

"I told you before you owe me nothing. We're square, okay?"

"Then I'd like you to come with me."

Nadine blew her bangs from her eyes. "Look, Prince, you don't have to—"

Suddenly one of his large, warm hands covered hers and her heartbeat jumped. "I want to, Nadine. Come on."

She knew she should resist him, that taking a ride alone with him would be emotionally dangerous. If she didn't heed the warnings of her mother and her classmates, she should at least listen to the erratic, nearly frightened, drum of her heart. But she didn't.

He tugged gently on her arm, helping her to her feet, and before she could come up with a plausible excuse, he was helping her into the boat.

"Hey!"

Ben's voice sounded far in the distance as Hayden yanked off the anchoring rope and opened the throttle. The boat took off with so much force, Nadine was thrown back into her seat and her hair streamed away from her face. From the corner of her eye, she saw Ben, running barefoot along the dock, yelling at the top of his lungs and waving his arms frantically. Served him right for ogling Patty Osgood!

"Nadine! Hey! Wait! Monroe, you bastard..." Ben's voice faded on the wind.

Nadine laughed over the roar of the powerful boat's engine. Turning, she waved back and forced a sweet smile onto her lips. Ben motioned with even more agitation and Patty, left on the blanket, was frowning darkly, probably because Ben's attention had been ripped away from her. Too bad. Nadine laughed again before she slid a glance to the boy...well, man really, standing at the helm. The wind blew his hair, revealing a strong forehead with a thin scar, chiseled cheekbones and a jaw that jutted slightly.

"Where do you want to go?" he shouted over the wind.

She lifted a shoulder and hoped that he couldn't see through her sunglasses to the excitement she knew was gleaming in her eyes. "You're the captain."

His white teeth flashed against his dark skin. "If you don't state a preference, you'll have to accept my decision."

"I do."

He laughed at that and the deep, rumbling sound surprised her. "Hope you're not disappointed."

She considered the rumors she'd heard about him, but dismissed them all. She felt carefree and a little reckless as the boat sliced through the water at a speed fast enough to bring tears to her eyes.

He followed the shoreline, turning back on the path they'd taken. On the south side of the lake, they passed by the old bait-and-tackle shop and the dock where Ben's boat still rocked with the waves. Ben was standing at the dock and his expression was positively murderous. Nadine smiled back at him. They passed the public park and moorage, as well as the old summer camp and chapel. Following the curve of the shoreline, the boat sped along the north bank, the rich side of Whitefire Lake. Nadine caught glimpses of huge mansions nestled discretely in thickets of pine and oak. Boathouses, patios, tennis courts and swimming pools flashed by. Every so often a private dock fingered into the clear water.

"You probably wonder why I'm driving this—" he said, motioning toward the boat, as if suddenly a little self-conscious.

"It's yours?"

"My father's," he admitted with a grimace, and then, as if guessing her next question, added, "Even though I didn't want the Mercedes, this is different. I can use the boat without having to worry about having any strings attached to it."

"No price to pay?"

"Not yet. But it could still happen." His smile faded. "With my old man you just never know. Everything comes down to dollars and cents with him." As if hearing the anger in his voice, he glanced at her. "Still want to hang out with me?"

"Talking about your father doesn't scare me off."

"It should."

"I've got two older brothers. I don't scare easily," she remarked, though her tongue nearly tripped on the lie. Truth to tell, she was frightened even now. Scared of being alone with him, scared of what she might do.

He laughed and shook his head. "You haven't come up against dear old Dad."

Seemingly convinced that she wasn't going to change her mind, he slowed the boat and edged the prow into a small cove on the north shore. Nadine's heart was thumping so loudly, she thought he could hear its uneven beat. What was she doing here, alone, with a boy she barely knew? A rich boy with a bad reputation? He decelerated the speedboat to a crawl, guiding the craft through a thin inlet that opened to a tree-shaded lagoon. "Ever been here?" he asked, and she shook her head.

She'd never been so close to all the expensive homes on this side of the lake. "Is this on your property?"

"My father's." A line of consternation formed between his brows for a second. "Garreth takes great delight in owning things and people."

"Like you?"

One side of his mouth lifted crookedly. "Well, I'm the one thing he can't buy. At least not anymore. It frustrates the hell out of him."

"And gives you great joy."

His white teeth flashed devilishly. "I do like getting his goat." Taking her hand, he guided her to a stretch of beach where sunlight pierced the canopy of pine boughs and pooled on the glittering sand. "I used to come here as a kid," he admitted, eyeing the berry vines that were beginning to encroach along the forest's edge. "But that was a long time ago, when my father could still buy me."

"You act as if your father's an ogre."

"Isn't he?"

"My dad doesn't think so." Nadine sat on a smooth, bleached boulder and wiggled her toes into the warm sand. "In fact, he thinks your father is a prime example of the American dream."

"By inheriting a sawmill or two?" Hayden snorted. "He just happened to be the son of a wealthy man."

She glanced at him pointedly, but didn't say a word.

"I know, 'like me.' That's what you were thinking, so you might as well say it."

"It's just that I don't see that you have all that much to complain about."

"But, then, you don't know my family, do you?"

She shook her head, her long hair sweeping across her shoulders. And when she looked up, he was staring at her, his feet planted wide apart, his muscles tense. She felt the undercurrent of electricity in the air, as surely as the breeze causing the branches overhead to sway. The air smelled of water and cut cedar, and over the erratic beat of her heart she heard the muted sounds of birds chirping and the distant roar of motorboats.

She swallowed against a cotton-dry throat and licked her lips.

"Do you know why I brought you here?" he asked suddenly.

Oh, God! She couldn't breathe. The air was trapped in her lungs.

"I couldn't stop thinking about you. Since the other day, when you gave me a ride."

She could hardly believe her ears and wanted to pinch herself to make sure that she wasn't dreaming. "You... haven't called."

"I didn't want to call. I didn't want to see you again." He advanced slowly and sat down next to her, his body bare inches away. "I mean, I told myself I didn't."

"Then why did you stop at the dock?" she asked, her blood pulsing wildly.

"Because I saw you again and I couldn't help myself." He dropped his sunglasses into the sand and stared at her with the bluest eyes she'd ever seen. Intense. Electric. Erotic.

She licked her lips, and he let out his breath in a whistle through his teeth.

"Why didn't you want to see me?"

Laughing derisively, he touched her arm. Her skin tingled with a heat so intense, she nearly jerked away as his fingers wrapped around her wrist. "Because it'll only cause trouble."

"I thought you liked trouble."

His gaze sparked a little. "Some kinds."

"But—"

"But not girl trouble." His fingers grazed the inside of her wrist. "Don't tell me you haven't heard all the stories about me—all the dark tales about my past."

"I . . . I don't believe everything I hear."

He gazed at her long and hard, and a warmth curled inside her, gently turning over and causing her skin to tingle.

"You had a nickname for me."

"What?"

"Prince."

"Oh." She smiled a trifle nervously. "You deserved it."

"Yeah, I suppose I did," he admitted, but he didn't remove his hand. Like a manacle, the fingers encircling her wrist tightened, only warmly, gently. "What about you?"

"Me?"

"Have you been thinking of me?"

She wanted to lie. She told herself she shouldn't give him an inkling of what she really felt, and yet she despised women who calculated every thought or speech to manipulate men. She tried to yank her hand away, but couldn't.

"Well, have you?"

"Thought about you? Not a whole lot." She forced the words over her tongue.

"Liar."

"Why would I lie?" Instinctively she inched up her chin a fraction and found herself staring into eyes so blue, the sky paled in comparison.

"Because I scare you."

"I already told you I don't scare."

His eyebrow lifted an inch and his fingers moved upward to the sensitive skin on her throat. "You're trembling."

"I'm not scared."

"What, then?"

"Cold," she threw back, refusing to acknowledge that his touch caused her skin to quiver.

Laughter danced in his eyes. "Today. When it's over ninety degrees. You're cold?"

"Yes—"

"Could be you're coming down with something. Chills and a fever," he said, with a slightly wicked grin.

"Could be," she agreed, though she guessed they both knew the reason a blush was stealing up her neck and her flesh tingled all over and her pulse was beating rapidly.

He tugged gently on her arm, pulling her closer, positioning her so that his face was bare inches from hers, his breath warm as it fanned over her cheeks. "Or it could be that you're scared," he said again.

"I'm not—"

Her protest was cut short when his lips settled easily over hers. His mouth was warm and hard and persuasive, and all Nadine's resistance faded as surely as the ripples moving slowly to the shore.

Wrapping strong arms around her waist, he pulled her closer and she gasped as they fell to the ground. His tongue found entrance to her mouth, touching and exploring, flicking against her teeth and gums.

A wanton warmth invaded her blood and she opened her mouth even more, tasting him, feeling him, smelling the scent of lake water on his skin. He was hard and male and virile, calling upon a feminine part of her that readily answered.

Her entire body responded to him. Her breasts seemed to stretch the fabric of her swimsuit, and when his chest rubbed against hers, her nipples grew taut and firm beneath the shiny aquamarine Lycra. Hayden groaned and pulled her so close to him that their bodies lying on the sand were pressed intimately together. Her breasts were crushed against his naked chest and her bare thighs fit snugly against his.

A tremor passed from his body to hers, and when he finally lifted his head, his eyes were fired with a passion she'd never witnessed before.

He kissed her again and this time her lips sought his. Desire scorched them, and she felt his hardness pressing into her abdomen. His fingers moved around her rib cage as his lips stole the breath from her lungs. Gently exploring, inching upward beneath her breasts, his hands caressed her.

Moaning, she moved instinctively closer to him and he cradled one breast in his palm.

Somewhere deep in her mind she knew she should stop him, that if she continued kissing him she'd end up in a kind of trouble she'd never even considered, but her body betrayed her and the light, branding touches of his fingers against her swimsuit convinced her that what they were doing was right.

He reached for the knot of her blouse and quickly untied it, parting the cotton fabric before shifting and pressing hot, wet kisses down her neck and into the cleft of her breasts. She arched against him and a wildness deep inside her turned into a molten beast. Her hands delved into the thick strands of his hair, and he ran his tongue slowly up her breastbone, causing her to shiver in delicious anticipation.

There was a dull roar in her ears, the slamming of her heart against her ribs as his fingers rimmed the neckline of her suit. Her breasts felt full and ached for his touch.

"Damn, Nadine, I knew it would be like this with you," he said, lifting his head. His eyes were glazed and his hair fell over his forehead to cover the scar that cut across one of his dark eyebrows.

She could barely speak. "Like what?"

He smiled, a sexy, boyish smile that touched her heart. "Like there could never be enough."

"Oh." She licked her swollen lips, and he kissed her again, harder this time, with a mounting passion that swept from his body to hers. Rolling her quickly onto her back, he threw one leg between hers and she clung to him, kissing him feverishly, dismissing any thoughts of denial. He rubbed against her and she moaned in a voice she didn't recognize as her own. One hand tangled in her hair while the other scaled her ribs. His lips were everywhere. Kissing her face, her neck, her bare shoulders. And she wanted more. He lowered the strap of her suit and the stretchy fabric gave way, allowing her breast to fall free.

Groaning, he lifted it, touching her nipple with his thumb, while staring at the line that separated tanned skin from the white veined flesh surrounding the rosy tip. "So beautiful," he said, his hot breath causing her nipple to stand erect. He touched the hard bud with his tongue and Nadine arched upward, forcing more of her breast into his eager mouth. Heat exploded in her veins as he began to suck and she moved against him, wanting more of his touch. His free hand curved around her waist and fitted over one of her buttocks.

She moaned low in her throat.

"Oh, Nadine, don't do this to me," he pleaded as he lifted his head and her nipple, suddenly surrounded by air, stiffened with the cold.

"Hayden?" she whispered, and he slammed his eyes closed.

"You don't want this," he said.

"I do—"

"Damn it, Nadine, you don't." His fingers, still molded around her hip, dug into her buttock, and he swore loudly. "I don't!" With a guttural sound, he shoved himself off her and ground his teeth together. "Damn it all, Nadine!" he muttered, rolling to his knees and shoving his hair away from his face with shaking hands. "We *can't* do this!"

Nadine, suddenly bereft, felt a tide of embarrassment stain her neck. As if coming here and making out had been her idea! "You wanted me to come here with you," she pointed out.

"Look . . . I didn't mean . . . oh, hell!" He pounded a fist into the ground, then rolled onto his back, staring up at the sky through the pine branches. The bulge in his jeans was still evident, as were the taut muscles of his jaw. "I wanted to be with you. I just didn't realize that things would get *this* out of hand."

"Don't worry," she said, hoping to hide the irrational disappointment that burrowed deep in her soul. She should be grateful for his self-control. Lord knew hers had fled.

Brushing the sand from her skin and the folds of her blouse, she forced a brave smile. "Nothing happened."

"*Yet.* Nothing happened yet. But it wouldn't take long." He sent her a look that fairly sizzled. "Don't try to pretend you didn't feel it."

"I think you should just take me back to the dock," she said, wondering how she could have acted so wantonly. She thought of Trish London and realized that all too easily, she could have been seduced by Hayden. Or was it the other way around? Had she inadvertently started to seduce him? Their newfound relationship was already too complicated and frightening to think about.

"Don't get the wrong idea," Hayden said. "I *liked* what happened between us. It was what I wanted. Or thought I wanted. But..." He opened and closed one fist in frustration. "We should think of the consequences."

The consequences of getting mixed up with a girl from the wrong rung on the social ladder, she thought with a bitter taste rising in her throat. "I don't think we should talk about it."

He shook his head. "And just pretend that what we feel for each other doesn't exist?"

What we feel for each other. Her throat clogged. "I...I don't know. Nothing like this has ever happened to me before!"

"Me, neither," he admitted, and with a shaky smile, drew her into his arms again. She wanted to resist, but when he placed a tender kiss upon her cheek, she melted inside. With a sigh he rested his forehead against hers. "Some mess, eh?"

She almost laughed.

"Come here," he whispered roughly and tilted her chin upward before capturing her lips in a kiss that was sweet and chaste and so tender, it nearly broke Nadine's heart.

"What the hell is this?" Ben's voice boomed through the woods, reverberating through the trees and causing Nadine to jump away from Hayden, but she couldn't go very far. With lightning swiftness he caught her wrist and held her fast. Ben, nearly six feet of towering rage, strode into the clearing. His near-black eyes snapped with anger.

"Ben, don't—" Nadine interjected.

"What the devil are you thinking?" His gaze scraped her up and down, and the lines around the corners of his mouth turned white as he stared at her hair and open shirt. Her suit covered her breasts but one strap was still dangling over her arm.

"Oh, God, Nadine, what're ya doing?"

"I don't see that it's any business of yours!" Nadine tied her blouse beneath her breasts.

"Like hell!"

"You weren't invited, Powell," Hayden said, his fingers still gripping Nadine possessively. "This is my sister."

"I can handle myself!" Nadine interjected.

"You're only seventeen!"

"That's no reason for you to think you're my keeper!" she shot back.

"Well, it looks like someone has to be!"

"That's enough," Hayden warned, his eyes narrowing.

Every muscle in Hayden tensed, but Ben didn't back down an inch. In fact, he seemed almost glad to have a reason to fight—an enemy he could pinpoint.

His fists curled menacingly. "Take your hands off my sister."

"Oh, stop it!" Nadine said, jerking out of Hayden's grasp.

Hayden's nostrils flared, and he looked more than eager for the fight that was simmering in the air. "Don't let him tell you what to do, Nadine."

"I won't!" Outraged, she marched up to her brother and jabbed a finger at his chest. "Leave me alone, Ben. I can handle myself! I'm a big girl now."

"Who's about to make a big mistake! If she hasn't already." Ben plucked a brittle twig from her hair and twirled it in front of her nose.

"My mistake to make."

"Damn it, Nadine. Use that thick skull of yours."

"And you take your macho, big-brother act somewhere else." So angry she was shaking, she stared Ben down.

"Nadine—"

"I said I can take care of myself."

"You always were too stubborn for your own good!" Mumbling a curse under his breath, he threw a killing glance over his sister's shoulder. "Don't you dare touch her, Monroe. Not so much as a finger—"

"Ben!"

Her brother glared at her, but beneath the rage she noticed a deep regret in his eyes. His words, however, cut like the bite of a whip. "Listen, Nadine, I expect you back at the dock in fifteen minutes. If you're not there, I'm not waiting. You can explain all...this—" he flung his arms wide "—to Mom and Dad."

Swiftly Hayden crossed the short distance and glared at Ben. Heat seemed to rise from his body, and the tension he used to restrain himself was visible in the vein pulsing at his temple. "Don't you ever threaten her," he ordered.

"Just as long as you leave her alone." With a scathing glance cast at the rich boy, Ben muttered a choice blue oath under his breath and turned quickly and disappeared down a path. A few seconds later Nadine heard the sound of his boat's engine grind, then roar away, leaving only a disturbing silence.

"I'm sorry," she said, as Hayden's face turned to stone. "I don't know what got into Ben—"

"I'd better take you home."

"You don't have to."

His jaw tightened. "Ben's right—"

"Ben's *never* right!"

"Look, you're not going to get into any trouble because of me. Come on." Without another word of explanation, he grabbed the mooring ropes and tossed them inside the boat. Nadine had no choice but to follow.

Chapter Three

Miracle of miracles, Ben managed to keep his mouth shut. Nadine didn't know if he was honoring their unwritten code not to tell on each other, or if, because he'd been with Patty Osgood, he was as guilty as she of being with the wrong person. The purple patches on Ben's skin, just below the collar of his shirt, were proof enough of Patty's passion. If the Reverend Harry Osgood ever found out that Patty had been showing off her body and kissing Ben in his boat, there was sure to be fire and brimstone in the service on Sunday.

At dinner, Ben had ample opportunity to let the family know that Nadine had been spending time with Hayden, but he'd studiously avoided talking about waterskiing at the lake. Though several times he cast Nadine a meaningful glance across the table, he never said a word. Not even to their older brother Kevin, when the subject of the sawmill came up.

"You'd think old man Monroe would provide a Coke machine or something out in the sheds," Kevin said as he pronged a slice of ham with his fork.

Their father, always the defender of Garreth Monroe, scooped macaroni salad onto his plate. "There's soda in the company cafeteria."

"Big deal." Kevin glowered at his father and hunched over his plate, even though their mother had told him often enough to sit up straight and at twenty-two, he was well past paying attention. In Nadine's opinion, Kevin was still a kid in a lot of ways. He liked younger girls, had lost all interest in college when he couldn't play basketball and he seemed restless, though he wouldn't give up living in Gold Creek. "All Monroe cares about is making money!" He reached for the salt shaker.

"And that's what he should be thinking about. Remember, I've got money invested with him."

At the mention of the dollars that had been "invested" with Garreth Monroe, Nadine's mother dropped her fork. The subject was touchy and a topic that was usually avoided during the dinner hour.

"It didn't help much when my basketball scholarship ran out," Kevin pointed out, and George bristled slightly.

He turned his attention to his ham and cut off a bite-size piece with a vengeance. "These things take time. The money'll be there—it's just a matter of being patient."

"Some of us are tired of waiting," Donna said.

"If you ask me, you'll never see that money again. Old man Monroe will find a way to keep it for himself," Kevin predicted.

"It'll pay off."

Nadine noticed a drizzle of sweat near her father's temple.

"Monroe's a bastard."

Donna gasped. "Kevin!"

"I'll hear no talk like that at my table," their father ordered, and the dining room was suddenly silent. Deafeningly quiet. Aside from the drone of the anchorman from the television set in the living room, no one uttered a sound.

A piece of ham seemed to lodge in Nadine's throat. She drank a long swallow from her water glass and met Ben's worried gaze over the rim. Their animosity dissolved instantly and once again they were allies in the war that seemed to be growing daily within the family. A war, Nadine was sure, in which no one would be a victor.

The next week was the Fourth of July. In celebration, and because of the escalating fire danger in the woods due to dry summer conditions, Fitzpatrick Logging Company and Monroe Sawmill Company were closed. The entire town was on vacation. A fever of excitement swept through the streets of Gold Creek in preparation for a parade led by the mayor, a city-wide barbecue put on by the churches and a dance held in the park.

In addition, the Monroe Sawmill Company picnic was slated for that weekend in the county park on the west shore of Whitefire Lake.

Long before she'd met Hayden, Nadine had planned to spend most of the weekend with Sam. Now, as the celebration approached, she couldn't find any enthusiasm for being with Sam. He was nice enough and he cared about her, but...if she were honest with herself, she knew she'd rather spend her free time with Hayden. Silly girl!

The day of the city barbecue dawned sultry. Thick, gray clouds huddled in the western sky and the air didn't seem to move. The house felt a hundred degrees as Donna baked three strawberry-rhubarb pies to take to the potluck dinner.

Nadine rode into town with her parents, watched the parade, then walked to the park where red, white and blue streamers had been tied around the trunks of the largest trees. Balloons filled with helium floated skyward, while children ran and laughed and adults set up the tables covered with butcher paper. Under a canopy, several women set out platters of corn on the cob, green beans, salads, Jell-O molds and every imaginable cake and pie. Men, sweating and laughing, stood barbecuing chicken and ribs.

There was a festive feel in the atmosphere, and even Nadine, glum because she'd agreed to meet Sam, was caught in the good mood. There was a chance that she would see Hayden at the picnic. She helped her mother serve desserts and watched as children ran in gunnysack and three-legged races. Some adults were caught up in a softball game and most of the teenagers were playing volleyball or sunbathing.

Nadine couldn't help scanning the crowd, searching for Hayden. Though she'd agreed to help pour soda into paper cups, her gaze strayed from her task so often that her hands were sticky near the end of her shift.

Sam showed up in the late afternoon. With a group of boys from school, he approached the soda station and suggested that Nadine find someone to take over her job.

"Can't. I promised that I'd work until seven," she said. "Unless you want to finish my shift and spend the next couple of hours pouring soda."

"Very funny," Sam replied, though he didn't smile.

"This is important to Mom. The proceeds go to the library book fund."

"Big deal."

She felt more than slightly irritated by his attitude. "It is if you're the part-time librarian."

"I suppose." Sam ordered a Coke, then hung around the booth's window while she continued to work. He even helped out when the dinner crowd showed up, but still she resented him. Ever since she'd been with Hayden, her interest in Sam had waned. She still liked him; he'd been her friend for years, but she knew she'd never tingle in anticipation when she saw him, would never feel the powerful surge of emotions that seemed to explode in her every time she looked into Hayden's eyes.

At seven o'clock, she was finally relieved by Thelma Surrett and her fifteen-year-old daughter, Carlie. Thelma worked as a waitress at the ice-cream counter of the Rexall Drugstore and Carlie was a couple of years behind Nadine in school. With raven black hair, round blue eyes and high cheekbones, Carlie was drop-dead gorgeous and had already attracted a lot of male attention. Even Kevin, who was twenty-two, had noticed her.

Nadine quickly showed them the cash box, how to change soda canisters and the portable cupboard in which the extra paper cups were stashed. She offered to work longer and help out, but Thelma waved her aside. "I've spent half my life serving these folks down at the store. I figure Carlie and I can handle a few cups of root beer. You two go on along." She shooed Nadine out of the booth. "Have some fun. Dance."

Sam didn't need any encouragement. Grabbing Nadine's hand, he headed toward the stage where a group of local musicians were tuning up and one of the technicians was trying to eliminate the feedback that screeched from the microphone.

She had no choice but to dance with Sam. She had promised that she'd be with him for all of the celebration, yet she wasn't comfortable in his arms, had trouble laughing at his jokes, avoided his lips when he tried to kiss her.

"Hey, what's wrong?" he asked as he held her close and swayed to the band's rendition of "Yesterday."

"Nothing's wrong," she lied, knowing that Hayden Monroe was at the heart of her discontent.

"Sure." He tried to pull her closer and rather than argue, she let him fold her into a tight embrace. How could she explain that she was falling for another boy—a boy she barely knew, a boy who would probably never look her way again? She closed her eyes and remembered the kisses she and Hayden had shared, the feel of his skin, the way his touch could turn her bones to water....

"That's more like it," Sam whispered against her ear. He kissed her temple and Nadine tensed. She felt like a Judas, dancing with him, holding him when her heart was far away with Hayden Monroe.

As the song ended, she disentangled herself and made an excuse about needing to go to the bathroom. Sam found his friends and she hurried off toward the rest rooms, intending to splash cold water on her face and find a way to tell Sam that she wasn't interested in him romantically.

"Having a good time?"

Hayden's voice stopped her short. She whirled, hardly daring to breathe and found him in the thickening shadows, lounging against the rough trunk of a massive cedar tree.

"I'm trying to."

"That your boyfriend?" He cocked his head in Sam's direction, where, along with a few of his friends, Sam was adding to his soda from a bottle hidden in a brown paper bag.

"He's . . . he's just a friend."

"Looked like more than that to me."

"You were spying on me?"

His teeth showed white in the coming darkness. "Just happened to see you." He stepped out of the shadows, and Nadine's heart lurched at the sight of him—his smooth, disjointed walk, his thick dark hair and blade-thin mouth. His eyes, midnight blue in the gloaming, held hers and the night seemed to close around them. Laughter, music and conversation grew suddenly distant, and the air, still and muggy, became thick. When his gaze shifted to her neck, she knew he could see the tempo of her heartbeat at the base of her throat.

"I'm surprised you're here," she said.

"Command performance."

"Who commanded?"

"The king." When she didn't smile, he explained, "You called me the prince. That would make my father—"

"The king," she said.

"So now I've done my duty."

Her heart dropped. "And now you're leaving."

Smoldering blue eyes held hers. "Want to come along?"

"And go where?"

"Does it matter?"

No! her heart silently screamed, but she knew she couldn't just take off. Not without an explanation to her parents and to Sam. "I can't."

"Why not?" He cocked his head toward the group of boys huddled in the parking lot. "Your boyfriend disapprove?"

"I already told you he's not—" He took hold of her shoulders, pulled her impatiently against him and cut off her explanation with a kiss. Hot and supple, hungry and anxious, his lips molded firmly over hers.

She didn't protest, but sagged against him, her arms encircling his neck. She drank in the smell and taste of him, felt the sweet wet pressure of his tongue as it insistently prodded her teeth apart and explored the dark inner reaches of her mouth.

When he dragged her deeper into the foliage, she followed willingly, her lips still pressed to his, her body beginning to respond in wanton, lusty abandon. His hands spanned her waist, and his lips claimed hers with such passion that her head spun and her body began to ache.

When one hand moved upward to cup her breast, she sighed into his mouth. His thumb brushed in eager circles over her nipples and her bra was suddenly far too tight. He slipped his fingers beneath the hem of her blouse, upward until he touched the webbing of lace that covered her breasts. Groaning, he pushed her back against a tree and she sagged as his fingers probed and plundered, massaged and sculpted the shape of her breast until she felt as if she were on fire. The ache between her thighs began to pulse.

"Why do you do this to me?" he whispered hoarsely, as if he were angry with the world. He still held her breast, but now his body was pressed against hers and he was breathing in deep, trembling gulps of air.

"Do... do what?"

"Torture me."

"I don't—"

"Oh, hell, sure you do! You've got to know it! I'm crazy when I'm around you." With his free hand he reached up and tilted her chin so that she was forced to look into his eyes, then slowly, deliberately, he circled her nipple with his other hand, gently rolling the taut bud in his fingers.

Nadine could barely breathe. Her diaphragm pressed hard against her lungs. His hips were snug against hers and his hardness was forced deep against her midriff. "You're all I've thought about for days," he admitted. "I want you, Nadine," he said simply. "And I can't have you."

She wanted to ask why, but knew the answer deep in her heart. He was the rich kid, the boy who was used to taking anything he wanted, and she was a poor girl whose father worked for his, a nobody, and therefore off-limits.

"Nadine?"

"Oh, God, that's Ben," Nadine said with a gasp as she pushed herself away from him. "What is it with your brother? Doesn't he trust you?"

She glanced back at Hayden and flipped her hair away from her shoulders. "I think it's you he doesn't trust."

Hayden's eyes narrowed. "He's smarter than I gave him credit for."

She looked back to the dance, the torchlights being lit, the streamers and balloons and Sam, standing a little less steadily, laughing with a group of his friends. Ben was walking crisply along the path leading toward them and if it weren't for the fact that Patty Osgood called out to him, he would have surely discovered his sister with Hayden.

"I want to come with you," Nadine said impulsively, and for a second, the ghost of a smile played upon his lips. He reached for her hand, then dropped it quickly.

"Forget it."

"But you invited me—"

Hayden stared at her so hard, she didn't dare say a word. "I want nothing more in the world than for you to climb into that car and go home with me," he said, shoving a handful of dark hair from his eyes. "But it would only get you into trouble again."

"I don't care."

"Your brother—"

"It's none of his business what I do!" she said indignantly.

"But your parents?"

"They'll never know if we come back quickly."

He hesitated, then let out his breath in a whistle. "You're not making this any easier, you know. Besides, what about your...'friend'?"

"I don't owe him anything."

"You came with him."

"I came with my folks."

"You know what I mean."

She did, of course. But she'd risk hurting Sam's feelings to be with Hayden. "It's okay."

He shook his head, though reluctance shone in his eyes.

"Hayden," she said, her voice throaty, "I want to be with you. Maybe it's a mistake, but if you want to be with me, then—" Impulsively she wound her arms around his neck and he groaned.

"You don't know what you're getting yourself into."

"Tell me."

He squeezed his eyes shut, as if closing out her image would push her from his mind, as well. "Nadine, don't—" He started to untangle her arms. Startled, she looked into his eyes and he moaned loudly. "I don't want to hurt you."

"You won't," she said. "I won't let you."

"Promise?" His face was so close she saw the tiny lines at the crinkle of his eyelids and inhaled the very essence of him.

"Promise."

His mouth captured hers and he gently tugged, pulling her lower lip into his mouth and touching it with his tongue. Liquid warmth rippled through her blood and her joints suddenly seemed to melt.

Hayden's tongue plundered and explored; his hands were hard and anxious, and she felt him tremble as he finally lifted his head and buried his face in her hair.

"What the hell am I going to do with you?" he ground out, his breath ragged and torn. "Just what the hell am I going to do with you?"

"Trust me."

The smile he flashed her was positively wicked. "I don't think either one of us should trust the other. And I *know* you shouldn't trust me. God, Nadine, I— This isn't going to work."

"I want to be with you," she said desperately.

His eyes searched her face and he smiled a little, though reluctance still shone in his gaze. "Meet me later."

"Nadine?"

Ben's voice again!

She froze. "Later?" she asked Hayden, desperate to see him again. Curse her brother for interrupting them. "But how—"

When he didn't answer, she stepped closer, surprised at her own boldness. She touched him lightly on the shoulder and he closed his eyes and gritted his teeth. "Where?"

"Don't—"

"Where?" she demanded.

He held her close and kissed her, appearing to accept their fate. "At the lake. Tomorrow night," he finally said, then turned and disappeared into the darkness. "In the lagoon where we were before."

Nadine shivered as he left. She rubbed her arms and wondered if she'd have the nerve to meet him again. What did she know about him? He was rich. He'd never known the meaning of want. He didn't have much respect for his father. And she lost all sense of reason when he kissed her.

She was acting like a ninny. She was no better than Patty Osgood or Trish London. But she couldn't help herself. Hell could freeze over and Nadine knew that tomorrow night she'd be waiting for him. *At the lake.*

The air was thick and heavy, the sky hazy for the Monroe Sawmill Company picnic. Unlike the day before, all the food and beverages were catered and served by a firm from Coleville. Compliments of Garreth Monroe.

A whole pig roasted upon a spit, and cloth-covered tables were arranged under a huge tent, where salads cooled in trays of crushed ice, and a huge electric freezer was churning home-made ice cream to top fresh strawberry shortcake.

Despite the threat of thunderstorms, the mood of the employees of the sawmill company was carefree. Laughter and conversation floated on the air tinged with the acrid scents of cigarette smoke and sizzling pork slathered in barbecue sauce.

Blankets were spread upon the grass and sunbathers soaked up rays while children splashed in the roped-off area of the lake and older kids swam farther out.

Nadine's entire family attended. Her mother, sipping iced tea, sat at a table and gossiped with other wives of the mill employees. George Powell threw horseshoes with some of his friends. They talked and laughed and sipped from cups of beer drawn from a large keg.

Kevin swam with the younger men he worked with and Ben linked up with Patty Osgood, who had come as a guest of one of the foreman's daughters.

The muggy air was cloying, and sweat collected on Nadine's skin as she sat on a blanket next to Sam. Her eyes, hidden behind dark glasses, continually scanned the crowd for Hayden. She knew she was being foolish, but she couldn't stop herself from searching the groups of people. Surely he would attend. His father was here, glad-handing and acting just like one of the men who worked for him. He pitched horseshoes, downed beer and told off-color jokes with his employees. Dressed in crisp jeans and a polo shirt, he squired his wife, Sylvia Fitzgerald Monroe, through the tents and games. Hayden's mother managed to smile, though no light of laughter lit her cool blue eyes. Her silver-blond hair was coiled into a French braid at the back of her head and the nails of her fingers were painted a dusty shade of rose, the same color of her jumpsuit. A delicate scarf was pinned around her neck and diamonds winked at her earlobes.

Hayden was nowhere in sight.

Nadine tried to hide her disappointment and pretended interest in a game of water volleyball, but she wished she'd catch a glimpse of him.

"You're still mad at me," Sam said, touching her arm.

"I'm not mad."

"Just because I tied one on. It was a stupid thing to do and I'm sorry. It won't happen again. Come on, Nadine, don't hold a couple of drinks against me."

"It was more than a couple."

"I got a little out of hand—"

"You threw up all over the back porch, Sam," she said, irritated. Even her parents had been angry.

"I'm sorry. Forgive me?" he asked.

"Nothing to forgive." She leaned forward and wrapped her arms around her knees. Sam had added liquor to his soda last night, and it was the first time Nadine had ever seen him drunk.

Leaning back on his elbows, Sam adjusted his sunglasses to protect his eyes. He had sobered up since the night before and was suffering with a hangover. His skin was paler than usual and two aspirin hadn't seemed to help to ease the pain of what he called a thundering headache. "Don't tell me. I know," he said, wincing as a ten-year-old boy set off a string of firecrackers against all park and company regulations. The kid was promptly scolded by his mother. "I deserve this." Sam reached for her hand and held it between two of his. "I probably wouldn't have gotten so drunk if you wouldn't have been in such a rotten mood."

"So now it's my fault?" she asked, removing her hand and feeling uneasy.

"What's going on, Nadine? Something's not right—and don't bother trying to deny it."

She couldn't. It was time to be honest with Sam. She owed him that much. "I...I just think we shouldn't see so much of each other," she said in a quick rush of breath.

Sam didn't move a muscle, just continued staring across the lake. "So much of each other?"

"Yes..."

"You want to date other guys?"

"I—"

"Who?" he demanded, suddenly facing her. His face suffused with color while his lips turned white.

"Who what?"

"Who is he?" he asked, his voice low. "There's someone else, isn't there?"

"No one special," she lied.

"Like hell! Dammit, Nadine, where'd you meet him?" he demanded, suddenly furious.

"I just think it's time we saw other people. That's all."

"Why now?" He glanced around, as if he expected one of the boys at the picnic to come up to Nadine and claim her as his own. "It's not like we're going steady or anything."

Nadine tucked a strand of hair around her ear and hoped their conversation didn't carry to other knots of people crowded around the stretch of beach. "In this town, two dates with one person is the same thing as going steady. You and I both know it. People couple up."

"And you don't want to be part of a couple."

She steeled herself. She didn't want to hurt him, but she couldn't live a lie. "Not right now, Sam."

His shoulders slumped as if with an invisible weight, and she felt instantly sorry for him. She liked Sam, she did. But he wanted their relationship to deepen, and he wasn't the boy for her. The sooner he knew it, the better for him, she reasoned, but couldn't help feeling like a heel.

And just who is the boy for you? Hayden Garreth Monroe IV? She frowned and picked up a small stone, skipping it along the surface of the lake and watching the rings of water ripple in perfect circles.

"I guess this is it, then," Sam finally said, his jaw set in stony determination.

"We—"

"Don't say 'we can still be friends,' Nadine, because we can't. At least I can't. Not right away."

"I didn't mean to—"

He waved off her apology, stood and without a look over his shoulder, found his way to a pack of his friends who were hanging out with Joe Knapp, Bobby Kramer, Rachelle Tremont and her younger sister, Heather. Rachelle was a striking girl with long, mahogany-brown hair, and hazel eyes that were as intelligent as they were beautiful. Heather was blonde and petite, but much more outgoing than her older sister. Though the youngest member of the group, she was the center of several boys' attention, including Sam's as he sidled up to them.

Nadine let out a sigh of relief and wiped the sweat from her forehead. Thunderclouds rolled over the mountains, gray and ominous and burgeoning with rain.

Tossing another stone into the water, Nadine closed her eyes, and silently wished that she'd see Hayden again soon.

Forty-five minutes later, as the pig was being carved, a speedboat jetted toward the dock. Nadine's heart leapt as she recognized Hayden steering the boat inland. But her euphoria was quickly doused as she noticed his passenger—a tall, willowy girl who hopped out of the boat before Hayden could set the moorings.

His date was gorgeous. Her short blond hair was thick and streaked in shades of gold. A white sundress showed off a tan and legs that seemed to go on forever. At five-eight or -nine, she was model-thin and radiant. An effortless smile played upon her full lips as she grabbed hold of the crook of Hayden's arm and made a beeline toward his parents.

Sylvia Monroe embraced her and Hayden's father winked and gave her an affectionate pat on her rump while Hayden glowered and the girl, Wynona Galveston, Nadine guessed, was still linked to Hayden. She said something clever, everyone but Hayden laughed and Garreth herded them into one of the shaded tents.

Nadine felt as if a trailerload of stones had been dumped into her heart. Wretchedly she sat alone on her blanket, pretending interest in the swim races being organized for the children, while inside she was miserable. How could she have thought he cared for her—a simple, not-all-that-pretty country girl—when he was used to such sophisticated beauty? She felt incredibly naive and wretched inside.

Avoiding Hayden, she wished she could think of an excuse to go home. She didn't have a ride, unless her father drove her, and from the looks of him, his face starting to flush with the combination of too much hazy sun and beer, a smile fixed onto his face, she doubted he would want to end the party.

Her mother, too, seemed content to sit and gossip with the other women while fanning herself with her fingers. Ben, with Patty Osgood, was having the time of his life. Even Kevin was laughing and joking with his friends and a few younger kids.

Sam was already gaining the attention of some of the girls, but Nadine didn't care. He deserved someone who could care for him more deeply than she could. As for Hayden, he didn't seem to be having much more fun than she.

She was shoving around the scalloped potatoes on her plate when Ben plopped down beside her at the picnic table. "So, it looks like Lover Boy has found someone new."

She shot him a look meant to convey the message *Drop dead.*

"Dr. Galveston's daughter. Big bucks." He picked up his corn on the cob. "She looks good, too—blond and sexy."

"Like Patty Osgood."

Ben scowled slightly. "I'm just pointing out that Wynona Galveston has looks and money. Who could want anything else?"

"Grow up," she muttered.

"Maybe you should take that advice." Ben ate a row of corn from his cob, then hooked a finger toward the tent where Garreth Monroe was holding court. "Face it, kid, you'd never fit in—and count yourself lucky for that. If Hayden marries Wynona, I'll bet she'll be miserable."

"Why?"

"If not because of her husband, then look at her father-in-law. He's had more affairs than you can count, and see the way he's all smiles whenever Wynona's around. What do you bet, he's already set his sights on her."

"That's gross. He's old—"

"Enough to be her father," he finished for her. "Or her father-in-law. Doesn't matter. He's a tomcat. Always on the prowl. That whole family is bad news, Nadine. You're better off with someone else."

"Like Sam?" she asked, but to her surprise Ben shook his head.

"Don't limit your options, kid. You could have the best. Don't get me wrong. Sam's a good guy, but . . . well, if you want to know the truth, he's got his share of problems."

"Is there anyone good enough?" she asked, a little hot under the collar. Where did Ben get off, trying to tell her how to run her life?

"Maybe not."

"How about Tim Osgood?" she said. "Patty's brother?"

Ben's good mood vanished and he dropped his corncob onto his plate. "I was only trying to help."

"Well, I can handle myself."

"Sure you can," he said, unconvinced. "Just don't do anything stupid."

"Nothing you wouldn't do," she replied, and his head snapped up as quickly as if he'd been stung. He started to say something, changed his mind and tore into the rest of his dinner. Nadine couldn't eat another bite. She disposed of the remains of her meal in one of the trash cans and started back to the lake again, but stopped short when she nearly ran into Hayden and Wynona, stuck together like proverbial glue.

"Nadine!" Hayden grabbed hold of her arm for just a second, as if he were afraid she might slip by.

"Hi." Her heart was thumping so fast, she could barely breathe. Surely they could both hear its erratic beat. Was she imagining things or did the tiniest smile touch the corner of his mouth at the sight of her? He made hasty introductions and Wynona, still clinging to his other arm, smiled brightly, as if she really was pleased to meet yet another one of Hayden's father's employee's family members. She had grit; Nadine would give her that much.

Hayden's eyes were hidden by sunglasses again, but Nadine felt the power of his gaze. Somehow she managed to make a few sentences of small talk before spying Mary Beth. "Look, nice to meet you, but I've got to run," she said, hoping to stop the awkward conversation.

"Nice meeting you, too," Wynona sang out as Nadine hurried past them. In the brief seconds Hayden had restrained her, Nadine had felt his fingers tighten possessively against the soft flesh of her upper arm, reminding her that they were supposed to meet.

Or was she just fantasizing? He was with Wynona, for God's sake, and though he didn't appear to be having the time of his life, that was easily enough explained. Considering his feelings for his father, he was probably looking for a way to escape this charade of a celebration.

She rammed her fists into the pockets of her shorts and decided there was only one way to find out how Hayden felt. Tonight. She'd meet him at the lake tonight as they'd planned. If he stood her up, then she'd understand that he was just using her for idle sport.

But if he showed up... Oh, Lord, what would she do then?

Chapter Four

"Don't you ever think of the children? Of me?" Donna Powell's voice carried up the stairs and Nadine squeezed her eyes shut, wishing she couldn't hear the snatches of conversation that filtered into her room. Though her door was closed and she was lying on her bed on the opposite side of her small room, the argument seemed to pulse around her, rising like heat to the rafters and ricocheting off the sloped, papered ceilings. She'd waited for two hours, hoping her parents would climb up the stairs and go to bed so that she could safely sneak out, but their argument had started a few minutes ago and had quickly escalated into a horrible fight.

"What about all the promises?" Donna went on. "All the dreams you've put into the kids' heads?"

Nadine barely dared breathe and put her hands over her ears, praying that they would stop, that this war that had been going on for the past few years would just end. But she knew it wouldn't, and her stomach knotted at the thought that someday soon her mother would file for divorce.

"Please, God, no," she whispered, fighting back tears. The room seemed stuffy and close and she had to get away. Away from the accusations. Away from the anger. Away from a house where love had died a long time ago.

To Hayden.

If he would still have her. If he wasn't tied to Wynona Galveston.

Still lying on the bed, she reached for her denim cutoffs, slung carelessly over the bedpost, and she heard her mother's sobs, broken only by well-worn phrases.

"How could you...everything we ever worked for...the kids...did you ever think once about them?"

Her father's reply was muffled and sounded apologetic. Nadine couldn't just lie on her sagging mattress, staring up at yellowed wallpaper, wondering if this would be the time her parents would wander up the stairs and tell their children that they were splitting up.

Besides, Hayden was waiting for her. He *had* to be.

She slipped out of bed, slid into the cutoffs and found a beat-up pair of Nikes her brother Ben had worn three years ago. Yanking a T-shirt over her head, she silently prayed her mother wouldn't come up and check on her.

As she had when she was still a student at Gold Creek Elementary, she opened the bedroom window and hopped onto the wide sill. The heavy branch of the maple tree was less than a foot away. Nimbly Nadine swung onto the smooth limb, crawled to the trunk and shimmied to the ground.

Though it was late, summer heat was still rising from the earth. The moon was full, but partially obscured by clouds, and far in the distance the lights of Monroe Sawmill winked through the trees. She cast a look over her shoulder at the two-storied frame house her family rented. The only light glowed from the kitchen, and through the gauzy curtains, Nadine saw her mother, shoulders slumped, hips propped against the counter. Her father sat at the table, nursing a beer and scowling as he peeled the label from the bottle. For the first time in her life Nadine thought George Powell looked old.

He'd been cranky ever since they'd returned from the company picnic, and Nadine couldn't help speculating if Hayden's father was to blame. Garreth had cornered George Powell just before the festivities ended, and instead of seeming buoyed by his employer's attention, George had been tight-mouthed and silent all the way home.

Biting her lip, Nadine turned and started walking through the sultry night, away from the anger, the hatred, the lying and heartache of that little house where once there had been so much love.

Dear God, what had gone wrong? She could still remember her mother and father in their younger years, while she and her two brothers were in elementary school. There had been hope and laughter and songs in their house on Larch Street in Gold Creek. Every Friday night, her mother had laughingly told her children she was "taking the day off." Her father had come home from working the day shift at the mill and the family had eaten sandwiches at the big, round kitchen table. As Mom had cleaned up, Dad had dragged out the cards and taught the kids how to play go fish, rummy, pinochle and even poker. Later in the evening, after the cards had been shoved back into the drawer, Mom had played the piano. The whole family had sat in the living room singing familiar old songs, everything from ragtime and big band music to soft rock. Even their father had joined in, his rich baritone contrasting to Mom's sweet soprano.

So when had it changed? Nadine kept walking. Fast. Her brow puckered and she bit hard on her lower lip. She began to sweat. A few cars passed, but, by instinct, she ducked into the shadows, waiting until the taillights, as two glowing red specks, disappeared in the distance.

Life had been good when the Powell family had lived in town, in their own house—a small ranch with three tiny bedrooms and a family room. It had been small, but cozy. Then, a few years ago, her father had decided that his family should sell their house in town and move to the rented place less than two miles from the lake.

Nadine's feet crunched on the gravel strewn between the asphalt road and the ditch. The night was humid and thick, but she kept walking. Soon she'd be at the lake. It would be cooler near the water. And Hayden. He'd be there. He had to be. She crossed her fingers.

The first indication that something wasn't right in her parents' marriage had happened soon after they'd moved.

Nadine remembered the day vividly. It had been one of those hot, lazy summer Sundays when the whole family had planned to be together. In the past those days had been wonderful. The entire family picnicked in the backyard and feasted on Mom's fried chicken, potato salad, berry pie and watermelon.

But that particular Sunday things had started out wrong. Ben and Kevin had been fighting, wrestling in their room across the hallway, and Ben, in an attempt to restrain his older brother, had thrown a punch that landed through plasterboard separating the boys' room from the staircase.

Dad had been furious and threatened the boys with his belt. Her mother, horrified, had blanched at the size of the hole in the wall and had fought a losing battle with tears. Nadine had stood and stared at the wall, while her father had rounded up the boys, forcing them downstairs. "We may as well go get that firewood today anyway," he'd said to his wife, as he'd herded Ben and Kevin to the pickup.

Mom hadn't said a word, just watched from the back porch as the old truck had rolled backward down the lane. Then, without glancing in her daughter's direction, had said, "You'd better get ready for church, Nadine."

Nadine, staring longingly after the plume of dust in the drive, had been about to protest, but her mother's eyes had narrowed quickly. "Now, don't give me any back talk. I'm not in the mood. I've got a headache coming on and we're late as it is, so hurry on upstairs!"

Nadine hadn't argued. She'd thrown on her one good dress and had pulled her wild red-brown curls into a ponytail. Her mother had hardly said a word as she'd driven into town. Her thoughts had obviously been miles away, but as she'd parked the old Buick wagon in the church lot, she'd turned her head suddenly and stared at Nadine so intently that Nadine had wiped her cheek, sure there was a smudge on her face.

Donna's eyes had been moist and red. She'd forced a trembling smile and touched Nadine's hair. "Take my advice," she'd said, fighting tears, "be careful who you marry. Don't believe in fairy tales."

Nadine had wanted to ask why, but had known from her mother's expression that the question was better left unspoken. Later, after listening to the Reverend Osgood's blistering sermon on the wages of sin, and catching a few curious looks from Mrs. Nelson, Donna had driven home without bothering to switch on the radio. She'd been so lost in thought, Nadine had been certain that she hadn't even seen the road in front of them.

At home, after changing into faded slacks, Donna had baked a strawberry pie and started frying chicken, but she'd cooked as if with a vengeance, ordering Nadine to fetch her the oil, and the flour and whatever else she'd needed. Worst of all, she hadn't sung. Not one solitary note. As long as Nadine could remember, Mom had sung while she worked in the kitchen. Just as she'd sung in the church choir, she'd sung while she'd hung up the clothes on the back porch, she'd sung with the radio when she drove to her part-time job at the town library and she'd hummed while flipping through magazines and dreaming. Music had always been a part of their lives. But that horrible Sunday, while prodding the sizzling pieces of chicken, Donna's lips had been tightly compressed and deep lines had furrowed her usually smooth brow.

Later, when her father and brothers had returned, Mom's grim expression hadn't changed. The chicken had simmered in the frying pan on the stove, the pies had cooled on the kitchen counter and Donna, frowning, had swept the back porch as if she'd thought her life depended upon it, only looking up when she'd heard the familiar crunch of gravel under the battered old pickup's tires.

The lines around her mouth had become firm and set, but she hadn't stopped sweeping. Nadine, whose job it had been to take the potato peels to the compost pile, had stopped dead in her tracks.

George Powell had seemed to have forgotten his sons' bad behavior. He had whistled as he'd parked the old pickup near the carport. His thick red hair had been wet with sweat, his face flushed. Kevin and Ben had torn out of the cab of the truck and found the hose. After taking long drinks, they'd taken delight in spraying each other and even casting a shot or two in Nadine's direction.

"Smells good," George had told his wife as he'd mounted the stairs and brushed her cheek with his lips. "Lord, am I hungry." He'd tried to wrap his grimy arms around his wife, but she'd sidestepped his embrace.

"Supper'll be ready in an hour."

Rebuffed, Nadine's father had rubbed a sore spot in his back and rotated his neck until it creaked. He'd caught sight of his daughter and winked. "You're the lucky one, gal! You won't have to work with your back, ever!"

"Don't talk nonsense to the children—"

With a wide grin, he'd grabbed hold of his daughter and scooped her into his strong arms. "You, missy, might just be the first woman president."

"I said, 'Don't talk nonsense to the children.'"

"Your ma's no fun," George had whispered into Nadine's ear before setting her on her feet. "We've all got us a little investment plan."

"With Garreth Monroe," his wife had pointed out, scowling as she'd swept the floor so hard, Nadine had wondered if the broom handle might snap.

"And Thomas Fitzpatrick," her father had defended, wiping the sweat from his ruddy face.

"With the money we had from that house of ours." Her lips had turned white. "Rich people don't make a habit of sharing their wealth."

"Well, you might be surprised." George had ignored his wife's disapproval and managed to wrestle the hose from his sons. "You'll see," he'd told them all with a conspiratorial smile as he'd twisted off the faucet and sauntered into the carport where he kept a case of beer in a rattling old refrigerator. "When you kids are famous lawyers and surgeons, we'll just see. Why, I might even buy your mother a new house or take her on a cruise."

The lines around Donna Powell's mouth had deepened. "That'll be the day," she'd mumbled under her breath, and Nadine had wondered why her mother was so cruel, why she didn't believe in Daddy's dreams. "I've never yet seen a Monroe or a Fitzpatrick doing a favor for anyone."

"Garreth Monroe's my boss. He wouldn't sell me short." George had wrenched the cap off his beer, set his boot on the fender of the family's old Buick and taken a long swallow. "Yes sir," he'd said, squinting at the small backyard. "We'll move out of here...maybe get one of those fancy houses on the lake. How'd ya like that, honey?"

Donna had stopped sweeping for a moment. She'd leaned on the handle of her broom and the lines around her eyes had softened a little. A smile had teased her lips, and Nadine had been taken with how beautiful her mother was when she wasn't worried.

"You'd have fancy dresses and jewelry and you wouldn't have to run around in this rattletrap of a station wagon." He'd kicked on the bumper to add emphasis to his words. "No way. We'd buy ourselves a fancy sports car. A BMW or a Mercedes."

"A Cadillac," she'd said. "One with leather seats, air-conditioning and a sunroof."

"You got it!" George had said. As if she'd been caught being frivolous, Donna had scowled suddenly and shoved the broom over her head and into the corner of the porch roof, jabbing at a mud-dauber's nest. The wasp had buzzed frantically around its attacker's head, but Donna hadn't given up, she'd just kept poking the worn straw of the broom into the rafters until the dried mud nest had fallen to the floor. Grimacing, Donna had swept the remains, baby wasps, larvae and all under the porch rail and into the rhododendron bushes.

"You'll be the richest woman in three counties," George had predicted as he'd finished his beer.

"That'll be the day," Nadine's mother had muttered, and her voice had rung with such bitter disappointment, Nadine's stomach had tightened into a hot little knot.

"Come on, Kev. Ben, we've got work to do. You two unload the truck and I'll split the wood. Nadine, you can bundle up the kindling."

As Nadine had walked to the back of the woodshed where her father's ax was planted on a scarred stump, she'd glanced over her shoulder at her mother, who had tucked the broom into a corner of the porch and walked stiffly through the screen door.

If only Mom believed she'd thought then as she'd thought oftentimes since. *If only she trusted Dad!*

Five years had gone by since that day. Five years of watching as the happiness the small family had once shared had begun to disintegrate, argument by argument. But the fighting wasn't the worst part. It was the long, protracted silences Nadine found the most painful, when, for days, her mother wouldn't speak to anyone in the house.

"Don't worry about it," her father had advised his children. "She's just in one of her moods." Or he'd blame his wife's sour disposition on "her time of the month." But Nadine knew that the problems ran much deeper. She was no longer a child, not quite so naive and realized that the root of her mother's discontent had more to do with her husband than her menstrual cycle.

Her father's dreams had begun to fade as, year after year, they still lived in the rented house outside of town. Now, not only did her father still work in the mill, but her oldest brother, Kevin, did, as well. Kevin had dropped out of college and returned to Gold Creek—a fatal mistake in Nadine's opinion. A mistake she'd never make.

She walked so quickly, her legs began to ache. Her skin was damp with perspiration. The forest around the road grew thick, and the only sounds in the night were the thump of her shoes on the pavement and the noise of her own breathing. She thought of Hayden and rubbed her sweaty palms on the front of her cutoffs. Was she on a fool's mission? What if he wasn't waiting for her?

The smell of water carried on the wind, and Nadine hurried unerringly to the sandy shore of Whitefire Lake. She grimaced as she considered the old Indian legend that every now and then was whispered in the streets of Gold Creek and wondered if she should stay here until morning, sip from the lake and hope the God of the Sun would bless her. Her lips twisted when she thought about the reverend and what he would say about her blasphemous thoughts.

Following the shore to a dock, she recognized Ben's boat. Ben had traded a summer's worth of work as a handyman and yard boy for the boat and he paid a moorage to the owner of the dock, the father of a friend of his. Nadine had no qualms about using the craft. She climbed into the boat and rowed, watching as moonlight ribboned the water and fish rose to the calm surface.

There was no cooling breeze off the lake. The waters were still and calm; the only noises were the lap of her oars as they dipped into the water, and the nervous beat of her heart. Somewhere, in the far distant hills, thunder rumbled ominously.

She rowed toward the middle of the lake, and once she'd put a hundred yards between herself and the shore, she started the engine. The old motor coughed and died before roaring to life. With the partially blocked moon as her guide, and help from a powerful flashlight Ben kept in the boat, she steered the craft toward the north shore.

Three times she passed the entrance to the cove before she found the break in the shoreline that led to the lagoon. Her hands were oily on the helm. Turning inland, she steered through the narrow straight and, as the lake widened again, cut the boat's engine. Slinging the mooring rope over her shoulder, she hopped over the side and anchored Ben's craft. If her brother guessed what she was doing, he'd kill her, she thought uneasily, but closed her mind to her family and her problems at home. For now, she had to worry about Hayden. If he didn't show up, she'd try to take Ben's advice and forget him; if he did appear, her life would become even more complicated.

Damned if you do. Damned if you don't. One of her father's favorite sayings suddenly held a lot more meaning.

Listening to the sounds of the night, she recognized the soft hoot of an owl, the rustle of undergrowth as some night creature passed, the sigh of a gust of sudden wind as it shifted and turned, moving the branches overhead. Nervously she checked the luminous dial of her watch every three minutes.

As the first half hour passed, her reservations grew. How long would she wait? An hour? Two? Until dawn? The first few drops of rain began to fall from the sky.

The snapping of a twig caused her to jump to her feet. Heart pounding in her throat, she whirled, facing the noise. What if it wasn't Hayden? What if his father . . . or some criminal escaping justice were hiding in the—

"Nadine?"

His voice made her knees go weak. "Over here."

She saw him then. His dark profile emerged from a path between two trees. Relief chased away her apprehension and she walked quickly to him.

"I didn't think you'd come," he said as she approached, and before she could answer, he swept her into his arms and his lips claimed hers with such hunger, she melted inside. She kissed him eagerly, her arms wrapping around him, her heart thundering. He'd come for her!

His kiss was hot and demanding, his tongue anxious as it parted her lips and easily pried her teeth apart. Together they tumbled to the ground, hands and arms holding each other close. "Nadine, Nadine," he whispered hoarsely over and over again.

"I was afraid you wouldn't show up," she whispered, tears suddenly filling her eyes.

"I said I would."

"But you were with—"

"Shh." He kissed her again. More tenderly. "I couldn't have not come here if I'd wanted to," he admitted, sighing as if his fate were sealed and he had no way to change it. "I was afraid you wouldn't be here."

"I told myself I'd wait until dawn."

"And then?"

"Then I'd figure that you didn't want to be with me."

"If you only knew," he whispered against her ear, his fingers twining in her hair.

He touched her chin, cupping her face, his eyes dark as a raindrop slid down his nose. "Nothing could have stopped me from being here. Not God. Not the devil. And not even my father."

She thrilled as his lips found hers again and she kissed him feverishly. He moaned into her mouth as the kiss deepened, touching her very soul. His hands were gentle, but firm, and one of his legs wedged between hers. Her fingers curled over his shoulders and her breath was hot and trapped in her lungs. An uncoiling warmth started deep within her, spinning in hot circles, and caused her to press against him.

His hands found the hem of her T-shirt and explored the firm flesh of her abdomen, searching and probing, moving ever so slightly upward, scaling her ribs. She thought she would go mad with want and her own fingers tugged his shirt free of his jeans and felt the hard muscles of his chest, the light springy hair, the flat nipples that seemed to move beneath her hands. Groaning, he reached into her bra, drawing out breasts that ached for his touch.

Nadine's nipples reacted and she wanted more. He yanked her T-shirt over her head and gazed down at her. Within seconds he'd disposed of the lacy scrap of cloth and was kneading her gently, his tanned hands dark against her white, veined skin, rain beginning to splash against the ground.

She moaned, and when he dipped his head to suckle, a shock wave caused her to buck against him, her hips instinctively pressing against his.

"God, you're beautiful," he said, his breath fanning her wet, taut nipple and causing an ache between her legs. She writhed as his tongue flicked across the hard tip. She wrenched off his shirt and her fingers dug into the sinewy muscles of his shoulders.

He took her hand and placed it on his fly. She reacted as if burned, her arm jerking backward. "It's okay," he insisted, and placed her palm squarely on the apex of his legs again. Her throat felt dry as a barren desert; her heartbeat thundered in her ears. Beneath his jeans, she felt him, hard and anxious. "That's what you do to me," he admitted, and she felt suddenly powerful.

Boldly she nuzzled his chest, her hand still in place against the soft fabric of his pants. She scraped her wet tongue across a nipple buried in downy hair and he made an animal sound.

She knew she was playing with fire, that soon this petting and kissing might get out of hand, but she didn't care. Despite the rain, the night was hot, Hayden was hotter still and she wanted, more than anything, to kiss him forever. With him, her problems disappeared. All that mattered was Hayden.

His arms surrounded her and he found her lips again. Kissing her until she couldn't breathe, crushing her naked breasts against his rock-solid chest, Hayden moved against her. His hardness, still encased in denim, pressed deep into her bare abdomen and he shivered, as if trying to restrain himself.

"I should never have asked you here," he said, breaking off the kiss and breathing hard.

Nadine's heart dropped. "Why?"

"Because I want to make love to you, Nadine." He sighed against her hair and all his muscles grew tight and strident. "Nothing else in my life is working and you're all I think about and I . . . I want you. In the worst possible way." He said the words as if they were vile.

"Is that so wrong?" Tipping her face up to him, she blinked against the rain.

He laughed, but there was no mirth in the sound. "Not usually, but my intentions aren't noble."

Her heart began to break. "What do you mean?"

Gritting his teeth, he held her at arm's length, his fingers digging into the flesh of her forearms, his eyes gazing deep into hers. "All I think about is making love to you. Here, on the beach, in my boat, in my bed, in some sleazy motel room. It doesn't matter where, but I want you. More than I've ever wanted any girl. It's driving me crazy. Right now, all I want to do is push you onto your back, kiss you until you can't see straight and touch your body in places no one ever has. I want to pry your knees apart with my legs and I want to lie on top of you and make love to you until I can't anymore.''

She knew she should be frightened, that his words were meant to scare her, but she wasn't afraid. Even in the darkness she noticed the tortured expression on his face, the lines of self-loathing in the turn of his mouth. The wind lifted his hair from his forehead and blew across Nadine's skin, but rather than cool her lust, the steamy breath of air seemed to further fan the flames of desire.

He rolled off her and sat on the ground, his arms slung over his knees, his muscular back to her. ''I'll take you home. Come back to the house and I'll get the car and drive you—''

''I don't want to leave.''

His muscles flexed. ''Really, Nadine, this isn't right—''

Reaching forward, she traced the outline of one wet muscled shoulder with her finger.

His breath whistled through his teeth. ''Don't!''

''I want to.''

Whirling, he grabbed her offending hand and held it tight in his. ''This could go too far.''

''I don't think it will—''

''Of course it will!'' He dropped her hand and plowed ten fingers through his hair. ''Are you a virgin?''

She felt as if she'd been slapped. ''What's that got to do with—''

''Are you a damned virgin?'' His hands were suddenly on her shoulders and shaking her.

''Yes, but—''

He swore and shoved himself upright. ''Get up.''

Suddenly embarrassed, she stood, but couldn't hold her tongue. ''Are you?''

''What?''

"Are you a virgin?"

He rounded on her. His eyes were black as the breathless night. "I don't see that it matters."

"You started this."

His mouth tightened. "No."

"Good. Then I don't have to worry about ruining your reputation, do I?" Standing on her tiptoe, she threw her arms around his neck and tilted her head upward. With a groan, he kissed her again, and lightning forked in the sky.

"This is wrong, Nadine."

"Only if you think it is."

He was already lowering himself to his knees, kissing her chin and neck, drawing her down and slowly dragging his wet tongue down her breasts as thunder cracked loudly through the hills. As they kneeled in the pooling moonlight, he cupped her breast and placed his mouth around the nipple. Slowly he drew on the dark bud, and Nadine shuddered to her very core.

"Is this what you want?" he asked.

"Mmm." She couldn't think or answer.

"Oh, Nadine." Every muscle in his body went rigid and he drew in a long, ragged breath. His arms surrounded her again and he held her close, resting his chin upon her head. "I think we'd better take this slow...or at least slower. If it's possible." He found her T-shirt and tossed it to her.

"Take me for a ride...in your boat."

"My *brother's* boat," she corrected, feeling slightly wounded. Had she done something wrong? True, she didn't know much about satisfying a man or even turning one on, but she'd thought, from Hayden's response and her own, that everything was right.

She fumbled with her T-shirt, then waded to Ben's boat. Hayden helped her guide the craft to the open water, and once in the middle of the lake, he reached over, turned off the ignition switch and let the boat drift. They kissed in the rain, lips touching as lightning sizzled through the air.

Throwing his jacket over her shoulders, he said, "We've got to get home. This isn't safe."

"I don't care—"

"You will." He guided the boat to the landing and cut the engine again. Helping her out of the boat, he slung an arm around her shoulders. As they walked to the county road, he shoved a lock of wet hair from her cheek. "Aren't you going to ask me about Wynona?"

"Do you want to talk about her?"

"Not particularly."

Nadine wasn't sure she wanted to hear about the other girls in his life and yet she was curious, about everything that touched him. Especially the women.

"She's the one my parents have chosen to be my wife."

Nadine's heart did a free-fall and hit rock bottom. "Your wife?" She was suddenly sick inside. He was going to marry someone else? Oh, God, how could she have behaved as she did? How could *he* have nearly made love to her?

"That's what the old man wants. That's what the car was all about. He gave me the Mercedes as an 'engagement present.' Trouble is, I'm not engaged."

"Yet."

He touched her arm. "Ever. At least not to Wynona."

"She's pretty."

He snorted. "Do you think so?"

"Mmm." She shivered. What was she doing out here alone with him discussing the physical attributes of the woman he was supposed to marry?

"Well, so does she."

"Does . . . does she think you're getting married?"

He scowled. "It's hard to know what Wynona thinks, but I have a feeling that she'd do just about anything to get a piece of the old man's fortune. Marrying me would be the easy way."

Nadine's heart shattered into a million pieces. Hayden talked about marriage as if it were a prize with which to bargain. She considered her parents' union and knew that wedded bliss was something straight out of fairy tales. Yet she was enough of a romantic to believe that somewhere true love had to exist. It just had to!

She thought of Hayden kissing Wynona, touching her as he'd caressed Nadine, and her stomach roiled painfully. A question loomed between them and she told herself not to ask it, yet she had to know the truth. "You said you weren't a virgin."

He didn't respond.

"Have you...did you...with Wynona?"

Clearing his throat, he grabbed her arm, causing her to stop walking. "Never."

"But—"

"There was another girl."

"Trish London," Nadine guessed.

"So the word got around." He started walking again, his fingers linked with hers. "Don't believe everything you hear, Nadine. At least in Gold Creek. People like to stretch the truth."

She knew instinctively that the subject was closed.

Hayden walked her home. Over her protests, he insisted on seeing that she was safely on her back porch where he kissed her gently, then jogged back toward the road. She watched until he disappeared into the night. After assuring herself that he was really gone, she ran through the drizzle to the tree and climbed to the branch near her window. Carefully, so as not to make any noise, she slipped over the ledge and landed softly on the bare floor.

Letting out her breath, she began yanking off her soaked Nikes, but stopped short when she heard the click of a lighter and watched in horror as her mother, leaning against the bureau, lit a cigarette. The tiny flame gave Donna's face a yellow, haggard appearance, and her lips were pulled into a deep frown as she drew in on the first smoke she'd inhaled in over five years.

Nadine's heart nearly stopped. She was caught. There was no way around it.

"Want to tell me where you've been?" Donna asked, white smoke drifting from her mouth and nostrils as she clicked the lighter shut.

"At the lake."

"With?"

"I went by myself," Nadine said, sidestepping the lie.

"What did you do there?"

"Took a ride in Ben's boat."

"Hmm." Another long, lung-burning drag on the cigarette. The tip glowed red, the only light in the room. The smell of burning tobacco mixed with rainwater. "Where?"

Shrugging, Nadine replied, "I just drove it around."

"Alone?"

Obviously her mother didn't believe her. "I...I overheard you and Dad. The fight. I...I had to get out." Nadine tossed her sodden hair over her shoulders.

"So you walked nearly two miles in the middle of a thunderstorm and then spent the next three hours cruising around Whitefire Lake in the dark. Is that what you expect me to believe?"

"Yes."

Sighing, her mother rested her forehead in her hand. "Of all my children, Nadine, you've given me the least amount of grief. Kevin...well, he's got his problems. When he couldn't play basketball anymore, he quit school and checked out—thought his life was over and took a job at that damned mill. As for Ben...we all know what a hothead he is. He thinks all problems can be solved with his fists or...in the case of girls, by opening his fly." At Nadine's swift intake of breath, she added, "I hate to admit it, but Ben's girl-crazy. As for you... Oh, Nadine..." Her voice trailed off and she drew long on her cigarette again.

Nadine felt miserable. She'd never intended to disappoint her mother.

"So, now, tell me. My guess is that you were meeting a boy. Was it Sam?"

Nadine shook her head wretchedly.

"Then who?"

"I...I can't say."

"Why not? Won't I approve?" When she didn't answer, Donna made a quick waving motion in the air. "Well, no, I suppose I won't. Meeting any boy this late at night is begging for trouble, Nadine." She sat on the edge of Nadine's bed, and the old mattress creaked. "I...I guess I should have told you this a long time ago. Maybe you've already figured it out, but Kevin wasn't premature. I got pregnant and had to marry your father." She worked the fingers of her free hand through her hair. "Oh, don't get me wrong, I probably would've married George anyway. But faced with having a baby, well, I just didn't have any options. So there was no way out. I was stuck." Blinking hard, she added, "I just don't want the same thing to happen to you."

"It won't," Nadine said, though her tongue tripped a bit when she realized how close she'd come to losing her virginity this very night. If Hayden had pushed her, seduced her, she wouldn't have argued the point. Contrarily, she *wanted* to make love to him.

"So who's the boy?"

"Mom, please, don't ask."

Stubbing her cigarette angrily in a dish on the bureau, Donna set her jaw. "Are you going to see him again?"

"I . . . I don't know."

"I'll make it easy for you. Don't see him again—ever." Her mother stood and advanced on Nadine. "I'll find out, you know. This is one helluva small town and someone will figure out who you've been sneaking around with. The truth will come out, Nadine, so don't protect him. He's probably not worth it."

Nadine's mind spun with thoughts of Ben. . . . No, he would never rat on her, but Patty Osgood would and so would Mary Beth Carter. A lot of people had seen her climb into Hayden's speedboat at the lake. Her mother was right. It wouldn't be long. But she wouldn't be the person to name him. No. Instead she'd warn him that her mother was on the warpath.

"Well?"

"I can't, Mom."

Her mother's lips drew into a disgusted line. "Well, whoever he is, I hope he's as noble as you are." She walked to the door, but stopped, her hands resting on the knob. "It goes without saying that you're grounded. For the next two weeks. And if I ever catch you sneaking out of this room again, I'll put a lock on the door and bar the windows."

"Mom—"

"Don't argue with me, Nadine. And believe this," she said, turning, her face a study in determination. "I'll do anything, *anything* I can to prevent you from making the same mistake I did."

She slipped through the door and slammed it, her warning echoing through the room.

"The bastard!" Donna threw her dish towel into the sink and tears began to run from her eyes. Her husband tried to comfort her, to place his big hands upon her shoulders, but she shrugged him off. "How could you, George? How could you believe Garreth Monroe?"

Nadine reached for the screen door, but let her hand drop as she heard the tail end of the argument. Ben was running up the back steps, Bonanza leaping and barking at his heels. Nadine's finger flew to her mouth. "Shh!" she ordered, but it was too late, her parents both turned and saw them huddled on the porch.

Nadine wanted to drop through the dusty floorboards, but Ben, oblivious to the argument still simmering in the kitchen, yanked open the door.

"You may as well both come in," their father said, and Nadine noticed that his normally ruddy complexion was ashen. He gnawed on his lower lip and his hands fidgeted along the dirty red-and-black elastic of his suspenders. Sawdust was sprinkled in his hair and his broad shoulders looked as if they were weighted by invisible bricks. "As this concerns everyone in the family, we'd better talk it out. Sit down." He kicked a chair away from the dining room table and, without a word, Nadine and Ben slumped into the worn wooden seats. "I'll tell Kevin when he gets home.

"You all know that I've been promisin' everyone in this family a whole lot of money. Education for you kids, a new house and car for your mother...everything." His jaw wobbled slightly, and he paused to clear his throat. No one in the room dared breathe. "Well, it's not gonna happen. The money I gave Mr. Monroe to invest is gone."

"Gone?" Ben cried. "Gone where?"

George shrugged. "The investment didn't pan out."

"What do you mean, 'didn't pan out'?" Ben demanded, and Nadine's stomach squeezed so hard, it hurt. "Where did it go? To old man Monroe's pockets? To pay for one of his mistresses? To send his son to a private school?" Ben's face was flushed, his eyes flashing fire.

"Now, hold on. I knew the investment was risky," their father admitted, and Donna made a small whimpering sound. She leaned against the sink for support. "That's the only way to make money—big money. The bigger the pay-off, the riskier the investment."

"*What* investment?"

"Oil wells."

"Oh, God," Donna whispered.

"You mean dry wells?" Ben demanded.

Nadine felt sorry for her father as he nodded curtly and said, "It appears that way."

"But who says so? Monroe?"

"I saw the geological survey," their father replied. "There's nothin' there but an empty hole."

"Oh, it's not empty," Donna said bitterly. "It's filled with every dollar we ever saved! It's filled with the house we used to own, and it's filled with our dreams, George, our damned, beautiful, foolish dreams!" Tears were tracking freely down her face, and Nadine wanted to run anywhere to get away from the awful truth and the doom she saw in her mother's eyes.

"How could you trust a Monroe?" Ben demanded. "Everyone in town knows old Garreth's as greedy and crooked as his brother-in-law. He was in on it, too, wasn't he? I'll bet it was Thomas Fitzpatrick's idea. Monroe doesn't have the brains to pull off a scam like this!"

"It wasn't a scam."

"Like hell!" Ben said, standing and kicking the table.

"Ben!" Donna's back stiffened, but he didn't listen to his mother.

He whirled, and planting his flat hands on the table, glared at Nadine. "Now you know what the Monroes are like, little sister," he snarled. "All of them. Cut from the same cloth. And your precious Hayden is no different than his old man.''

"Oh, God,'' Donna whispered. "Nadine. Not Hayden Monroe!'' The lines of her face carved deep into her once beautiful skin, and Ben, realizing what he'd done, gritted his teeth.

Nadine's spine stiffened, and though her eyes burned hot with unshed tears, she wouldn't break down. She cared for Hayden, probably even loved him. And, deep down, he felt the same for her. She knew it.

"He's the boy you were sneaking out with?'' Donna demanded.

"Oh, hell,'' Ben grumbled, apparently sick with himself.

"Who's been sneaking out?'' Kevin wanted to know as he shoved open the screen door.

"Nadine. With Hayden Monroe.'' Donna's condemning stare landed full force on her daughter. Her fingers curled around the edge of the table. "There's just one thing I want to know,'' she said, her voice trembling, and Nadine braced herself for the blow. "Tell me the truth, Nadine. If you lie I'll find out anyway.''

Nadine lifted her gaze to meet her mother's. "What?''

"Are you pregnant?''

"Pregnant?'' Kevin repeated, shaking his head. "What's going on here?''

Their father eyed his firstborn. "What're you doing home so early?''

"I'm home for good, Dad,'' Kevin replied as he flopped into a chair. "I got laid off today.''

"Laid off?'' Donna said, and Nadine hated the disappointment in her parents' eyes.

"Don't you know? They're cutting back shifts. The newest guys like me got pink slips.''

Nadine felt the doom settle over the roof of the little frame house.

"If you ask me,'' Kevin said, "old man Monroe has lost it. And it's probably because of his son. The kid's gone 'round the bend, I guess.''

"Hayden?'' Nadine whispered.

"You don't know?" Kevin's eyes scanned everyone in the room. "Hayden Monroe is in the hospital. He wrecked the old man's boat this afternoon and the girl he was with, his fiancée, she's been life-flighted to San Francisco. There's a question whether she'll make it or not."

Nadine's life splintered into a million pieces. "And Hayden . . . is he . . . ?"

"Oh, he'll be all right. Those Monroes are lucky bastards. The way I hear it, he broke a couple of ribs and tore up his leg, but he'll survive."

Donna was already reaching for the telephone, no doubt to confirm the story. Nadine crouched lower in her chair, her eyes hot with unshed tears.

The kitchen seemed to disappear, but she could still hear her mother's quick questions to a friend of hers who worked at County Hospital. It was true enough; Hayden was lying in the hospital emergency room, in pain, perhaps more seriously hurt than Kevin knew.

She heard the receiver click and slowly raised her eyes to meet her mother's. Donna nodded. "The Galveston girl is critical—crushed pelvis, possible internal injuries, but Hayden Monroe will be fine. There's a question about him ever walking without a limp, but he'll survive."

"He's at County?" Nadine asked, involuntarily reaching for her purse.

"That's right."

She felt her father's hand on her shoulder. "I hate to do this, Missy," he said, his voice rasping with regret, "but you're not going anywhere."

"I've got to go. . . ." She felt everyone's eyes on her.

"You're grounded," her father said. "Don't even ask me for how long 'cause I can't begin to tell you. Now you listen hear, young lady. There'll be no more sneaking out. Until Hayden Monroe is transferred to a hospital in San Francisco to be with his own doctors, you aren't going anywhere."

"But—"

"Don't argue with me, Nadine. Believe me, I know best." His faded eyes held hers. "I've learned my lesson about the

Monroes the hard way, and I'm not going to stand by and see you get hurt.''

Panic surged through her. "I won't—"

"You heard me. That's it. We won't speak of it again. As far as I'm concerned, you're to forget you ever met Hayden Monroe.''

BOOK TWO

San Francisco, California

The Present

Chapter Five

Mist gathered over the tombstone, and the sod, recently turned, smelled fresh and earthy. Chilled to the bone, Hayden shoved his hands in his pockets. Sleet drizzled past the upturned collar of his old leather jacket and dripped from his bare head and nose.

He stared at the final resting place of his father, strewn with roses and carnations and lilies, and he whispered under his breath, "I hope you got what you deserved, you miserable bastard."

A lump filled his throat and his eyes burned with tears he refused to shed. Hayden Garreth Monroe III had been a pathetic excuse of a father. He'd shown his son no love, nor kind words—only strict discipline and upper-crust values.

From his pocket, Hayden withdrew a leather baseball, autographed by Reggie Jackson, and hurled it into the soil. The ball wedged deeply, nearly buried with the old man. Fitting, Hayden thought bitterly. His father had paid a fortune for that baseball, given it to Hayden and never once played catch with his only son. He'd never had the time, nor the inclination.

"Rest in peace," Hayden muttered, before turning and never once looking over his shoulder.

His old Jeep was idling at the curb, and Hayden slid into the torn driver's seat, wrenching the wheel and gunning the accelerator. Leo, a battle-scarred Lab and his best friend in the world—perhaps his only friend—was seated in the back seat. "One more stop," Hayden informed the dog. "Then we're history around here."

Driving through the gates of the cemetery, he headed into the city for yet another ordeal—a meeting with William Bradworth, of Smythe, Mills and Bradworth, his father's attorneys.

Bradworth's private suite fairly reeked of blue blood and big bucks. From the mahogany walls to the leather club chairs situated stiffly around a massive desk, the rooms were meant to invite conversation about money, money and more money. Even the view of San Francisco Bay didn't disturb the Wall Street atmosphere that some high-priced decorator had tried to transfer from East Coast to West.

The phony ambience made Hayden sick.

Shifting restlessly in his chair, he glanced from the balding pate of William Bradworth to the window where sleet was sluicing down the glass and the sky was the color of steel.

Bradworth's voice was a monotone droning on and on. "...so you see, Mr. Monroe, except for the money that's been set aside for your mother, her house, her car and jewelry, you've inherited virtually everything your father owned."

"I thought he cut me out a few years back."

Bradworth cleared his throat. "He did. Later, however, Garreth had a change of heart."

"Big of him," Hayden muttered.

"I think so, yes."

"Well, I don't want it. Not one damned piece of rough-cut lumber, not one red cent of the old man's money, not one stinking oil well. You got that?"

"But you've just been left a fortune—"

"What I've been left, Bradworth, is a ball and chain, a reminder that my father wanted to control me when he was alive and is still trying to run my life from the grave." Hayden gave a cursory glance to his copy of the last will and testament of Hayden Garreth Monroe III, lying open on the polished desk. He slid the damned document toward his father's arrogant son-of-a-bitch of an attorney. "It won't work."

"But—"

Standing, Hayden planted both of his tanned hands on William Bradworth's desk and leaned forward, his gaze drilling into the bland features of a man who had worked for his father for years. "I didn't want the company when the old man was alive," he said in a calm voice, "and I sure as hell don't want it now."

"I don't see that you have much choice." Always unflappable, Bradworth leaned back in his chair, putting some distance between himself and Hayden's imposing, aggressive stance. Tenting his hands under his chin, like a minister ready to impart marital advice, he suggested, "You can sell the corporation, of course, but that takes time and you'll have to deal with your uncle—"

Hayden grimaced at the mention of Thomas Fitzpatrick.

"Tom owns a considerable amount of shares. Meanwhile the employees will want to keep getting paid and, unless you want to close the doors and put those people on the unemployment rolls, Monroe Sawmill Company will keep turning out thousands of board feet of lumber from the mills."

Hayden's back teeth ground together. Even from the grave, the old man seemed to have him over a barrel. Hayden didn't have much love for Gold Creek, where the oldest and largest of the mills was located, but he didn't hate the people who lived there. Some of them were good, salt-of-the-earth types who'd worked for the corporation for years.

Thrown out of work, they'd have no place to turn. A fifty-five-year-old millwright couldn't be expected to go back to school for vocational training. The whole damned town depended upon that mill one way or another. Even the people who worked at Fitzpatrick Logging Company needed a sawmill where they could sell the cut timber. The banks, the shops, the cafés, the taverns, even the churches depended upon the mill to keep the economy of that small town afloat. It was the same with the other small towns around the smaller mills he now owned.

With the feeling that he was slowly drowning, Hayden said, "Look, Bradworth, I know about selling companies. I just got rid of a logging operation in Klamath Falls, Oregon. So there must be some way to get rid of the mills around Gold Creek."

The attorney drew back his lips in what Hayden surmised was supposed to be a smile. "Your Podunk logging operation in Klamath Falls—what did it consist of? A few trucks, maybe a mill or two and some timber? Handling a small-time business is a lot different than running an operation the size of Monroe Sawmill, son."

"Doesn't matter. I just don't want it. I don't care if I ever see a dime of the old man's money."

Bradworth's eyebrows raised a fraction. "So you want to donate the corporation, lock, stock, barrel and green chain to—whom? The homeless? The Cancer Society? Needy children?"

Hayden's lips flattened against his teeth. "That's a start."

"How?"

"You're the attorney—"

"Right. So that's why I'm telling you. We can't go out and donate a wood chipper to the Salvation Army. You know, most people would jump at a chance to own a company like this."

"I'm not most people."

"Obviously." Bradworth's gaze raked down Hayden's body, taking quick appraisal of his soggy jeans, flannel shirt and battered running shoes. His wet jacket had been cast casually over the back of one of the attorney's stuffed leather chairs. Water dripped onto the expensive burgundy-hued carpet. "As for the charitable organization of your choice, I'm sure the board of directors would be more than happy to take your money—but not in the form of the corporation, so you can sell Monroe Sawmill Company to a rival firm, if there is one that wants it, or raffle it off piece by piece to some corporate raider who'll close up shop and put the employees out of work. Your choice. But for the time being, you are, whether you like it or not, the majority stockholder and CEO of the firm, and the next board meeting is scheduled for January 15." Bradworth glanced meaningfully at his desk calendar. "That's barely a month away. I doubt that anyone will buy the company from you by then." He reached behind him, opened a sleek walnut credenza and pulled out several binders. "These," he said with quiet authority, "are copies of the company books. I suggest you study them. As for the town house in the Heights, here are the keys, along with a key to the Mercedes, BMW and Ferrari. There's also the summer place at—"

"Whitefire Lake," Hayden supplied, thinking of the remote house on the shore, the only place he remembered from his youth with any fondness. He'd enjoyed his few years on the lake and the summers thereafter...until his entire life had been turned inside out. "I know."

Bradworth's lips pursed. "As for the money and company stock, it will just take some time to go through probate and transfer everything to you. I've already started putting things in order—some of the buildings need to be cleaned and repaired, leases need to be transferred. Some of the assets of the corporation are personal and—"

"I don't give a damn!" Lead weight seemed to settle over Hayden's broad shoulders. "This is ludicrous," he remarked, though the attorney probably thought the same. It wasn't a secret that Hayden and his father had never gotten along. But the old man insisted on cursing him, even from the ever-after.

"I couldn't agree with you more," Bradworth admitted as he shoved the will back across the desk. "But there it is. Now, how will I reach you?"

"You can't. Just take care of everything 'til I get back."

"But I'll need to know where you are so I can keep in touch—"

"Don't worry. I'll call you." Grabbing the damned documents, the notebooks and the keys, Hayden snagged his jacket with his other hand and strode over yards of expensive carpet to the door. He paused with his fingers resting lightly on the knob. "What's going to happen to Wynona?" he asked, eyeing the attorney.

"Who?" But the lawyer's face tightened spasmodically and Hayden's stomach turned sour.

"Wynona Galveston," Hayden replied without a trace of bitterness.

"I don't know who—"

"Save it, Bradworth. Just let her know the old man's gone. She'll be interested."

Bradworth cleared his throat. "She's been provided for—"

"Bought off, you mean. Like all the rest." Casting a disgusted glance over his shoulder, he added, "Dear old dad left a helluva mess, didn't he?" Without waiting for a reply, he strode through the door, slammed it shut behind him, and walked quickly through the maze of corridors lighted by recessed bulbs. At each intersection in the labyrinthine hallways, original paintings and sketches in pastoral country scenes graced the walls. The whole effect was reminiscent of an Englishmen's club. Brass lamps and oxblood leather chairs, mahogany tables strewn with copies of *Forbes, GQ,* and the like were grouped in intimate circles in the reception area, decorated much as Hayden remembered his father's den. All that was missing was the old man himself and the ever-present, sweet smoky scent of his father's private blend of pipe tobacco.

Strange that he should feel a sense of nostalgia for a man he'd grown up hating. Shoving his arms through the sleeves of his jacket, he rode the elevator to the parking garage where his old Jeep stood waiting. Leo's tail thumped against the back seat as Hayden slid behind the wheel. The dog tried to scramble into the front seat, but Hayden ordered him to stay, and Leo, with a sniff, settled down, head between his legs, liquid-brown eyes staring straight at Hayden. "We're going on a vacation," Hayden told the dog as he glanced in the rearview mirror and fired the engine.

Backing the Jeep out of its parking place, he maneuvered through the garage and into the drizzly light of a wintry San Francisco afternoon. The wet streets were crowded with bustling cars and pedestrians. Holiday lights blinked red and green in the windows of major department stores and bell-ringers stood near the doorways, asking for donations for the needy this holiday season. Slowly traffic inched out of the city. "Whitefire Lake," Hayden said, catching Leo's reflection in the rearview mirror. "Believe me, you're gonna love it there." As if the dog could understand him! God, he was losing it.

Frowning at the reminder of the small town, he flipped on the radio. He's spent most of his summers at the lake hanging out with his cousins, Roy, Brian and Toni Fitzpatrick. Roy was dead now and Brian's wife had finally proved to be Roy's killer. Hayden scowled. Nope—not many fond memories in Gold Creek.

There had been a girl once. Nadine Powell. She'd been different—or so he'd thought. She'd turned his thinking all around until, like the others, she'd shown her true colors and when offered money to stay away from Garreth's son, she'd eagerly reached out her greedy little fingers.

He grimaced at the thought of her hands and the way they had touched his body. Good God, he'd almost seduced her a couple of times. No doubt that had been what she'd been hoping for. When he thought of the way she could turn him on....

"Hell!" He ground the gears and the Jeep slid a little. The familiar notes of "Santa Claus Is Coming To Town" filled the vehicle's interior. Hayden turned the radio dial to an all-news station. He didn't want any reminders of the holiday season as his memories of Christmas were tangled up in emotions he didn't want to dissect.

Though Garreth had proclaimed Christmas as the one time the family was to spend together, he had, often as not, shown up hours late to a goose that was cold and to barely flickering candles that had burned down to stubs of dripped wax.

Even as the spoiled son of Garreth Monroe, Hayden hadn't wanted to become a man like his father. Though his name promised the same wealth and financial wizardry as that of his predecessors, Hayden had no interest in making money. Hell, he'd already done that with the lousy mill in Oregon.

Maybe, he thought, his mouth thinning in repressed anger, he should change his name. Wouldn't that tick the old man off?

Except it didn't matter now. Hayden alone was the sole survivor of the Monroe line—no brothers to carry on the tainted Monroe name. The H. G. Monroe lineage was destined to die with him because he'd sworn to himself over and over again, he'd never become another Monroe mogul.

He wouldn't marry and he'd never father children. No one really gave a damn, anyway. He knew that he'd been conceived for the express purpose of carrying on the Monroe line and, had he been born a girl, his mother would have been pressed to produce a male child—an heir.

Female after female would have been born until a boy had finally come along. Fortunately for Sylvia Fitzpatrick Monroe, who really wasn't all that interested in motherhood, she'd come through with a male. Saints be praised, the line would continue! Hayden could imagine the magnums of Dom Pérignon that had been uncorked when his father's manhood had been proved and his son had been delivered into the world to preserve the family name.

What a joke, he thought, as the Jeep bucked up the steep hills of the city before merging onto the freeway heading north. He laid on the horn when an old white sedan tried to swerve into his lane ahead of him. "Idiot," he muttered, and Leo snorted in agreement.

The windshield wipers slapped away the rain and the engine thrummed as Hayden shifted down. Cold air seeped in through the windows that didn't quite close, and rain drizzled down the inside of the glass. Hayden barely noticed. He wasn't about to return to his father's house and take the damned Ferrari.

"Damn you, Garreth," he growled, as if his father could hear him. "Leave me alone." *The way you did when I was a kid.*

If having a son were such a big deal, why hadn't the old man taken any interest in him until he could read the market quotes in the *Wall Street Journal?*

"Bastard." Hayden had grown up all alone, and that's the way he planned to live the rest of his life. Alone.

He could think of worse company.

Hands on her jean-clad hips, Nadine stood near her idling Chevy and stared at the fortress that protected the Monroe summer home. In all her thirty years—even in the few weeks when she'd been secretly seeing Hayden—she'd never walked through the sturdy wrought-iron gates that led to what was rumored to once have been the fanciest house on the lake, built by a movie star in the late twenties and purchased—or, more likely, stolen—by the thieving Monroe family in the fifties.

Her lips turned down at the corners as she eyed the rock wall that stretched around all fifteen acres of prime lakefront property. Only the uppermost branches of the tallest pines were visible over the eight feet of stacked basalt and mortar.

And now, she was allowed—as a servant, she reminded herself—access to the fabled estate. The code she'd been given by the hotshot attorney in San Francisco worked. She punched out the numbers on a keypad and electronically, with a loud clang and groan, the gates swung inward.

Ironic, she thought, that she should be here, called upon to clean up the old manor, get it ready for its new inhabitant. It seemed that the attorney who had hired her didn't know about her connection to the Monroes. All the better.

She slid behind the wheel of her Nova and disengaged the emergency brake. The little car sprang forward, as if as eager as she to view the mansion owned by the man who had nearly single-handedly ruined her family.

The drive was overgrown with weeds, but still seemed inviting as it curved through a forest of sequoia, oak and pine. Pale winter sun streamed through the leafless branches and spattered the ground with pools of shimmering light.

As she glanced in her rearview mirror, she noticed the huge gate swing closed again, cutting her off from the stretch of road that wound through the hills surrounding Whitefire Lake.

She'd thought often of leaving Gold Creek, but after her shattering experience with Hayden, and what had happened to her as a direct result of her short-lived romance with him, she'd never left again. Her family, or what was left of it, still resided in the town, and she wasn't the kind of woman who would fit into the suburban sprawl or the hectic pace of the city. She'd learned that lesson the hard way. So, after being shipped off to a boarding school her parents could barely afford, she'd returned to Gold Creek and her battered family. Through her parents' divorce, through her eldest brother's death and through a bad marriage, she'd stayed.

She'd even, for a brief period, fancied herself in love with Turner Brooks, a rough-and-tumble cowboy whose house she cleaned on a weekly basis.

Nadine squelched that particular thought. She hadn't let herself think of Turner for several months. He was happily married now, reunited with Heather Tremont, the girl of his dreams. He'd never even known that Nadine had cared about him.

Why was it that she always chose the wrong men?

"Masochist," she reprimanded herself, as the lane curved and suddenly the lake, smooth as glass, stretched for half a mile to the opposite shore. Mountains rose above the calm water, their jagged snowcapped peaks reflected in the mirror that was Whitefire Lake.

Nadine parked and climbed out of her old car. She shoved her hands into her pockets and shivered as a cold breeze rushed across the water and caught in her hair. Rubbing her arms, she stared past the gazebo, private dock and boathouse and tried to see her own little house, situated on the far banks of the lake, but was only able to recognize the public boat landing and bait-and-tackle shop on the opposite shore.

Her small cottage was a far cry from this, the three-storied "cabin" that had once been the Monroe summer home. The manor—for that's what it was, in Nadine's estimation—looked as if it should have been set in a rich section of a New England town. Painted slate gray, with navy blue shutters battened against the wind, it was nestled in a thicket of pines and flanked by overgrown rhododendrons and azaleas.

This was where the Monroes spent their summers, she thought, surprised at her own bitterness—where Hayden had courted Wynona Galveston before the accident that had nearly taken the young socialite's life. He'd never called Nadine, never written. Nadine had told herself that the pain and disappointment were long over, but she'd been wrong. Even now, she remembered her father's face when he'd come home and caught her trying to sneak out and visit Hayden before he was transferred to San Francisco. She'd begged and pleaded until Ben had agreed to take her over to County Hospital while her mother had been working at the library, but George Powell, his shift shortened that day and for many days thereafter, had come home early and caught them. Thin lines of worry had cracked her father's ruddy skin, and anger had smoldered bright in his eyes.

After sending Ben out of the room, he'd rounded on his daughter. "Didn't I tell you to stay away from him?"

"I can't, Dad. I love him."

She'd been banished to her room, only to come down later and find her parents engaged in another argument—a horrid fight she had inadvertently spawned.

"I'll kill that kid," George had sputtered.

"Daddy, you wouldn't—"

He changed tactics. "Well, I'll let him know how I feel about him using my daughter. No one's going to get away with hurting my little girl."

"You think you can stop him?" Donna had interjected bitterly, pinning him with a hateful glare. "Haven't you learned yet that those people have no souls? How could you

hurt a man like Hayden Monroe? The way you hurt his father? By giving him everything we ever owned.''

"Stop it!" Ben had snarled. "Just stop it!"

At that point Nadine's father had nearly broken down; it
was the only time Nadine had seen him blink against tears
in his usually humor-flecked eyes.

Now, years later, she saw the irony of the situation. Obviously, because her name was no longer Powell, the attorney who'd paid off her father hadn't recognized her.
Instead, he'd offered to hire her at an exorbitant rate to
clean the place from stem to stern. "...and I don't care how
much time it takes. I want the house to look as good today
as it did the day it was built," Bradworth had ordered.

That would take some doing, Nadine thought, eyeing the
moss collecting on the weathered shingles of the roof.

She'd almost turned down the job, but at the last minute
had changed her mind. This was her chance to get a little of
her father's lost fortune back. Besides, anything to do with
the Monroes held a grim fascination for her. And she needed
to prove to herself that she didn't give a fig what happened
to Hayden.

So now she was here.

"And ready to wreak sweet vengeance," she said sarcastically as she grabbed her mop, bucket and cleaning
supplies.

The key she had been sent turned easily in the lock, and
the front door, all glass and wood, opened without a sound.
She took two steps into the front hall, her eyes adjusting to
the darkness. Cloths, which had once been white and now
were yellow with age, had been draped over all the furniture and a gritty layer of dust had settled on the floor. Cobwebs dangled from the corners in the ceiling, and along the
baseboards mice droppings gave evidence to the fact that she
wasn't entirely alone.

"Great. Spiders and mice." The whole place reminded her
of a tomb, and a chill inched up her spine.

To dispel the mood, she began throwing open windows,
doors and shutters, allowing cool, fresh mountain air to
sweep through the musty old rooms. *What a shame,* she

thought sadly. French doors off the living room opened to an enclosed sun porch where a piano, now probably ruined, was covered with a huge cloth. Plants, long forgotten, had become dust in pots filled with desert-dry soil.

It looked as if no one had been to the house in years.

Well, that wasn't her problem. She'd already been paid half her fee in advance and spent some of the money on Christmas presents for the boys, as well as paying another installment to the care center where her father resided. The money hadn't gone far. She still had the mortgage to worry about. Soon John would probably need braces and God only knew how long her old car would last. But this job, which would take well over a week, quite possibly two, would stretch out the bills a little. And the thought that she was being paid by Monroe money made the checks seem sweeter still.

Covering her head with a checked bandanna, she decided to work from top to bottom and started on the third floor, scouring bathrooms, polishing fixtures, sweeping up cobwebs and airing out the rooms that had obviously once been servants' quarters. Paneled in the same knotty pine that covered the walls, the ceiling was low and sloped. She bumped her head twice trying to dislodge several wasp's nests, while hoping that the old dried mud didn't contain any living specimens.

As she turned the beds, she checked for mice or rats and was relieved to discover neither.

By one-thirty she'd stripped and waxed the floors and was heading for level two, which was much more extensive than the top floor. Six bedrooms and four baths, including a master suite complete with cedar-lined sauna and sunken marble tub.

Summer home indeed. Most of the citizens of Gold Creek had never seen such lavish accommodations.

In the master bedroom she discovered a radio and, after plugging it in and fiddling with the dial, was able to find a San Francisco channel that played soft rock. Over the sound of rusty pipes and running water, she hummed along with the music, scrubbing the huge tub ferociously.

As she ran her cloth over the brass fixtures, a cool draft tickled the back of her neck.

Suddenly she felt as if a dozen pair of eyes were watching her. Her heart thumped. Her throat closed. She froze for a heart-stopping second. Slowly moving her gaze to the mirror over the basin she saw the reflection of a man—a very big man—glaring at her. Her breath caught for a second, and she braced herself, her mind racing as she recognized Hayden.

Her insides shredded and she could barely breathe. He looked better than she remembered. The years had given his body bulk—solid muscle that was lean and tough and firm.

"Who the hell are you?" he demanded, his blue eyes harsh. His face was all bladed angles and planes, arrogant slashes that somehow fit together in a handsome, if savage, countenance. His hair was black and thick and there was still a small scar that bisected one of his eyebrows. And he was mad, so damned angry that his normally dark skin had reddened around his neck.

Her heart broke when she realized he didn't remember her. But why would he? He must've been with a hundred girls—maybe two hundred—since they'd last seen each other in the middle of a sultry summer night.

"I was hired to be here," she said, still unmoving. Her voice caught his attention and his eyes flickered with recognition.

"Hired?" he repeated skeptically, but his eyes narrowed and he studied her with such intensity that she nearly trembled. "By whom? Unless things have changed in the past four hours, this—" he motioned broadly with one arm "—is my house."

"I know that, Hayden."

He sucked in his breath and he looked as if he'd seen a ghost. "I'll be damned."

"No doubt." Slowly, never moving her gaze from his reflection in the mirror, she turned off the water. Struggling to her feet, she was aware, as she turned to face him, that the front of her sweater and jeans were wet, her hair hidden, her face devoid of makeup. "What I'm doing is cleaning your bathtub," she said calmly, though she was sure her eyes were spitting fire.

"That much I figured." An old dog, golden and grizzled, sauntered into the room and growled lowly. "Enough, Leo," Hayden commanded, and the retriever obeyed, dropping onto the floor near the duffel bag Hayden had apparently carried inside.

Hayden, satisfied that Leo wouldn't give him any more trouble, swung all his attention back to the small woman who stood like a soldier in front of his tub. He couldn't believe his eyes. "Nadine?"

"In the flesh," she quipped, though she didn't smile.

"Why are *you* here?"

Her jaw slid to one side, as if she found him amusing—some kind of joke. "I was hired by William Bradworth to clean this place and—"

"Bradworth doesn't own it," he cut in, sick to death of the pushy attorney. "I should have been told. Oh, hell!" He shoved his hair from his eyes. "What I meant was—"

"Save it, Hayden," she replied quickly. "I don't care what you meant." Her clear green eyes snapped in anger, but she didn't back down. She looked ridiculous, really. The front of her clothes wet, an old bandanna wrapped around her head. Gloves, much too big, covered her hands and yet...despite the costume, she radiated that certain defiance that had first caught his attention all those years ago. She tipped her little chin upward. "Bradworth paid me to finish the job."

"Consider it done."

"No way. I realize this isn't the way you do things, Hayden, but when I agree to do a job," she assured him, those intense eyes snapping green flames, "I do it. Now, you can stand there and argue with me all day long, but I'm really busy and I'd like to finish this room before I go home."

"You're a maid?" he asked, and saw her cringe slightly.

"Among other things. And right now, I have work to do. If you'll excuse me..." Quickly she leaned over the tub and twisted on the faucets again. Water rushed from the spigot and she swished the last of the scouring soap down the drain.

"What other things?" he asked as she turned off the faucet.

Sliding him a glance that was impossible to read, she explained, "Oh, I have many talents. Scrubbing tubs and waxing floors and setting mousetraps are just a few." She yanked off her gloves, and this time she dropped them into an empty bucket. Bending her head, she untied her bandanna and unleashed a tangled mass of red-brown curls that fell past her shoulders and caused his gut to tighten in memory. "Now, I've got to get home, but I'll be back in the morning."

"You don't have to do any more—"

"Oh, yes I do," she said firmly, and the determined line of her jaw suggested she was carrying a sizable chip on her slim shoulders. "I guess I didn't make myself clear. I never leave a job unfinished—no matter who's paying the bill."

"What's that supposed to mean?"

"Figure it out, Hayden," she said, as if she were harboring a grudge against him—as if *he* had done *her* a severe injustice when she had been the one who had used him.

Seethingly indignant, she grabbed her mops, pails and supplies and walked briskly past him. Her flaming hair swung down her back and her jeans hugged her behind tightly as she bustled out of the room and clomped noisily down the stairs. Hayden was left standing between the bathroom and bedroom to wonder if she was going home to a husband or boyfriend.

He heard the front door click shut and moved to the window, where he saw her load her supplies into a trashed-out old Chevy, slide behind the wheel and then, without so much as a look over her shoulder, tromp on the accelerator. The little car lurched forward, and with a spray of gravel from beneath its tires, disappeared through the trees.

"I'll be damned," he muttered again.

Well, at least she was gone. For the time being. He should be grateful for that. He reached for his duffel bag and a flash of light, a sparkle on the rim of the tub, caught his eye.

He moved closer to inspect the glitter and saw the ring that she'd obviously forgotten. Frowning, he walked into the bathroom and picked up the tiny band of gold. A single blue stone winked up at him. Simple and no-nonsense, like the woman who wore it.

He wondered if this were a wedding band or an engagement ring, and told himself it didn't matter. He'd take the damned piece of jewelry back to her and write her a check for services rendered as well as those not rendered. He didn't need a woman hanging around right now, especially not a woman who, with a single scalding look, could set his teeth on edge and his blood on fire.

Hayden Monroe! Back in Gold Creek! Nadine couldn't believe her bad luck. She never should have agreed to work for the bastard, and she had half a mind to wring Aunt Velma's long neck! But she couldn't afford to say no to the sum of money that attorney Bradworth had offered. And she'd never expected to come face-to-handsome-face with Hayden again. She'd known, of course, that someone would be staying in the house, but she thought it was probably going to be rented or sold. She hadn't expected Hayden. The last she'd heard about him, he'd moved to Oregon and was estranged from his father.

Ben had been right about Hayden and his dad. They were both cut from the same cloth—dangerously handsome, extremely wealthy; men who didn't give a good goddamn about anything or anyone. Just money. That's all they cared about. What was the saying? Fast cars and faster women? Whatever money could buy.

Hands clenched over the steering wheel, she mentally kicked herself. It was all she could do not to take him up on his offer and quit. But, in good conscience, she couldn't tell him to take his job and shove it, as she'd already spent a good part of the money. And she didn't want her two sons to lose out on the best Christmas they'd had in years because of her own stupidity.

"Damn, damn, damn and double damn!" she swore, her little car hugging the corners as she headed back to town.

She frowned as she guided the Chevy beneath the railroad trestle bridge that had been a Gold Creek landmark for over a hundred years. Hayden Monroe! As handsome as ever and twice as dangerous. She steered through the side streets of town and stopped at the Safeway store for groceries. Christmas trees were stacked in neat rows near the side entrance, fir and pine trees begging to be taken home, but she didn't succumb. Not yet. Not with the windfall she'd so recently received. Just in case she never finished the job. The trees would go on sale later. She picked up a few groceries, then climbed back into her car again, heading to the south side of Whitefire Lake.

She was irritated at having been caught by Hayden again, and was discouraged by the heady feeling she'd experienced when she'd stared into his blue eyes. But she was over him. She had to be. It had been years. Nearly thirteen years!

She only had to deal with him for a week or two. She rolled her eyes and bit her lower lip. Fourteen days suddenly seemed an eternity.

She had no choice, so she'd just make the best of it and avoid him as much as possible. She would simply grin and bear Hayden Monroe with his sexy smile, knowing eyes and lying tongue until the job was finished.

Then it was *sayonara*.

Veering off the road that circled the lake, she drove down a single lane that served as a driveway to several small cabins built near the shore. She slowed near the garage, a sagging building filled with cut cord wood and gardening supplies, and snapped off the ignition. Grabbing both sacks of groceries and her purse, she stepped onto her gravel drive. "Boys!" she sang out, not really expecting to hear a response as both bikes, usually dropped in the middle of the driveway, were nowhere to be seen and the raucous sound of their voices didn't carry in the cool mountain air. "Boys! I'm home."

Nothing.

Well, it was early. They were probably still pedaling from the sitter's.

Juggling the groceries, she reached into her purse for her keys and opened the screen door, only to find that her sons had, indeed, been home from school. The back door wasn't locked and book bags, sneakers and jackets were strewn over the couch and floor.

She left the groceries on the counter, then headed back outside. "John? Bobby?" she called again, and this time she could hear the sound of gravel crunching and bike wheels spinning.

She was carrying her mops, buckets and cleaning supplies into the house when she heard the sound of tires slamming to a stop.

"You're a liar!" Bobby's voice rang through the house, and Nadine walked to the window in time to see her youngest son, his lower lip thrust out stubbornly, throw a punch at his brother.

John, older than Bobby's seven and a half years by a full eighteen months and taller by nearly four inches, ducked agilely away from Bobby's wild swing and managed to step over Bobby's forgotten bike. Wagging his wheat blond head with the authority of the elder and wiser sibling, John announced, "*I* don't believe in Santa Claus!"

"Then you're just stupid."

"And *you're* the liar." John leered at his brother as Bobby lunged. Sidestepping quickly, John watched as Bobby landed with an "oof" on the cold ground near the back door.

Leaning down, John taunted, "Liar, liar, pants on fire, hang them on—"

"Enough!" Nadine ordered, knowing this exchange would quickly escalate from an argument and a few wild punches to a full-fledged wrestling match. "Look, I don't want to have to send you to your rooms. Bobby, are you okay?"

"We only got one room," John reminded her.

"You know what I mean—"

"John's makin' fun of me," Bobby wailed indignantly. A shock of red-blond hair fell over his freckled face as he looked to Nadine as if for divine intervention. "And I saw Santa Claus last year, really I did," he said earnestly.

"Tell me another one," John teased, sneering. "There ain't no such thing as Santa Claus or those stupid elves or Frosty or Rudolph, neither!"

Bobby blinked hard. "Then you just wait up on Christmas Eve. You'll see. On the roof—"

"And how am I s'posed to get there—fly?" John hooted, ignoring the sharp look Nadine sent him. "Or maybe Dancer or Vixen will give me a lift! Boy, are you dumb! Everything comes from Toys "Я" Us, not some stupid little workshop and a few lousy elves!"

"I said 'enough!'" Nadine warned, wondering how she would survive with both boys for the two weeks of Christmas vacation that loomed ahead. Right now, her sons couldn't get along and Nadine's already busy life had turned into a maelstrom of activity. John and Bobby seemed hellbent on keeping the excitement and noise level close to the ozone layer and they couldn't be near each other without punching or kicking or wrestling.

"You're not really gonna send us to our room, are you?" Bobby asked, biting on his lower lip worriedly.

"Well, not yet—"

"He's such a dork!" John called over his shoulder as he found his rusty bike propped on the corner of the house. "A dumb little dork!"

"John—"

"Am not!" Bobby screamed.

But John didn't listen. He peddled quickly down the sandy path leading to the lake. His dog, a black-and-white mutt named Hershel, streaked after him.

"I'm not a dork," Bobby said again, as if to convince himself.

"Of course you're not, sweetheart."

"Don't call me that!" He pulled himself up, dusted off his jeans and kicked angrily at the ground. His eyes filled with tears and dirt streaked his face. "John's just a big...a big jerk!"

This time Nadine had to agree, but she kept her opinion to herself, and hugging her youngest son, asked, "Are you okay?"

"Yeah." But his hazel eyes glistened with unshed tears.

"You sure?" Nadine asked, though she suspected little more than his pride had been bruised. "How about a cup of cocoa, with marshmallows and maybe some cookies?"

"You got some at the store?" he asked, brightening a bit.

"Sure did."

He blinked and nodded, sniffling as he tagged after his mother into the house.

Nadine heated two cups of water in the microwave while Bobby climbed into one of the worn chairs at the scratched butcher-block table. When the water was hot, she measured chocolate powder into one cup and said, "And as for Santa Claus, I still believe in him."

"Do you?"

"Mmm-hmm. But Oreos won't do for him. No siree. You and I'll have to bake some special Christmas cookies and leave them on the hearth."

Bobby sent her a look that said he didn't really believe her, but he didn't argue the point, either. "Thanks," he muttered when she handed him a steaming cup and a small plate of Oreos. "John can't help us make the cookies, neither."

"Well, if he has a change of heart—"

"He won't. He's too...too...dumb!"

Nadine blew across her cup, not wanting to condemn her eldest quite yet, but needing to placate Bobby. "Look, honey, I know how tough it can be with John. I'm the youngest, too, you know," she said, thinking of Ben and Kevin. A knot of pain tightened in her chest at the memory of Kevin, the eldest of the Powell siblings, a golden boy who'd once had it all, before his dreams and later his life had been stolen from him. Now there was just her and Ben, she thought sadly, then, seeing her son's expectant face, she forced a grin. "Remember Uncle Ben?" She dunked a tea bag into her cup, and soon the scent of jasmine mingled with the fragrance of chocolate, filling the cozy little kitchen.

"Is he a creep?" Bobby asked, his little jaw thrust forward as he dunked an Oreo into his hot chocolate.

"Ben?" She laughed, her melancholy dissolved as she stared at the hopeful eyes of her son. "Sometimes." Nadine wished that Ben were still around. He'd be home soon, after ten years in the army and she couldn't wait to have him back in Gold Creek. Ben was the only member of her fractured family to whom she still felt close.

Bobby seemed placated slightly. "Well, John doesn't know anything! I saw Santa Claus and I'm not gonna say I didn't!" he stated with a firm thrust of his little chin. He dropped a handful of marshmallows into his cocoa and watched them slowly melt.

To her son's delight, Nadine broke open an Oreo and ate the white center first, licking the icing from the dark wafer. "And what was Santa doing last year—when you saw him?"

Bobby lifted one shoulder. "Dunno," he muttered. "Prob'ly tryin' to figure out which present was mine." His brow puckered again. "I hope he gives John a lump of coal!"

"I don't think that'll happen," Nadine said as he gulped his cocoa then wiped one grubby hand across his mouth.

"Sure it will. Santa knows when John's lying. He knows everything."

"I think it's God who knows so much," she corrected.

Her son lifted a shoulder as if God and Santa were one and the same, and she didn't see any reason to start another argument. Obviously Bobby's imagination was working overtime. But she loved him for his innocence, his bright eyes and that mind that buzzed with ideas from the moment he woke up until he fell asleep each night.

"Come on, you," she said, touching him fondly on the nose. "You can help me dig out all the Christmas decorations and wrapping paper. I think most of the stuff is in the closet under the stairs—"

"Mom, hey, Mom!" John's voice echoed through the small house.

Bobby rolled his eyes and sighed theatrically. "Oh, great. He's back."

"Hey—there's someone here to see you! Says you left somethin' at his place," John yelled.

Nadine glanced out the window to see John, riding his old bike as if his tail were on fire. Hershel galloped beside him, barking wildly.

Nadine froze for an instant when she recognized the reason for all the commotion. Her back stiffened to steel. Behind the boy and bike, striding purposefully up the path to the house, his angled face a mask of arrogance, was none other than Hayden Garreth Monroe IV.

Chapter Six

Bracing herself, she walked onto the front porch, arms crossed over her chest. In his beat-up jacket, flannel shirt and faded jeans that fit snugly around his buttocks and rode low on his hips, he didn't look much like the multimillionaire he'd become overnight. He was still too damned sexy for his own good. Or hers.

"I think you forgot something," he said as he strode up the slight incline to her house. His gait was a little uneven, but that was probably due to the rocky ground rather than the result of his boating accident years before.

"Forgot something?" she repeated, shaking her head. "Believe me, Hayden, I haven't forgotten anything." She glared at him, and all the bitter memories of her youth washed over her in a flood.

His eyes narrowed and his anger was visible in the hard angle of his jaw. Digging into the front pocket of his jeans, he withdrew a ring. Her ring. Instinctively she touched her fingers, assuring herself that the band with its imitation stone was really missing. "Yours?" he asked as he climbed the two long steps of the porch.

"Oh." She felt suddenly foolish. And trapped. He was too close. Too threatening. Too male. Squaring her shoulders, she managed to find her voice. "Thanks. I didn't realize I'd left it." She took the ring from his outstretched hands, careful not to touch him. "You didn't have to go to all this trouble. I would've been back for it tomorrow."

His eyes held hers for a heart-stopping second and her lungs squeezed. Quickly he glanced away. "I wasn't sure you'd be returning."

"I said I would—"

"You've said things before, Nadine," he pointed out and the comment cut her as easily as the bite of a whip. He was insulting her, but why? She'd never done anything to hurt him. Or his family.

"Hey, mister, is that your boat?" John's eyes were round with envy as he stared at the dock where a speedboat—shiny silver with black trim—was rocking on the waves.

"It is now."

"Oh, wow!"

"You like it?"

John was practically drooling. "What's not to like? It's the coolest."

"Is this your son?" Hayden asked.

Was it her imagination or was there a trace of regret in his question? Reluctantly, she made introductions. "Hayden Monroe, my oldest son, John," Nadine introduced, and spying Bobby peeking through the window, waved him outside. Bobby came cautiously through the door. "And this is my baby—"

"Don't call me that," Bobby warned.

"Excuse me." Nadine smiled and rumpled his red-blond hair. "This is my second son. Bobby. Or are you Robert today?" she asked, teasing him.

"Hello, Bobby. John." Hayden shook hands with each of the boys, and Nadine wondered if the shadow that stole across his summer-blue eyes was a tinge of remorse.

"Are you the guy who owns the sawmill?" John asked, and Nadine's polite smile froze on her face.

"For now."

"The whole mill?" Bobby asked, obviously impressed.

Before Hayden could reply, John said, "My dad says that the owner of the place is a goddamned mean son of a—"

"John!" Nadine cried.

"Your dad is right," Hayden replied with a glint in his eye.

John's forehead creased into a frown.

"Hayden just inherited the mill from his father," Nadine guessed, glancing at Hayden for reassurance. "He hasn't owned it all that long. Daddy wasn't talking about him."

"You don't like your dad?" Bobby wanted to know, and Nadine sent up a silent prayer. She didn't want to get involved with Hayden, didn't want her children feeling comfortable with him, didn't want to know anything about his life.

"My dad's gone," Hayden said flatly. Then, as if seeing that the boy was still confused, he added, "We didn't get along all that well. Never saw eye to eye."

"My dad's the greatest!" John said proudly as he threw his mother a defiant look.

Hayden's lips turned down a fraction. "That's how it should be."

Satisfied that he'd made his point, John waved to his brother. "C'mon, Bobby. Let's check out the boat!" John was already running down to the dock.

"Be careful. Don't touch any—"

Hayden's hand clamped over her shoulder and she gasped. "They'll be fine," he said. "No need to over-mother them."

"But—"

"I'll wager they know how to handle a boat and what to steer clear of."

"You don't even know my boys," she shot back indignantly.

"Maybe not. But I do know about mothers who are overprotective."

His hand was still resting upon her shoulder, but she shrugged the warm palm away from her. "It's none of your business how I raise my children, Hayden," she said crossly.

"Just a little free advice."

"Then it's worth exactly what I paid for it—nothing."

"Boys need to explore, check things out."

"Is this something you've read or are you talking from experience?"

"I was a boy once."

"I know," she said, her heart thumping unnaturally. "I remember."

His gaze sliced into hers, and though he didn't say a word, the air seemed charged with silent accusations. To her disbelief she realized again that *he* seemed to be holding a grudge against *her*. As if in that faraway other lifetime she'd wronged him! As if he and his father hadn't altered irrevocably the direction of her life! As if he hadn't walked away from her and never so much as cast a glance back over his shoulder! Her insides were shredding, and she bit down on her lip so that she wouldn't start throwing angry accusations his way.

Standing on the porch, being so close to him was awkward. Being near him was uncomfortable. And yet she had to be polite. He was, after all, her boss as well as her ex-husband's employer. She dragged an invitation over her tongue. "If you're not worried about the boys damaging your boat, why don't you come in and have a cup of coffee?"

His dark brow arched. "Your husband won't mind?"

"Not at all," she replied quickly, and decided not to tell him that she was divorced. Not yet.

"A peace offering?"

"We got off on the wrong foot. I think we should try again." The minute the last syllable left her lips, she wished she could call the words back, but she couldn't. Silent, painful memories of their youth stretched between them.

His jaw tightened and he hesitated, glancing back at the boat. Nadine felt like a fool. Of course he wouldn't take her up on her offer. He was just returning her ring and had probably delivered it himself to fire her in person. No doubt the minute she'd left his house, he'd phoned William Bradworth, set the attorney straight in a blistering conversation, managed to find out her address and had jetted across the lake hell-bent to hand over her walking papers. Well, she'd be damned if she'd make it easy for him.

"Okay. You're on." He surprised her by accepting and following her into the small cabin.

She poured coffee into two ceramic mugs, offered cream and sugar, then followed him back outside where she could sit on the porch and watch the boys.

Nadine blew across her cup and sat on the old porch swing. Hayden balanced his hips against the weathered rail, his back to the lake, his long legs crossed at the ankles. The stiff wind ruffled his hair and brought her the scent of him— clean and male, no trace of after-shave or cologne.

"Bradworth said your name's Warne now," he observed. "You married Sam," he said without a trace of emotion.

"That's right."

"I thought he was just a friend."

"He was. Then he got to be a better one." She didn't have to explain anything to Hayden, especially something as difficult and complex as her relationship with Sam. Sam, who had once adored her. Sam, who had wanted to marry her and father her children. Sam, who even early in their marriage had shown signs of being unable to control his alcohol consumption. Nadine had thought she could help him with his problem; he'd denied that there had been a problem at all.

She swallowed a long drink of coffee, feeling the warm liquid slide down her throat. Long ago, Sam had been her friend, Sam had been safe, Sam had been there when Hayden and her family had not. Though their marriage hadn't always been happy, she didn't regret marrying Sam, not when she considered her sons. Even with the trouble John and Bobby gave her, she loved them both with all of her heart. Nothing would ever change that. Sam had given her those precious boys.

She felt Hayden's gaze upon her, and she cradled the warm cup in her fingers as she looked up at him. "What about you, Hayden? I read somewhere you were engaged to marry Wynona."

He snorted. "Didn't happen."

"You never married?"

His eyes turned an angry shade of blue. "Never." He didn't bother to explain and she didn't ask. The less they knew of each other, the better. She had a job to do and their relationship was strictly professional. The fact that she felt nervous around him was easily explained and she'd just have to get over it. Whatever they'd shared long ago had been fleeting and was definitely over.

He drained his cup as the boys tired of their exploration. John ran up the narrow path to the porch. "That's a great boat, Mr. Monroe."

"You think so?"

"Yeah, the best!" Bobby chimed in.

"I bet it goes real fast," John hinted, and Nadine wanted to die.

"You boys had better go inside—" she said.

"Would you like a ride?" Hayden asked suddenly.

Nadine nearly dropped her cup. "No!" she said, her stomach doing a somersault as she sloshed coffee on her hand.

"Would I?" John echoed gleefully. "You know it!"

"Me, too!" Bobby chimed in, jumping up and down.

This, whatever it was, couldn't happen! "Now wait a minute. You have homework and chores and—"

"Aw, Mom, just for a little while?" John asked, some of his earlier belligerence disappearing, his face flushed with anticipation. "Please?"

"Mr. Monroe is a busy man." She glanced at Hayden for help out of this one, but found him grinning at her discomfiture. She wiped her hand on her jeans. "I just don't think it would be such a good idea tonight to—"

"I'm not that busy," Hayden replied. "It's okay with me. If, of course, it's okay with you."

Both boys started begging and pleading at once. Nadine felt her cheeks flush and saw the silent laughter in Hayden's eyes.

"You don't have a great track record with boats," she said, and saw his countenance grow deathly still at the mention of the boat wreck that had nearly taken Wynona Galveston's life.

His skin stretched tight over his face, but he didn't back down and Nadine knew she'd said too much. Deep in her heart, she realized that he wouldn't hurt her children—not intentionally. And yet letting them go with him was difficult. "Do you have life jackets?" she finally asked.

"Life jackets are for babies!" John declared.

"I even have one for you," Hayden replied stonily, and Nadine had to grit her teeth. It wasn't that she wanted to deny the boys a good time, she just didn't want to get involved with Hayden in any way, shape or form.

"I don't have time," she said. "And the boys really should get started on their—"

Bobby's eyes filled with tears. Silently her youngest beseeched her. She didn't know if he was putting on an act or not, but he'd been so unhappy lately, she couldn't find it in her heart to say no to him. "I suppose it would be all right for a little while," she said, caving in and knowing that she was not only treading in dangerous waters by allowing Hayden any insight into her or her family's life, she was diving in wholeheartedly! Bobby, the little con man, was suddenly all smiles. His tears seemed to evaporate into thin air. "Be back before dark," she insisted, still trying to assert her authority. She was, after all, still the mother and therefore still the boss.

"We will!" Her sons were already running back to the dock.

Hayden slowly set his empty cup on the rail. "Thanks for the coffee—I'll bring them back soon," he assured her, but there was no warmth in his voice.

Nadine felt instantly contrite. He was just giving her children a much-needed thrill and a little male attention. "Look, I'm sorry for the crack about the boating accident, it's just that—"

"Don't worry about it," he snapped.

She glanced to her boys, already climbing into the speedboat. "I hope you know what you're getting yourself into."

"It's just a ride. Don't read anything more into it, Nadine," he said, and she felt her cheeks flush. "Believe me, I'm not getting into anything."

The kids were rambunctious and excited. They could hardly sit still, and each kept pushing the other out of the way so that he could be in the front and therefore in command. The wind tore at their hair and eyes and they laughed with an uninhibited abandon that surprised Hayden. There had been few times in his childhood when he had felt as carefree as these two rowdy boys. Maybe if he'd had a brother or even a sister to share some of the scrutiny and expectations from his two parents, he would have been able to cut loose a little as a kid and would have avoided the rebellion that had slowly become his guiding force as he'd entered high school and had stuck with him through college.

He glanced over his shoulder and saw that the little house Nadine occupied was far in the distance.

Frowning, he realized she'd changed. She was different from the girl he remembered. She had filled out and matured, her hair had darkened and her hips and breasts were curvier. Her green eyes still snapped with intelligence but her tongue had become sharper over the years, her cynicism surprising. There was a deep-seated bitterness toward him. She seemed to blame him for some injustice she'd suffered at his hand. But what?

He gnawed on his lips and his eyes narrowed. True, he'd never called her after the accident. His parents had made it crystal clear that she wanted nothing to do with him, that she'd only cared about his money. He hadn't trusted them of course, but he'd seen the canceled check, the "hush money" of five thousand dollars that his father had paid George Powell in order that his daughter didn't cry "rape."

But that was crazy. They'd never made love...not that he hadn't wanted to. They'd come close a couple of times, and Nadine had seemed more than willing, but they'd never consummated their lust because Hayden had held back, thinking that he was protecting her honor, never wanting her to go through what Trish London had endured.

He shoved the throttle all out and the boys whooped in glee. Their faces were red with the wind and spray from the water and their hair was damp against their heads. "I don't suppose either of you would like to drive," he said, and was met with loud shouts from each boy proclaiming that he should be the first to helm the boat.

"Hold on. You first," he said to Bobby. Slowing the craft, he balanced behind Bobby, ready to take over the wheel at a second's notice. The boy laughed as they cut across the choppy water, gaining speed near the center of the lake.

Impatiently, John demanded his turn at the wheel. By the time they'd circled the lake five or six times, the sky had turned a dark pewter hue. Lights glowed from Nadine's cabin, and smoke, barely visible in the fading light, curled from the chimney.

"Better drop anchor," Hayden said over loud protests from both boys.

"Just one more turn," John pleaded.

"And have your mother on my neck? No way." Hayden guided the speedboat inland and shut off the engine after mooring the rocking craft. He walked behind the boys as they scurried up the path to the front door and met their mother on the front porch.

"Look at you," Nadine said, eyeing their wet clothes and ruddy faces and clucking her tongue. "You're chilled to the bone."

Standing in the doorway, the light from the fire casting her hair in its fiery glow, she touched each boy fondly on the head. Hayden felt his diaphragm slam hard against his lungs. Her skin was creamy white, dusted with a few freckles across the bridge of her nose and her cheeks were two spots of apricot that contrasted with the deep, searing green of her eyes.

"Go on. Into the shower. Both of you," she ordered.

"But we're not dirty," John argued.

"You're wet and cold."

John looked about to argue further, but thought better of it as he tried to brush past her.

"And leave your shoes out here—"

"Yeah, yeah."

Dutifully both boys kicked off their sneakers and yanked off soggy socks before tromping inside. John turned just inside the doorway. "Oh, Mr. Monroe. Thanks."

"You're welcome."

"You can stay for dinner!" Bobby said, and Nadine's complexion paled.

Hayden, glancing at Nadine, shook his head. "I don't think so."

"Please," Bobby insisted.

"Another time." Hayden's gut twisted, and for the life of him he wondered why it was that dinner in this cramped, cozy cabin seemed so appealing. Maybe it was the house. Maybe it was the kids. Or maybe it was the woman. Another man's wife. His mouth filled with a bitter taste that wouldn't go away.

"Mom, make him stay." John pleaded.

"I don't think anyone can *make* Mr. Monroe do anything he doesn't want to."

"But he wants to. He's just bein' polite!" Bobby said, exasperated at his mother for being so blind.

"You could stay," she said, though there was more than a trace of reluctance in her voice.

"Wouldn't your husband object?"

She hesitated for a second, as if wrestling with her conscience, then shook her head. She looked about to say something, then held her tongue.

Hayden's jaw tightened. Was she the kind of woman who kept secrets behind her husband's back? Hayden had never liked Sam Warne, thought the guy was a whining, self-indulgent slob, but if Nadine had married him, she should honor her vows. Irritated, he stared at her. God, she was sensual—not in a model or Hollywood manifestation of beauty, but in a purely earthy, feminine way that bored right to his soul. Gritting his teeth, he swore to himself that he'd have nothing more to do with her. She was married and that was that. If she wanted to cheat on Sam or entertain men behind his back, so be it. But not with Hayden.

"I've got to get back anyway," he lied, trying to tell himself that the pine-paneled cabin with its river-rock fireplace and glowing coals held no appeal for him. No more appeal than the woman standing in the doorway. Before he changed his mind and decided that adultery wasn't such a sin, before he did something they'd both regret for the rest of their lives, he turned on his heel and walked rapidly back to the dock. Plunging fists deep into the pockets of his leather jacket, he bent his head against the wind. He'd go back to that morgue of a summer home, pour himself a stiff drink and try to make some sense of the corporate records of Monroe Sawmill Company. Somehow, some way, he'd shove all thoughts of Nadine from his mind.

The last person he expected to find waiting for him was his uncle. But there he was, big as life—Thomas Fitzpatrick himself, unfolding his tall body from the interior of a roomy new Cadillac that was parked near the garage. The Caddy's white finish gleamed in the light from a security lamp over the garage. Leo, barking furiously, neck hairs standing upright, ran toward Thomas.

"Stop!" Hayden commanded, and the dog, snarling lowly, did as he was bid.

"He looks like he could take your leg off," Thomas observed.

"Only when provoked." Hayden hadn't seen his uncle for a few years and he was struck again by Thomas's ageless quality. His hair was thick and white and there wasn't an ounce of extra padding on his trim body. His trademark mustache was neatly clipped and his eyes were shrewd.

Somewhere around sixty, Thomas was as sharp as he'd ever been.

"Thought you'd probably show up sometime," Thomas said as he smoothed the flat of his hand over his hair. "That's why I waited. Bradworth said you called and I thought I could clear up a few company matters."

"I can handle it," Hayden replied, slightly rankled that his uncle thought he needed help deciphering the company books.

"Well, that's good to hear." Thomas rewarded Hayden with a wide smile. "The way Bradworth talked, I thought you might be turning the whole damned operation over to charity."

"Bradworth talks too much," Hayden said, retrieving a key from his pocket and unlocking the door. He shoved it open, and Leo, nails clicking, ran through the foyer.

"He only talks to the right people." Thomas accepted Hayden's silent invitation to walk into the house. As he did, his practiced smile fell. Hayden guessed that a host of memories crept through his mind. Absently Thomas touched the rail of the stairs and his lips rolled inward. Hayden could only guess what Thomas was thinking. This had been where Jackson Moore had hidden out overnight all those years ago when the whole town of Gold Creek thought he'd murdered Thomas's son, Roy. Just this past summer, the truth had finally come out and not only had Thomas's younger son's wife, Laura, confessed to the crime, but the entire town had learned that Jackson was Thomas's bastard son.

Hayden, never close to his uncle, was at a loss for words. "Mom told me about Laura," he said, as much to break the ice as anything. "I'm sorry."

"Not half as sorry as I am," Thomas admitted as they walked into the den. "Brian's never gotten over it, I'm afraid.... He still works for the company, but..." Thomas shrugged, and his shoulders seemed a little more sloped. His life hadn't turned out as he had planned, Hayden knew. His son Roy had been killed; Brian had embezzled from the company and his wife had been found to be Roy's murderess. Toni...well, stubborn, strong-willed Toni was off to college back East and Thomas's political ambitions had all but died in the scandals involving his children. The rift between Thomas and Jackson, his bastard son, would probably never be repaired and he was estranged from his wife.

Hayden almost felt sorry for his uncle. Almost. He still didn't trust the guy. Thomas was as slippery as a seal in a tank of oil. Opening the old liquor cabinet, Hayden found a bottle of Irish whiskey with an unbroken seal. "Can I buy you a drink?"

Thomas nodded. "Guess you can afford it now."

Hayden pulled two crystal glasses from the cupboard, wiped them out with the tail of his shirt and splashed amber-colored liquor into each one. "To Roy," he said, handing his uncle a glass.

Thomas frowned, then touched his glass to Hayden's and downed his shot. "I wish that boy would've lived," he said.

"Me, too." Roy had been Hayden's friend. True, they'd oftentimes quarreled, and just before his death, Roy had proved himself to be a royal pain in the backside, but there had been years...many years while Hayden was growing up a lonely rich kid when Roy and Brian had been his only friends.

Hayden gulped the fiery liquid, feeling the heat slide down his throat. Thomas tossed back his drink, as well, and accepted another shot of whiskey in his glass.

"To your father," Thomas said, and Hayden gritted his teeth. "May he rest in peace."

"And get what he deserves." Again the glasses clinked, but Hayden sipped his drink slowly this time.

"You're still blaming him."

Hayden's muscles tightened. "I just don't like anyone trying to run my life."

The silence between them stretched to the breaking point before Thomas, in an effort to change the conversation, asked, "Where were you tonight?" He threw off a dustcover and settled into a worn leather chair. Placing the heel of his shoe on the matching ottoman, he eyed his nephew as Hayden opened the damper of the fireplace and lit the dust-dry logs that had sat for years in the grate. "I heard the boat."

Hayden tensed a little. For an unnamed reason he didn't want to discuss Nadine. "Bradworth hired a woman to clean the place. She left a ring here and I took it back to her."

"By boat?"

"She lives across the lake."

Thomas scowled and glanced through the windows to the darkness beyond. The lake wasn't visible through the glass, but lights on the distant shore winked in the night. "Who is she?"

"Someone Bradworth got from an agency in town. HELP!, I think it was."

A shadow flickered in Thomas's gaze and the corners of his mouth tightened almost imperceptibly. "Nadine Warne?"

"That's right."

Thomas's eyes darkened, but he didn't comment and Hayden was left with the feeling that their conversation was unfinished, that Thomas knew something about Nadine that he didn't. Not that he cared, he reminded himself. What she did with her life, other than cleaning this damned house, didn't affect him.

Finishing their drinks, they discussed his mother and how she was coping since Hayden's father's death. Then the conversation turned to the string of mills he'd inherited. Though the largest sawmill was located in Gold Creek, there were other smaller operations in northern California as well as in southern Oregon.

"Those mills have been in the family for decades," Thomas said, leaning back in his chair. "Especially the one here, in Gold Creek. It was the first. Monroe Sawmill is a way of life—practically a tradition—to the people of Gold Creek. When times were tough during the depression, the company store or the sawmill and the logging company kept this town afloat. Even employees whose hours had been cut back were given credit to buy food and clothing for their families.

"Gold Creek depended upon the mill and the logging operation to keep it alive."

"That was a long time ago."

Thomas waved dismissively. "I know. But in the intervening years, through two world wars as well as the troubles in Korea and Vietnam, timber provided for the people of Gold Creek. Generations have depended upon the logging company and the sawmill for their livelihoods. That all may come to a grinding halt soon enough if the government tightens up on clear-cutting and logging old growth— but in the meantime we owe this town."

"Sounds like a bunch of political bull to me," Hayden observed. "I thought you had decided against running for public office a few years back."

Thomas placed his hands on his knees and stood. His joints creaked audibly. The fire cast shadows on his patrician face and his expression was stern. "I can't tell you how to run your life, Hayden. Hell, even your father wasn't able to do that. But, one way or another, until you find a way to get rid of it, you own a majority interest in some valuable mills. Now, you can look at the corporation one of two ways—either you want it because it makes money for you, or you want it because it's the lifeblood of this community."

"I don't want it at all." Hayden studied his uncle a minute. "I thought you'd come here to try to buy me out."

Thomas's lips curved beneath his mustache and his eyes glimmered. "You remind me of Roy. He always cut right to the chase."

Hayden rolled his glass in his palms. "So what's it going to be?"

"I need a little time. Most of my cash is tied up in oil wells, at least temporarily. I'm still trying to buy some land north of here. I was interested in Badlands Ranch, but the owner is being stubborn." Thomas's eyes shadowed. He didn't like to be bested. "I'm interested in diversifying," he explained. "I've got enough invested in logging and sawmilling and I don't believe in putting all my eggs in one basket."

"Seems to me you've diversified a lot. Timber, sawmilling, real estate and oil."

"It's just a start." He clapped Hayden on the back. "I'm not going to pressure you, though. This company is in your blood whether you like it or not."

He walked out to his Cadillac before pausing at the car door. "The woman who Bradworth hired...?" Thomas asked, and Hayden felt his spine stiffen slightly.

"What about her?"

"Maybe you should tell me what's going on with that little piece," Thomas said, and Hayden's fists balled as the older man laughed. "Seems as if there's something more than the company in your blood."

"I got two days' detention," John announced at breakfast the next morning.

"For what?" Nadine asked, though she didn't really want to know. She wasn't in the best of moods. Ever since seeing Hayden again, she'd been on edge, her nerves jangled. She had to face him in less than an hour and wasn't looking forward to the day.

"Lack of respect," John answered. "Mrs. Zalinski hates me."

"She doesn't hate anyone," Nadine replied as she bit into a piece of dry toast she really didn't want.

"Oh, she hates me all right. Me and Mike Katcher. She hates us both."

Nadine chewed thoughtfully. Mike Katcher was trouble. No doubt about it. That kid reminded her a lot of Jackson Moore, a boy she'd gone to school with years before. Jackson, too, had been a troublemaker, a kid who had gotten into more than his share of fights, a boy who was constantly walking a thin line with the law. Years later, he'd risen above his past, returning to Gold Creek as a prominent attorney, a man who had cleared his murky reputation.

Nadine didn't think Mike Katcher would ever shape up. Mike's mother, too, was a single parent and she spent more time looking for another husband than she did with her son.

"Look, John, why don't you give Mrs. Zalinski a break?"

"You'd better," Bobby advised. "Her husband's a cop and he might arrest you."

"You don't get arrested for locking girls in the bathroom," John said, and then turned a deep shade of red.

"Is that what you did?" Nadine asked. "John—"

"It was Mike's idea."

"Well, maybe you should come up with your own ideas." She glanced at the clock and gritted her teeth. "Look, we're going to talk this out this afternoon. And I'm going to call your teacher and Principal Strand and Mike's mother to straighten out this mess."

"Aw, Mom, *don't!*" John cried, horrified.

"We'll talk tonight."

"Promise me you won't call."

"Tonight," she replied, as the boys clambered down from the table and hurried out the back door. Despite the first drops of rain falling from the sky, they climbed on their bikes and headed toward the sitter's home to wait for the bus.

Nadine cleared the dishes and stacked them in the sink. John was becoming more and more defiant. Until this point, she'd been lenient with him, convinced that she couldn't come down on him too hard or he'd want to live with Sam. He couldn't, of course—she had custody. But Sam had been making noise about wanting more time with the boys and if he went to court again and John pleaded to live with his father... "What a mess!"

She'd have it out with John tonight and lay down the law. If he brought up living with his father again, then she'd deal with it. Hopefully it wouldn't come to that.

She placed a call to the school asking for a conference with John's teacher, then started collecting her cleaning supplies. Before she could concentrate on her son, she had to spend the day dealing with Hayden.

She passed by the small room that had been the pantry and she frowned. Inside, the shelves were filled with scraps of leather, buttons, paint and beads. In her spare time she created earrings and pins, hair clips, studded jackets and even tie-dyed shirts, whimsical designs of her own making; she'd begun to sell some of her work and had orders stacking up for more of her "wearable art." But lately it seemed that she didn't have an extra five minutes in each day, and she needed to devote hours to her craft if she ever wanted to make enough money from it to support herself and the boys.

"Someday," she told herself as she shut the pantry door and picked up her bucket of soaps and waxes.

She climbed into her old Nova, sent up a prayer that it wouldn't die and smiled wretchedly as the engine turned over on the first try. Wheeling out of the drive, she turned toward the north shore of the lake.

And Hayden.

Chapter Seven

Hayden's Jeep, the one Nadine had seen when she'd left yesterday, wasn't parked in the drive. Though the electronic gates were open, there was neither hide nor hair of him on the grounds. She knocked on the door, and when she didn't get a response, let herself in with the key she'd received from Bradworth.

"Hayden?" she called, and his name echoed back to her through the empty rooms. Strangely, she felt more alone in the house today than she had yesterday. She observed evidence that he'd been in the house. Drink glasses had been left in the den beside an opened bottle of Irish whiskey, a sleeping bag had been tossed across the top of the huge bed in the master suite and the shower stall was still wet with drips of water. She swiped at the shower sides with a towel and wondered how long he planned to camp out here. A couple of days? A week? A month? As long as it took to sell the place? Not that it mattered, she reminded herself.

Chasing wayward thoughts of Hayden from her mind, she spent three hours on the second floor, sweeping away cobwebs, cleaning two fireplaces and polishing the floors while she washed all the bedding she'd found in the closets. She plumped and aired out pillows and kept notes of repairs that were needed, from the leaky faucet in one of the bathrooms to the gutters that were overflowing with pine needles and downspouts that were clogged and rusted.

She also created a list of supplies and was oiling the banister leading to the first floor when the front door opened and a rush of winter-cold air swept up the stairs. Startled, Nadine nearly jumped out of her skin.

Hayden, carrying two sacks of groceries, strode into the foyer and stared up to the landing where she was working. His gaze was cold as a glacier in January. "You lied," he said, his lips white with rage.

"I . . . what?"

"You lied to me!"

"I didn't—"

He dropped the bags and took the stairs two at a time to loom over her. She felt as if she were stripped bare. "I don't know what you're raving about, but you scared the devil out of me just now," she said, feeling color stain her cheeks. "I didn't hear your car—"

Grabbing her wrist, he said, "I think the devil's still in you, woman."

"You're talking in circles."

"You're not married," he said flatly, and she stiffened. His gaze raked down her body to glance at her left hand which was covered with a latex glove.

So that was it. She braced herself. "Not anymore. But I never said I was married," she replied hotly. "You jumped to conclusions."

"Then what was all that talk about your husband not minding if I stayed for dinner?" His nostrils flared in suppressed rage and his lips tightened in silent fury.

"He wouldn't."

"Of course he wouldn't!" Hayden whispered hoarsely, his face pushed so close to hers that she could see the movement of his nostrils as he breathed. "He walked out on you two years ago."

"I don't see that it's any business of yours—oh!" He jerked her roughly to him. He was so close that a wave of his breath, hot and angry, fanned against her skin.

"I don't give a good goddamn whether you're single, married or a bigamist," he snarled, his nose nearly touching hers. "But, as long as you're working for me, I expect you to be honest."

Her temper grew hot. "You're a fine one to talk of honesty, Hayden!"

"I never lied to you."

"You left—"

She heard his back teeth grind together. "Did I promise you differently? Did I say I'd stick around?" His fingers dug into her upper arms. "Damn it, woman, I ended up in the hospital and by the time I was back on my feet you were gone—vanished into thin air!" A cold smile touched his lips. "But you had what you wanted, didn't you?"

"I—wha—"

"The money, Nadine. I know about the money."

"What money?"

Dropping her hand as if it were acid, he hurried down the stairs and kicked the door shut. The door banged against the casing. "Don't you ever, *ever* make me look like a fool again!"

"I don't think I have to help you. You seem to do a fine job of that yourself."

"Son of a—" He grabbed his sacks of groceries and stormed into the kitchen.

"You arrogant, self-serving bastard!" Nadine hissed after him. "How *dare* you come storming in here full of half-baked accusations and lies!"

A crash sounded from the kitchen and a string of swear words followed.

Furious, Nadine told herself to remain calm. Usually, she could keep a level head. Even when she imagined herself in love with Turner, she'd managed to stay composed. But every time she was near Hayden, her emotions were wound tight as a clock spring, her temper ready to explode. She clamped down on her teeth and picked up her dust rag. The smart thing to do, the reasonable thing to do, was to hold her tongue and cool off. Think before she acted.

But despite her arguments to the contrary, she half ran down the stairs and dashed into the kitchen where he was picking up a coffee cup that he'd knocked over. The ceramic mug had shattered and coffee and chips of pottery had sprayed upon the floor.

"Watch out!" he warned.

"I can handle this. I'm used to dealing with spills and broken—"

"Just leave it the hell alone," he cut in. "And while you're at it, leave me the hell alone, too!" He glowered up at her, swept the pieces together with a wet towel and, under his breath, muttered something about pigheaded women.

"You know, Hayden, if you're trying to impress me with this macho routine, it's not working."

"I'm not trying to impress anyone."

"Good. Now, maybe you can explain about the money you accused me of wanting."

He threw her a dark, scornful look.

"What money?" she repeated, ready to strangle him with her gloved hands.

"The blackmail money!" He slammed a cupboard door shut. "The damned hush money."

"Are you crazy? Blackmail? What're you talking about?"

He shoved two sets of fingers through his hair. "You know, Nadine, I told myself that you were different, convinced myself that your *family* was different, but in the end you proved that you and Trish and Wynona are the same kind of women—cut from the same greedy cloth. Maybe there isn't any other kind!"

"I don't know what you're talking about—"

"Like hell!" He strode over to her and ripped his wallet from his back pocket. His face was a dangerous shade of red and his lips flattened against stark white teeth. Eyes crackling with fury he yanked out a thick stack of bills. "Here you go, Nadine. Take it and leave. Consider your job here finished!'' He slapped the bills into her hands, and she just stood there, too dumbfounded to speak. "If it isn't enough, if your deal with Bradworth is for more—just call him. He'll send you the rest.''

"I haven't finished—''

"Oh, yes, you have, Nadine. You were finished a long time ago.''

"You miserable—''

"You know where the door is.''

"I mean the job. It's not finished.''

He smiled coldly, cruelly. "Think of this as getting your walking papers.''

"You'd like that, wouldn't you? Well, forget it. I intend to do what I was hired to do.'' With strength born of fury, she flung the bills back at him. "I signed a contract to clean this house and clean it I will, whether you like it or not! If I bother you, Mr. Monroe, you can make yourself and your ridiculous accusations scarce!''

"If you bother me? You quit bothering me a long time ago.''

"Good! Then we don't have a problem, do we?''

His eyes narrowed a fraction. "I think we'll always have a problem.'' The air seemed to simmer between them. Nadine's pulse quickened and she gritted her teeth so as not to strike him. "I've got a job to do,'' she said, turning on her heel and heading back to the stairs. "And I'll get it done. All you have to do is stay out of my way!''

Easier said than done, Hayden thought as he strode to the den. Why did he let her get to him? He'd known a lot of women since he'd last dealt with Nadine. He'd worked with women, befriended few, slept with fewer still, but he'd never really trusted them. The women in his life, his mother, Trish, Wynona and Nadine had taught him from an early age about their priorities: money, money and more money.

There had been a few females that he'd met that hadn't seemed all that interested in his wealth. The women he'd dealt with in Oregon had had no idea that he was heir to a fortune, but he had been the boss—the owner of the logging company—and, for a small mill town, even the money he'd managed to make there had seemed a fortune to many of them. He'd never trusted their motives. Whenever a woman, a friend or lover, had gotten too close to him, he'd managed to cut ties with her.

Not that he cared. He whistled harshly to Leo and walked outside. A pale November sun was trying to warm the ground, but fog, in long, disappearing fingers, climbed up the trees and settled in a thick blanket over the lake.

Hayden kicked at a stone and sent it rolling toward the water. What was it about Nadine that made him see red? She wasn't always disagreeable, though he'd never met a more stubborn woman in all his life, but she had a way of rankling him to the point that he wanted to shake some sense into her or throw her on the ground and take her in a very primal way. He fantasized about her submission and realized it was his fantasy because she wasn't the kind of woman who would submit—those kinds of women turned him off. No, Nadine was a woman who knew her own mind, with a short fuse and a powder keg of emotions that was just waiting to be set off. It was the challenge in her eyes, the defiant lift of her chin and her sharp words that tied him in knots.

But she was dishonest. She'd already proved that much by lying about her marital status and trying to deceive him about the bloody money his father had paid her. Damn, what a mess!

Despite her deception, she fascinated him, intrigued him in a way that was as dangerous as it was impossible to ignore.

What was wrong with him? Just one look at her pouty lips, and he was ready to kiss her so hard, she'd have trouble breathing for days. Fool! Idiot!

Bradworth had contracted with her to work two weeks. Thirteen days were left. Surely he could rein in his emotions, manage to keep his hands off her and find a way to be civil to her for thirteen lousy days.

Shaking his head, he reached down and scratched Leo behind the ears. "I've never been a saint," he admitted. An understatement. "Dealing with that woman is probably going to kill me, but I can't let her win. If she can stand it, so can I."

Leo whined and thumped his tail.

His temper cooled, Hayden walked back to the house and locked himself in the den, trying to concentrate on the corporate records, but he heard her footsteps as she made her way to the kitchen. He called Bradworth, and asked a few questions, but was distracted by the sound of her humming an old Roy Orbison tune as she worked.

He drummed his fingers on the desk, tried to block her out of his mind and was half-crazy by noon. Angrily he slammed the books shut and convinced himself it was time for a break. Striding into the kitchen, he caught her, on her hands and knees, facing away from him, cleaning out a cupboard under the stove. His gut tightened as he noticed the way her jeans stretched across her rump and his mouth went dry when she looked at him over her shoulder, her red hair falling around her face and neck in untamed curls. "Is there something you want?" she asked him, and his vocal cords seemed to freeze.

He tried and failed to shift his gaze away from her. "I'm going out. Lock up when you leave."

"Yes, boss," she drawled, her eyes defiant. "Anything else?"

He shoved his hands into the pockets of his jeans and ignored the sensual curve of her lips. "Can't think of a thing."

She arched a fine mahogany brow, then turned back to her work.

"If you need me, you can get hold of me at the mill."

"I'll manage," she replied, never even glancing back at him and scouring the bottom of the cupboard as if her life depended upon it. She heard his keys jangle and his footsteps fade away. Once the back door slammed shut, she rocked back on her heels and blew her bangs from her eyes. She'd been able to sound cool and indifferent to him, but knowing he was in the house set her nerves on edge. She had listened for him, had expected to run into him at every corner, had found herself wondering what he was thinking. *He's thinking that he's the boss and you're the maid. That's*

*all. And you're not even a maid he wanted. So get over it
already. He's not worth it!*

If only she could.

Three hours later, she'd locked the house and driven to
Gold Creek Elementary. She hadn't seen Hayden again and
had shoved any thoughts of him aside as she sat in a small
chair at a round table in Wanda Zalinski's classroom.
Nearing forty, Wanda was slightly plump and her long black
hair, pulled back with two colorful barrettes, was streaked
with gray.

Wanda's smile was genuine. "John's not a bad kid," she
said, moving her hands as she talked. "He's just got a lot of
energy and sometimes that energy isn't expressed in a positive manner. On the playground he's a ringleader and always in the middle of trouble if there is any. He doesn't
always cause the trouble, mind you, but if there's a fight
brewing, John's there.

"He's also back talked the music teacher and been dis-
ruptive in the library."

Nadine's shoulders slumped a fraction.

"On the other hand, John's extremely bright. In fact, a
lot of times I suspect he's bored. I've given him a couple of
special assignments and he's done very well with them. Right
now, he's helping another student who's struggling."

Nadine cringed inside. John, who always taunted his
younger brother, didn't seem a model teacher's assistant.

"Oh, don't worry," Wanda said, as if reading her worried mind. "He's doing well. The boy, Tim, is improving."
She smiled encouragingly. "Academically, John's at the top
of the class, and we're working on his social skills. If you
reinforce at home, what we're trying to do here at school, I
think we'll see a vast improvement by the end of the school
year."

Nadine only hoped so.

"I . . . I, uh, was hoping John's father would come to this
meeting."

"He had to work," Nadine said quickly.

"Well, please let him know. John needs strong role models, and you can't do it alone."

"Sam will help out."

Wanda managed a pleasant smile that didn't quite reach her eyes. She knew Sam, of course. Most of the people in town did. There had been gossip at the time of their divorce; no doubt Wanda Zalinski had heard it. Wanda's husband, Paul, a deputy for the sheriff's department, had even hauled Sam into jail one night when he'd been partying too late, been pulled over and failed a breath test for alcohol.

Gold Creek was a small town. Everyone knew everyone else's business. However, if Nadine, or Sam for that matter, ever needed anyone's help, they had a web of friends and relatives that seemed to go on forever. Nadine could suffer the gossip for the security. It was more than an even trade.

His father's office felt uncomfortable. Though Garreth had only spent one or two mornings a week at Monroe Sawmill in Gold Creek, he had the most spacious office in the building. At that, the room wasn't fancy—not like his office in San Francisco—but, by the standards of this mill, the room was impressive. Carpeted in commercial grade sable brown, the office boasted built-in metal shelves and a large wooden desk. Two chairs, worn orange vinyl, were situated near the window and a battered olive green couch had been pushed against the far wall. There were three filing cabinets and the walls were covered with pictures of Little League teams who had been sponsored by the sawmill company. Hayden wasn't in any of the pictures of the smiling boys dressed in uniforms of varying colors, but he recognized some of the boys he'd known as a kid. Roy Fitzpatrick was in several, along with his brother, Brian. Scott McDonald, Erik Patton, and Nadine's older brothers, Kevin and Brian, were on some of the teams from over ten years ago. Their pictures had faded with time, but there were more recent colorful pictures of kids who were probably still in school today. Without realizing what he was doing, he checked over most of the photos, his eyes scanning the grinning faces of boys dressed in uniforms that looked as if they were made by major league manufacturers. Nadine's boys weren't among the eager group in any of the shots.

Why had she lied about being married? he wondered for about the hundredth time.

His father's secretary, a small birdlike woman of about sixty named Marie Inman, was more than eager to bring him old files and reports and keep his coffee cup filled. She refused to call him Hayden, though he'd told her several times he preferred it to "Mr. Monroe."

Most of the company's accounts, payroll records and general information were on the computer, but Hayden was calling up old information—information from thirteen years before, so he sifted through dusty, yellowed printouts and general bookkeeping records, hoping that he would discover that his old man had lied, and that the check he'd waved at him under his nose was phony.

His gut grew tight when he found what he was looking for: a check made payable to George Powell for five thousand dollars. The notation was "return on investment." Some investment. Hayden's stomach soured as he remembered lying in the hospital in San Francisco, his leg in a cast, his body racked with agony between mercifully numbing shots of painkillers.

His father had visited him. Garreth's face had been florid, his blue eyes as cold as the bottom of Whitefire Lake. "This is what that little tramp wanted, Hayden." He waved a check in front of his son's nose. "Money. That's all. When women look at you, that's what they see—dollar signs."

Hayden had tried to protest, but Garreth raged on.

"I hope to God she's not pregnant! That would kill your mother, you know. And Wynona, Lord only knows what that sweet girl thinks."

"I don't care 'bout Wynona," Hayden had managed to say. Strapped down to the bed, he felt cornered, like a bear in a trap.

"Well, you'd better care, son. Because she's planning on marrying you. That is *if* she survives. She's still in ICU, you know. Thanks to you! I don't know what you could've been thinking telling her you weren't going to marry her.''

Hayden bit back the sharp retort forming on his tongue. The truth would only enrage his father further.

"Thank God for Dr. Galveston and all his connections. Wynona's getting the best care possible."

"I'm not going to marry Wynona," Hayden said firmly as a tiny dark-haired nurse swept into the room and added something to his IV.

"Just rest," his father insisted. "We'll discuss this later."

"I'm not—"

But Garreth had already huffed out of the room and soon the medication had dulled Hayden's pain as well as his mind. He had slipped away to blissful, painless unconsciousness.

In the intervening years, Hayden had hoped that his memory had been clouded, that the check that had been shoved under his nose either had never existed and was a figment of his foggy mind or had never been cashed.

From Nadine's reaction when he'd brought up the check, he'd hoped that his faith in her could be restored. But the notation in the general accounting books was right where it should have been, written two days after the accident.

Marie bustled into the room. "Can I get you anything else, Mr. Monroe? More coffee?"

"Not now. Thanks. And it's Hayden," he said. As she left the room as quickly as she'd entered, he looked around the office, smelled the remnants of stale tobacco in his father's humidor and wondered what the hell he was doing here.

The next few days at the Monroe house were tense. Hayden and Nadine tried to avoid each other, but even in a three-storied house the size of a manor, two people did bump into each other and Nadine dreaded each meeting.

He spent some of his time at the mill, some of his time on the phone, and a little of his time outside, doing a few of the repairs that she'd brought to his attention. Nonetheless, there was still a lot of hours when they were alone in the house, and Nadine, as if she had a sixth sense, knew where he was at just about any given second.

Which irritated her. She wanted to ignore him, to pretend that he wasn't around. But she heard the scrape of his boots, or the softer step of his running shoes, and sensed when he was in the room next to hers. Several times she'd caught him gazing at her, staring at her with those intense blue eyes that seemed to scrape down her body and penetrate her soul.

There was a new anger in him, a deep rage that he tried to hide, but was evident in the harsh set of his jaw and the tense cords in his neck that bulged whenever she spoke to him.

On Friday, she couldn't stand the strain a moment longer. She had just finished cleaning the fireplace in the living room. The ashes had been hauled outside, the andirons gleamed, the mantel had been polished and the brass candlesticks actually sparkled for the first time in years.

Wiping her hands on her jeans, she glanced into the oval mirror over the mantel and caught Hayden openly staring at her. Propped by one shoulder, he leaned against the heavy woodwork of the arch separating the dining room from the living room. His frown was deep, his eyebrows drawn together and if looks could kill, she would have already been laid in a coffin by now.

"Don't tell me—this doesn't pass the white-glove test," she said, watching a tic near his scarred eyebrow.

"I don't give a damn how clean it is."

"Then you shouldn't have hired me."

"I didn't."

"I'll be done by the end of next week," she said, and hid her disappointment that he didn't seem to appreciate any of her labors. She'd spent hours polishing the piano, washing the windows and dusting the chandelier while standing on a ladder and hand-rubbing each crystal teardrop of glass. The oak floors were waxed to a deep patina, and once the crew came out to shampoo the carpets, the living room would look as grand as it had years ago when Hayden's parents had thrown parties here. However, she wasn't going to let Hayden's pessimism infect her. She'd done a good job and she was proud of it.

"You know, Hayden," she said, unable to hold her tongue a minute longer, as she ran her fingers down the keys of the piano and the room seemed to shiver with the sound, "I don't understand why you're so hostile."

"I'm not."

She held his gaze steadily. "You act as if I did something horrible to you. Something unthinkable. Or else, you're substituting your guilt for rage."

"My guilt," he repeated, unfolding his arms. "*My* guilt?"

She walked a few steps closer to him. "The other day you mentioned money—blackmail money or hush money. I thought you'd really gone off the deep end at the time, and I tried to forget about it, but I can't. Just what is it you think I did?"

"I know about the five thousand dollars."

"*What* five thousand?"

Hayden's eyes darkened in anger. "The money my father paid yours so that you wouldn't come chasing after me, or spread rumors about us or claim that we'd slept together."

"W-what—?" Nadine's mouth dropped open, and she felt the blood drain from her face.

"That's right, Nadine, I found out. The old man brought me the check, shoved it under my nose in the hospital." His lips twisted into a cruel grin. "I thought you were different."

"There . . . there was no money. Your father lied."

"I thought so, too," he admitted. "Hell, I wanted him to have told me the biggest lie of all time. But he didn't, Nadine. The check was cashed. I saw the records when I went into the company office. The check was written two days after the boating accident and it was cashed three days later. Your hush money."

"No!" Her knees felt weak, and she placed the flat of her palm on the piano, making a horrid noise, to support herself.

"There's no reason to try to cover it up—"

"I never saw a dime of your damned money, Hayden," she said, stiffening her spine. "And your information is all wrong. We lost everything—our house, our savings, even our family—because of some investment scam your father dreamed up." Shaking inside as she thought about how they'd suffered, she grabbed her pails of polish and headed for the front door. "I never thought I'd say this, Hayden, but you're just like your father!"

She tried to barrel past him, but he caught her arm and swung her around. The pail flew out of her hand, clattering to the floor. One bottle of polish crashed, the plastic containers rolled crazily upon the hardwood and Hayden placed her between himself and the wall.

"Don't you ever compare me to him," Hayden warned.

"Then stop acting like him. Stop believing lies that are all bound up in money! For God's sake, Hayden, be your own man!"

She saw his eyes blaze and the muscles in his face tense. He was breathing unevenly and his body was shoved hard against hers. Swearing, he suddenly covered her mouth with his and kissed her brutally. His lips ground over hers and he shoved his tongue between her teeth, tasting, touching, exploring.

Nadine's emotions were ragged, her patience worn thin. The assault caused her bones to turn to liquid and yet she didn't want to kiss him; she *didn't!* She tried to fight him off, but her hands, balled into tight fists ready to strike, slowly uncoiled and he captured her wrists, holding each by her side.

Her breasts were crushed, her abdomen flattened, her hips pinned intimately to his. Her mind closed to her arguments and she kissed him back, accepting his hungry tongue, her body thrilling at the feel of his hands as they released her arms and wound around her, dragging her closer still, until her clothes were suddenly too tight and she imagined herself making love to him, just as she'd imagined it years before.

He released her as suddenly as he'd taken her into his arms, and though she felt suddenly bereft, she wouldn't let him know that she tingled for his touch. "Was that supposed to convince me of something? Was I supposed to be tamed into believing all your lies? Did you think I would turn submissive because of one stupid kiss?" she threw back at him.

His eyes seared straight into hers.

"Don't ever touch me again," she warned. "As for your father's check. It never existed. You can balm your conscience any way you please, but I know the truth!"

"So do I, Nadine."

She glanced at her spilled bucket, thought the hell with it, and marched out the front door. Her hands were trembling as she started her little Nova and tears stung the back of her eyes, but she wouldn't back down and believe his horrible lies.

She thought of her father living in a retirement center; she thought of her mother, remarried and raising her teenaged children in Iowa; she thought of her oldest brother, Kevin, now dead; and she thought of Ben, wounded in the Gulf War and finally being discharged from the army. He would return to Gold Creek to nothing. Her fingers tightened over the wheel and she nearly sobbed. She could lay the blame for her fragmented family directly at the feet of Garreth Monroe.

Tears drizzled down her cheeks but she sniffed them back. She had the weekend in front of her. A long, lonely weekend. The boys would be with Sam and she would try to forget about Hayden and the emotional havoc he wreaked upon her and her family.

Could he have made a mistake?

Hayden kicked the empty pail and sent it rolling noisily toward the den. His muscles were tight, his mind cluttered and he wanted a woman. But not any woman. He wanted Nadine Powell Warne. He'd kissed her to punish her, to put her in her place by the most primal of means. Thinking about it now, he was embarrassed that he'd been so dominantly male, so savagely physical. And yet he'd enjoyed it. Kissing Nadine had turned him inside out and he'd wanted more. So damned much more.

Muttering a stream of oaths, he walked through the kitchen and out the back door. The wind was cold as it knifed through his shirt, but he didn't bother with a jacket. Inside he was hot, boiling. He headed to his Jeep. One drink at the Silver Horseshoe and then he'd decide what to do— whether to chase her down or not. Kissing her had been his first mistake.

He was about to make his second. Following her showed an incredible error in judgment, so he'd have to fight his natural instinct to take off after her.

However, as he climbed into the Jeep, he felt as if destiny had already tossed the dice. Deep in his heart he accepted the fact that later he'd wind up at Nadine's house.

"Just forget him," she told herself as she pinned up her hair, peeled off her robe and stepped into the warm tub of water. But keeping Hayden out of her thoughts would be near impossible. Even two glasses of Chablis hadn't helped. She drank the first in anger and brought the second to the bathroom, hoping that a little alcohol and a warm bath would ease her aching muscles and dull the pain in her heart.

Why she cared about Hayden, she didn't know. He was often brooding, sometimes downright surly. Oh, sure, he could be charming, even funny, but those moments were rare.

During the past week she'd caught him watching her and each time her heart had taken flight. She'd seen the passion simmering in his eyes, known he'd felt the same damned electricity charging the air between them.

But why? Why was she drawn to men who only caused her pain? She took a long swallow of wine and wished she'd forget him, that his face and body wouldn't invade her dreams and that during the day she could ignore him.

She sank down to her chin and let the water soothe her sore muscles and balm her wounded ego. She still felt the warm imprint of Hayden's kiss, though it had been hours since she'd seen him. She took a cloth, dipped it in the water and rubbed it over her lips, as if to erase any impression or memory of the feel of his mouth against hers, but the rough terry-cloth fabric only served to remind her of the taste and feel of him. She'd turned to putty in his hands and now she felt ashamed that she had. He'd treated her roughly, pulled a male-domination act that should have soured her stomach. Instead she'd nearly collapsed onto the floor and begged him to make love to her.

"Stupid woman!" she whispered, tossing the cloth into a hamper in the corner of the bathroom and finishing off her wine in one long swallow. She detested women who were involved with men who didn't respect them and she'd vowed long ago never to join that pathetic club. And yet Hayden, with one forceful kiss, seemed to have easily stolen all of her brains along with her self-respect. "Idiot," she murmured, lathering her body and letting the warmth from the water invade her tired muscles. Only one more week, then she could kiss Mr. Big Bucks goodbye—or at least walk out the door. Kissing him would only prove dangerous.

Hershel started barking on the front porch, and Nadine scowled. Maybe the boys had left behind something they needed. With a last longing look at the bath, she drained the tub and stepped onto the mat just as the pounding began.

"I'm coming, I'm coming! Hold on to your pants!" she yelled as she cinched her robe around her waist and hurried through the living room.

She yanked hard on the door and a blast of cold air rushed into the house, billowing her robe around her bare legs and causing the fire to glow. Nadine's heart lodged in her throat as her gaze collided with Hayden's.

He was windblown, his face ruddy, his hair falling over blue eyes that were dark and dangerous. Without a jacket, he stood, hands braced on his hips, his features hard and set.

Since she was paralyzed, he pushed on the door and walked into the room. "I think we need to talk."

"Didn't we do enough of that already?" she taunted, and he caught her elbow, spinning her to face him as she tried to breeze past.

"We yelled at each other."

"That's how we communicate best."

"Oh, no, lady, you're wrong," he said, his eyes catching the light of the fire. He kicked the door shut, and she visibly jumped. "We communicate best another way." To prove his point he drew her into his arms and his lips settled over hers. He tasted of whiskey. The scents of tobacco and fresh air clung to him and he kept walking until her back was pressed against the wall.

She wanted to push away, but his supple mouth moved easily over hers, not hard and demanding as it had been earlier in the day, but hot and hungry, with a desperation that caused her blood to heat and her heart to pound. Her hands were placed flat against his shoulders, but she couldn't shove him away; her strength seemed to seep from her.

"Nadine," he whispered roughly as he lifted his head and gazed into her eyes. His hands moved upward to cradle her face and he kissed her again, so tenderly she thought she might cry. His fingers found the pins in her hair, and he gently tugged until her flame-colored curls, still damp, fell around her face.

His features were suddenly tortured, as if all his well-built barriers had tumbled to the ground.

"I told myself I shouldn't come here."

"I told you not to touch me again."

"I can't stop myself."

"Willpower, Hayden," she advised, though her own was flagging. She tried to concentrate on the hateful things he'd said this afternoon, to focus her anger at him.

He traced her lips with his thumb and she shivered. "I never forgot you. I tried. But I never forgot you."

That was the alcohol talking. "You didn't recognize me that first day."

"You . . ." He touched her hair. "You've changed."

"So have you. We shouldn't—"

He pressed tender lips to hers, then lifted his head. "Where're the kids?"

"Don't worry, we're alone, but..." Her heart twisted. "...Hayden, this is wrong," she forced out, her lungs tight, her skin beginning to tingle with his touch.

"It can't be. It feels right."

That was the truth, but Nadine was afraid the wine and Hayden's sheer maleness had gone to her head. She couldn't think straight, couldn't make him understand. "You said awful things."

"So did you."

The past reared its ugly head. "You didn't call. Years ago, after the accident, I waited, believing in you, but—"

"You didn't visit."

"I couldn't...my folks...oh!" His lips trailed down the slope of her neck and his hands found the knot of her belt. Her abdomen constricted.

Stop him! Stop him now while you still can!

He slipped one hand between the folds of velour and cupped her breast. Her skin tingled. It had been so long...so painfully long. A soft moan escaped her throat as his thumb brushed over the tip and her nipple responded, puckering and causing an ache to spread deep within her.

"Hayden," she murmured as he dropped to his knees, pulling her forward and off balance enough that she had to rest her weight against him in order not to fall. "Hayden, no..." But she didn't stop him when the robe parted and his lips captured that waiting bud. Deep in the hazy recesses of her mind, she realized that she was naked, that the robe covered only half her body, that his strong hands were kneading the small of her back as he took more of her breast in his mouth and suckled. Heat swirled at the apex of her legs, and when he lifted his head, leaving her nipple moist to the cool air, she groaned.

He pressed his face into her abdomen and she felt liquid fire between her loins. Her legs seemed to spread of their own accord as he kissed the downy triangle below her navel. "Let me love you," he whispered, his breath fanning that most sensitive part of her.

A small strangled cry escaped her as he kissed her intimately. Braced against the wall, she arched closer to him, to the sweet torture of his tongue, to the ministrations of lips and teeth that sought and found, teased and conquered. She wasn't aware that her robe had fallen away and in the firelight her naked body was visible to him. She didn't realize that his shirt had been cast aside and that her fingers were digging into the sinewy cords of his shoulder muscles. She began to shudder and quake, and he slowly pulled her down on the floor, to lie with him. His hands molded over her, and he kissed her lips before tasting of the sweetness of her nipples again.

"I've dreamed of this," he admitted. "Oh, I've dreamed of this so many times...." His lips found hers again, and he guided her hand to the waistband of his jeans. Her fingers worked of their own accord, and soon he was free of clothes, his body supple and sleek. She noticed several scars on his legs before her gaze landed on the length of him, hard and proud.

"Beautiful, beautiful, Nadine," he said, poised above her.

She writhed beneath him, feeling the soft scratch of his chest hair against her breasts, smelling him and tasting the saltiness of his skin.

"I've waited a lifetime for this," he admitted.

Tears touched the backs of her eyes as his knees gently prodded her legs apart. "Me, too, Hayden. Me, too."

Their mouths met, tongues mated and Nadine lost all perception of time and space. He plunged downward and she arched up to meet him, eager for the feel of him. His movements were firm and hard, nearly angry, and she met each of his virile strokes with her own savage hunger.

The lights dimmed, the world seemed to spin, and in a breathtaking final surge, he thrust into her, falling against her and flattening her breasts as she shuddered with her own release. Thoughts reeling, her breath released in short pants, she clung to him and wished that she was thirteen years younger.

Then, they had had a chance. A future. But now they could have nothing. The course of their destinies was already set on vastly different paths. The best she could hope for was a short, passionate affair, the worst, a one-night stand.

Chapter Eight

Nadine stretched and sighed contentedly. Her dreams had been so wickedly sensual. She'd been with Hayden.... Her eyes flew open and she felt the weight of his arm around her waist, realized that the comforting warmth against her back was his chest and that the slight tickle at the back of her neck was Hayden's breath. His downy legs were angled beneath hers and she was as naked as a baby jaybird.

Oh, Lord!

She tried to scramble to a sitting position, but the hand splayed beneath her breasts pinned her close to him. "Awake?" he mumbled against her hair, and Nadine blushed.

"I can't believe that I...that you...that we—"

"Believe it," he whispered huskily, and the timbre of his voice caused a tingling to spread through her skin.

"Hayden, this is insane!"

"Maybe." He lifted her hair off her neck and placed a soft kiss against her nape.

Her silly body responded by trembling and she silently cursed herself. Sleeping with Hayden! Making love with him! Becoming one more of the women in his life who could be bought with a fancy trinket, a piece of jewelry or a few kind words. Just as her mother had predicted. A blush rose up the back of her neck as she remembered how easily, how eagerly, how desperately she'd wanted him. "This can't happen!"

"It already did." He kissed her ear, and she shuddered.

"Stop it! I'm serious—"

"So am I." He gently rotated her, forcing her to stare into slumbrous blue eyes. The hint of a smile played in the darkening shadow of his beard and for the first time since seeing him again she caught a glimmer of the boy who had captured her heart so many years before.

"We've behaved horribly," she said, but couldn't help the grin that tugged at the corners of her mouth.

"Wantonly," he agreed, his face a sudden mask of mock-seriousness. But his eyes twinkled.

"Without any responsibility whatsoever."

Nodding, he said, "We should be punished."

"Punished?"

"Mmm." He threw back the covers and his gaze raked down her body. "Let's start with you."

"Me?" she said nervously.

"You've been very, very bad." He brushed his lips across hers softly, deepened the kiss, then when she responded, drew back his head. "Uh-uh." Rolling her onto her back, he took both her wrists in one hand and held them over her head.

"Hey, wait a minute—"

"You wait," he said, his eyes darkening. "In fact, be as patient as you can." He kissed her again, longer this time, his tongue flicking into her mouth and scraping over her teeth. Nadine tried to return the kiss, to mold her mouth to his, but he lifted his head. "Patience," he growled.

"I'm not a patient person—ooh!"

Still holding her hands over her head, he ran his tongue down the length of her neck, leaving a slick impression. Her body arched upward and her nipples stood erect, anticipating his touch. So slowly she thought she might go mad, he kissed the cleft between her breasts and rimmed each nipple with his tongue. Heat exploded within her and the center of her womanhood felt empty and moist. Thoughts of their lovemaking long into the night filled her head.

His teeth found the tip of one nipple and nibbled. Nadine moaned. Her hips lifted anxiously. "Hayden."

"I'm here." To prove his point, he kissed her other breast, while his free hand lowered along her side, tickling the curve of her waist before settling against her hips. His fingers dug into the soft flesh of her rump.

An explosion deep inside rocked her and she bucked. Gazing up at him, she saw his pupils dilate and the sweat upon his forehead. So this was hard on him. Good. His muscles were tense, gleaming with perspiration.

"Patience," she whispered up at him, and with a groan, his mouth closed over hers again. His hand moved to part her legs and touch the soft wetness buried within. Her eyes closed and she lost track of time. Hayden's mouth and fingers seemed to be everywhere.

Small shudders rippled through her and she cried his name. Growling under his breath, he withdrew his hand and released her wrists. She arched upward, clinging to him, and he delved into her waiting moistness.

"Patience," she whispered throatily again.

"Like hell!" His thrusts were long and fierce and desperate as he joined with her. With a savage passion he cried out her name before collapsing against her, his sweat mingling with her own dewy sheen. "My sweet Nadine," he rasped against her hair as he breathed in thick gulps of air. "What're we going to do?"

Still wrapped in the gentle cloak of afterglow, she didn't worry. Not now. She kissed his sweat-soaked cheek, and her palms rubbed against his flat nipples. His chest hair was springy and soft.

As he rolled off her, she whispered, "Not so fast."

"What? Nadine? Again?" he said in wonder as she ran her tongue over his nipples and he shuddered. "So soon?"

His abdomen flexed as she kissed his navel, and when she lowered herself he groaned her name and gave in to the rising passion that was always simmering just under the surface whenever he was with her. Her lips and tongue played a special magic on him, and he knew in a moment of truth and ecstasy that he'd never get enough of her.

"Tell me about your marriage." Hayden was seated at the small table in the kitchen, one bare foot propped on a nearby chair as he watched her pour coffee into two mugs. He noticed her robe move with her as she worked, the hem skimming the floor, offering him a peek at long slim legs, wrapping around her breasts and nipping in at her waist. Her hair was tied at her nape and her cheeks were still pink from a night of making love.

"There's nothing much to tell. It failed," she admitted, her lips pinching a little.

"Why?"

She set both mugs on the table and, gently pushing off his foot, sat in the chair he'd used as a stool. "We grew in different directions."

"Bull."

"It's true."

"Did you love him?"

She was in the process of blowing the steam across her cup, but looked up quickly at the question. Hesitating, she set down her mug and cradled her chin in one palm. "I don't know. I... well, I believed that it didn't matter if you loved someone or not. The important thing was to like and respect the person you married. Sam was... steady, or I thought he was. And he loved me. He told me I would learn to love him the same way, that all we needed was time." She sucked in her lower lip and shook her head. "Now," she said, "I realize that I was looking for a way to escape."

"From?"

"The problems at my house. When I was finished with boarding school, my mother had already left my dad and I felt that if... if I stuck around, I'd never get free." Guilt seeped into her green eyes. "I didn't have the money for college so I decided to get married." She avoided his gaze. "People had always called me a 'romantic,' but I guess I proved them wrong." Frowning, she climbed to her feet, snapped a couple of slices of bread into the toaster and turned her back on him.

He sipped the coffee and listened to the clock tick from the living room. Each second that passed reminded him of the years he'd spent away from her. Empty years. Wasted years.

Rubbing his jaw, he decided to gamble. Until they cleared up the past, there was no way they could even think about a future. Not that he was. He had no intention of falling in love with Nadine Warne or becoming a husband to her and a father to her kids. Yet here he was, comfortable as you please, drinking coffee and waiting for toast and eggs that she cooked for him. It bothered him a little as he watched her crack eggs into a skillet. She didn't want a quick affair any more than he did. But what else was there? Maybe, if they made love enough, the excitement would wear thin, the fantasy of their youth would be replaced by harsh adult reality. Because they were just playing out their teenage frustrations, weren't they? He took a long swallow of coffee and watched her rump sway beneath the robe. In his mind he saw her white, lightly veined flesh, felt her muscles rubbing anxiously up against him like a mare in heat. Clearing his throat, he forced his gaze to the window, away from the exciting movement of her body. She was only cooking eggs, for crying out loud!

Yet, dressed from shoulder to ankle in that damned robe, Nadine Warne was sexier than most women wearing string bikinis. "Damn," he muttered, and she visibly started, spattering grease on her wrist.

Swearing softly, she turned to the faucet and ran cold water over her arm.

Hayden was on his feet in an instant and when he reached for her arm, she drew it back. "I can handle this," she said, when he tried to touch her again.

"I just want to see—"

"If you want to help, watch the damned eggs." Spinning quickly out of his grasp, she headed for the bathroom and slammed the door behind her.

Hayden felt like a fool as he slid the eggs in the pan. What the devil was he doing here anyway? If he had any sense whatsoever, he'd climb into his Jeep and head back around the lake before he got himself caught in the mystery and mystique of a woman he barely knew yet felt as if he'd known for a lifetime.

"Eggs are done," he yelled, and when she didn't reply, he set the pan off the burner and turned off the stove. He buttered the toast and slid the eggs onto small plates and had settled down to wait when she emerged from the bathroom dressed in a long denim skirt and blue sweater. Her hair was braided away from her face and a dusting of powder colored her cheeks.

"You okay?"

"Right as rain."

"And your wrist?" He glanced at the red burn mark on the inside of her arm.

"I'll survive," she replied.

"I could kiss it and make it better."

She grinned a little. "I'll bet." Then, as if the subject were already too intimate, she glanced at the table. "So you do know how to cook."

"Just the basics."

"I'm surprised," she admitted as she sat down.

"Why?" He reached for the blueberry jam and slathered a spoonful onto a piece of toast.

"I thought you had cooks and nannies and governesses to do all that."

"I did." He munched the toast and grinned, dabbing at a spot of jelly near his mouth. "But I walked out on my family after the accident and I learned by trial and error."

"Walked out?" She had been pronging a piece of egg, but her fork paused in midair. "Why?"

"The old man and I had a falling-out."

She waited, watching his facial muscles alter. Gone was his good mood, and in its stead was the same darkness that she'd begun to recognize. "You fought."

"More like a war."

"Over what?"

His eyes glittered with pent-up fury. "Over the worst possible thing—a woman."

"Wynona," she said aloud.

"Bingo."

"He thought you should marry her."

He hesitated for a beat, then nodded quickly. "That was the gist of it. I didn't think he should tell me who I should marry or when or even why. We started shouting at first, then, before you knew it, I threw a punch at him. That was it. By the time my mother found us, we were both panting and swearing and had done significant damage to the other. Mother tried to send me to my room. I was nearly nineteen, and instead I walked out the front door."

"But you returned?"

"Not until I'd proved myself, my own way."

"What about your parents—?"

"I hurt them," he said quietly. "Especially my mother. The old man, he had it coming, but I should've thought of my mom. She wasn't the best mother in the world, but, in her own way, she tried, and for the first six months after I left, I let her wonder if I was alive or dead. They sent out private investigators, of course. Eventually one of them caught up with me, a slimy bastard named Timms, but there was nothing they could do. I was legally an adult. So I told the P.I. to take a hike and then called my mother." He tossed a scrap of his toast into his partially congealed eggs. "I agreed to keep in contact with her if she'd call off her dogs. So we came to an understanding. I lived my life my way—they lived theirs differently. My dad was predictable. He cut me out of his will."

"But then how—?"

Hayden's mouth twisted into a cruel grin. "I guess he had a change of heart. Either that, or he knew that by giving me most of what he'd worked for all his life, he was taunting me from the grave.''

''Oh, Hayden, you can't really believe he would do anything so cruel.''

''You didn't know my old man, though, did you?'' he spat out, his lips flattening over his teeth. ''What was it you said the other night, something about him scamming your father?''

She swallowed hard.

''What was that all about?''

Nadine saw no reason to lie. She'd spent the night making love to him, the least she could do was explain to him why he was the last man on earth she should have taken to her bed. ''As I said, my father handed every dime he'd ever earned to your dad, invested in some oil wells that were nearly guaranteed to make him rich. He had plans that wouldn't quit. College for all three of us kids. A new house and car for Mom. Retiring with money in the bank. But he came home one day and told us that it wasn't going to happen. That the well was dry, so to speak.''

His eyes narrowed. ''Go on.''

She shuddered at the memories, and the cold spot in her heart seemed to grow. ''It was as if all the life went out of my folks' marriage. Mom kind of clammed up. Not too long after that my oldest brother, Kevin, decided he couldn't handle life anymore and ended it.''

Hayden's face was grim. ''Because of the money?''

She shook her head quickly. ''Because of a girl he was in love with. She didn't love him back.

''Kevin's death was more than my mother could handle. She divorced Dad and left us. Ben was through with high school and had joined up with the military and I was still away at school. Mom offered to take me to Iowa with her, but I decided I'd rather come home to be with Dad.''

''And Sam?'' he asked.

''And Sam.''

He rubbed his temples with his fingers as if suddenly tired, but he didn't say a word and she felt compelled to continue. If he really didn't know the truth, it seemed imperative for him to understand her.

"I don't know what happened to your five thousand dollars, Hayden. If my dad got it, he never let me know about it. I assume that the money went to pay some bills or maybe for my schooling. We were always behind. However, there's always the chance your father lied."

"I saw the notation in the company books."

"Books can be fudged," she pointed out. "Did you see the check—the endorsed check—that proved my father got the money? And what does it matter if he did? It wasn't hush money, Hayden. It was repayment of a very small part of a debt. That's all."

Tipping his chair back, he stared at her. "I wonder what would have happened to us if there had been no check."

She wasn't a fool and knew he wasn't, either. She shook her head and swallowed a gulp of coffee. "Nothing would have changed. You were from one world, I was from another. I'd like to believe that circumstances kept us apart, but I know better. If we had really wanted to be together, our families wouldn't have mattered.

"As for right now, we both know that what happened between us last night was probably a mistake." She felt her throat catch on the words, but had to go on. There was no reason to delude themselves, much as she wanted to. "We both felt . . . pent-up sexual energy. That's all."

He scraped back his chair and carried his plate to the sink. "We're wrong for each other. We both know it."

"Or so we've been told," he pointed out.

Her silly heart fluttered a bit and her palms began to sweat. She should leave well enough alone. She knew it. But she couldn't. "Are you trying to say that you want something more permanent? A woman with two preadolescent boys?"

He whipped around, his eyes dark. "I'm not the marrying kind," he said gruffly.

"Just the quick roll in the hay, let-me-show-you-how-we-communicate kind, right?" She felt her temper beginning to rise.

"I didn't make any promises."

"Good. Then you don't have any to break, do you?"

He strode over to her and physically lifted her from her chair.

"Without a doubt, you're the most beautiful and frustrating woman I've ever—"

"Put me down!" she commanded, her eyes snapping fire, her heart breaking a thousand times over, though she wouldn't let him know it, not while she had an ounce of pride left. As he removed his hands, she furiously wagged a finger in his face. "I may be a lot of things, Hayden, but I'm not a woman who likes to be manhandled or shoved around or treated like a member of a lesser sex. I've spent the past two years standing on my own, making my way in the world, taking care of my boys—and no man, not you or anyone else for that matter, has the right to physically restrain me or tell me what to do in my own house." So angry she was visibly shaking, she added, "I don't remember inviting you over, Hayden, so rather than insult me any further, why don't you just walk out the door?"

His jaw tightened and the muscles in his neck bulged.

"I mean it. You obviously are looking for a way out of this.... Well, you've got one. I didn't seduce you and I didn't make any promises, either. So there's no reason for you to think that just because we spent the night together I expect some claim of undying love. I'm not seventeen anymore, Hayden. I'm a full-grown divorced woman with two boys. Believe it or not, I don't want a husband any more than you want a wife!" She flung her arm wide, taking in the expanse of her small cabin. "This may not look like much to you, but it's mine. Mine and my boys', and we've done just fine without you all these years. So just because you showed up on my doorstep, took the kids for a boat ride and somehow ended up in my bed, don't think I expect or *want* anything more."

"You're satisfied with an affair?" he asked, his features granite-hard.

"It's hardly an affair. An affair indicates that we cared for each other and the truth of the matter is we hardly know each other. I believe in telling it like it is, and it's history. It was nice, don't get me wrong. I enjoyed it, but it was only a one-night stand and it's over." Her insides were crumbling as she said the words, but she held her head high, intent upon making him believe her. She didn't want him to think that she did care for him, that she always had. She believed in clean breaks, even if the result was a cracked heart and shattered dreams.

"A one-night stand," he repeated, his lips barely moving. "A 'nice' one-night stand. You 'enjoyed it.' Do you hear yourself? What we did didn't even brush 'nice.' It was hot and wild and probably the best sex of my life. But it wasn't 'nice.'"

She cringed inwardly, but tilted her chin up. "And we both agree it's over."

"No way." He grabbed her again, and this time he kissed her, his lips clamping over hers, his hands manacling her wrists so that she couldn't push him away. Her knees threatened to turn to water, her heart pumped, her blood pounded in her temples at the assault of his tongue and mouth, and tears threatened her eyes. She stood stiff as a board, refusing to respond, denying that he had any power over her whatsoever. When he finally lifted his head and released her hands, she reacted swiftly, slapping him so hard that the smack resounded through the room and Hershel, from his position under the table, growled.

"It takes two for a relationship, Hayden, and I'm not going to be a part of something just for the sex. One-night stands and affairs aren't my style. You're the first man I've slept with in years...the only man I've slept with besides my ex-husband. I really don't believe in hopping into bed without some emotional commitment."

"There's that word again."

"I'm not talking marriage, Hayden," she said, managing to keep the sound of misery from her voice, though she felt wretched. "I just think two people should know each other, like each other, respect each other, before they take their relationship a step further."

"But you told me we don't have a relationship."

"That's right, we don't. What we have is a mistake. I work for you. You're my boss. But you're not my lover. At least not any longer." Her heart was thudding so loudly, she thought he could hear it; her fingers were clenched into fists that ached.

Slowly Hayden turned and walked to the back door. "It doesn't have to end this way."

Her heart was shredding into tiny little pieces. "Of course it does."

"Nadine—"

Knees threatening to crumple, she said, "Look, Hayden, let's be honest. You're not staying in Gold Creek forever and I'm not leaving. The most we could have together is a few weeks." Tears threatened her eyes but she held them at bay. "That's just not good enough. Not for me."

His eyes narrowed. "You do want marriage."

"Maybe," she had to agree. "Someday. But more than that, I don't want to be the talk of the town. I have a reputation and children to consider. Goodbye, Hayden." Her voice nearly caught as she watched him walk out the door. A few seconds later, she sagged against the wall and wondered if she'd made the worst mistake of her life. Last night she hadn't considered the fact that she could get pregnant, or that he could unwittingly pass a disease to her. She'd been foolish... beyond foolish, but she wouldn't be again. She was a mother, for crying out loud. She had responsibilities. She couldn't act so rashly. She couldn't let passion or lust sweep away all her common sense.

"Never again," she vowed, and wondered why that horrid thought scraped the bottom of her soul.

The huge summer house looked like a tomb. Inside, it was cold and dark. Flooding the house with electric light didn't add an ounce of warmth. Compared to Nadine's small cabin, filled with the scents of banked fires, meals once cooked, fresh coffee and Nadine's perfume, this rambling old summer home came up short. Big and beautiful, it was like every other object in his father's life: ostentatious and frigid.

Her cabin had been cluttered with shoes left on the back porch, jackets hung on pegs near the door, bicycles propped against the garage and afghans tossed carelessly over the arms of the couch and backs of chairs in the small living room. Cozy. Warm. Lived-in. *Loved.*

There had been life in that small cabin and, of course, there had been Nadine. He remembered her as she'd answered the door, still damp from the bath, her wet hair curling around her face, her robe allowing him a provocative glimpse of her skin.

"Hell," he ground out. The walls of the house seemed to close in on him. He considered a drink, but it was still hours before noon. Besides, the last time he'd had a drink he'd ended up at Nadine's house making love to her.

Spoiling for a fight, he whistled to Leo and walked back to his Jeep. He'd forget her by throwing himself into the problem at hand: what to do with the damned mills.

He didn't want to think what he was going to do with her.

He drove like a demon, hoping that speed would dull his need of her, hoping to shove all thoughts of her from his mind. He would spend a few hours with the books in his father's old office, then he'd walk through the sheds and talk to some of the employees, get a real feel for this cog in the operation of the chain of sawmills that were spattered around the state as well as in southern Oregon. He planned on visiting each individual operation, and this was as good a time as any. If he timed it right, the trip would take about two weeks, hardly long enough to get Nadine Warne out of his system, but a damned good start.

She'd made it clear how she felt about him, and he wasn't going to try and change her mind. He'd never forced himself upon a woman and didn't intend to start now, no matter how much his body wanted her. Shifting down, he took a corner too fast, eased up on the throttle and managed to round the hairpin curve and keep the Jeep in once piece. "You've got it bad, Monroe," he told his reflection in the rearview mirror. He'd never had to chase a woman down and charm her into his bed. More often than not, he was the

one who'd been seduced. No woman had seemed worth the
trouble and challenge.

No woman except Nadine.

But she was out of his life.

Forever.

Chapter Nine

Hayden was gone. His Jeep wasn't parked in the drive, the old dog had disappeared, an answering machine, its red light already blinking, was hooked up to the telephone in the den and the sleeping bag he'd flung over the bed in the master bedroom was missing. He'd left. Without a word.

Nadine frowned to herself. This was what she'd wanted, wasn't it? A life without Hayden. She'd told him as much. So why should she feel any sense of depression? She usually wasn't a person to dwell on her mistakes, but she'd spent the remainder of her weekend thinking about Hayden and all the ramifications of making love to him. She'd kicked herself for not considering all of the problems that might arise *before* she'd tumbled into bed with him, but what was done was done, and now she had to live with the consequences.

Still, she felt a deep disappointment that he'd left. True, that without him her work would be easier; she could finish cleaning the old house more quickly and she wouldn't have to deal with the embarrassment of facing him again. Yet she was frustrated. No doubt about it. She'd put a little extra care into choosing her work clothes, fixing her hair and applying her makeup, silent testimony to the fact that she did care about him, if only just a little.

She spent the day finishing her intense cupboard-by-cupboard cleaning of the kitchen, then stripped all the floors. The stain in the foyer where Hayden had kicked over her bucket and some polish had spilled took hours of elbow grease. The telephone had rung several times while she was working, but she'd ignored it, and the answering machine had always clicked on. She hadn't heard the messages as she'd always been in another part of the house, but as she flung her jacket over her arm and picked up her supplies to leave, the telephone jangled again. This time she was near the den and couldn't help but overhear the one-sided conversation.

"Hayden?" A female voice asked, and then paused. "You there? It's me again. Wynona."

Nadine's heart seemed to slam through the floor.

"Hayden? If you're there, pick up," Wynona commanded. A few tense seconds of silence. "Great." Another pause followed by a lengthy sigh. "There's no reason to avoid me. You can't. You *owe* me." Nadine sagged against the wall, and Wynona's voice turned wheedling. "We've been through a lot together, baby. Let's not fight now. Give me a call. I'll be home all night, waiting to hear from you." After a few seconds, she clicked off, and Nadine, unaware that she'd been holding her breath, expelled the air in her lungs in a rush.

So Hayden was still involved with Wynona Galveston. Nadine's stomach soured at the thought, but she told herself not to jump to conclusions. The call was ambiguous and could mean anything. Besides, it didn't matter; Nadine had no claim to Hayden's affections or his attention. Just because they spent one night of lovemaking together... She let out a little strangled sound and then mentally kicked herself. She wasn't a simpering, love-besotted female, and she had lived long enough to accept that humans were sexual creatures. Her night with Hayden was either an act of rebellion or sexual fantasy, but it had nothing to do with love, so whatever his relationship was with Wynona, it didn't matter.

She argued with herself during the drive home and tried not to think of the last man she'd cared for. Hadn't Turner Brooks ignored her affections and fallen in love with his long-ago lover? Hayden would probably do the same and turn back to Wynona.

Yes, but you didn't sleep with Turner. You didn't make love with Turner. You didn't fantasize about living the rest of your life with Tur— "Stop it!" she ground out, switching on the radio and listening to a Garth Brooks recording of love lost.

Furious with herself, she snapped off the radio and pulled into the drive. She was too busy to dwell on Hayden or Wynona or anything but her sons, who, already home, tore out of the house at the sound of her car. They both flung themselves into her arms, and for the first time since hearing Wynona's voice, she felt better. As long as she had John and Bobby, who needed Hayden Monroe?

"I got an A on my math test!" John crowed. "And Tim, the kid I'm helping, he got a C, his best grade ever."

"Good for you." Nadine gave her oldest a squeeze.

"I didn't have a test," Bobby chimed in, not to be outdone. "But I made a new friend. His name is Alex and he just moved here from . . . from . . ."

"From Florida, you dweeb. His sister's in my class."

"I'm not a—"

"Of course you're not," she intervened, throwing her older son a warning glare. "And you, John, quit insulting your brother." Nadine kissed Bobby's forehead and rumpled John's blond hair. "Come on, you guys can help me fix dinner."

"What're we having?" John asked suspiciously.

"Hot dogs with whatever you want on them."

"All *right!*" Bobby shouted, seeming to have forgotten his older brother's insults.

After dinner, she helped the boys with their homework, then forced them into showering before they fell into bed.

She spent the next three hours sewing and gluing studs and beads on a faded denim jacket that was an integral part of her collection. By the time she'd cleaned the kitchen and read her mail, it was one o'clock in the morning. Her head sank into the pillow and she hoped for exhaustion to claim her. It didn't. Though she was so tired she ached, she couldn't sleep. Wynona's message played and replayed in her mind, and Nadine was left to wonder why she should care so much about Wynona Galveston.

Each day she expected Hayden to return, and each day she was disappointed. On Wednesday she received a letter from her brother, Ben, telling her that he was returning to Gold Creek before Christmas.

Thursday, she met her father downtown for lunch. He lived in a retirement center that was within walking distance to the heart of Gold Creek, but she always drove him to the restaurant. George Powell, at sixty, was no longer strapping. He walked with a cane, courtesy of a slight stroke several years earlier, and his hair was thin and gray. His apartment was small but adequate and he seemed comfortable if not happy.

As he eased his bulk into a worn red vinyl booth of his favorite restaurant, the Buckeye, he looked at his daughter. "Heard you been working for Monroe's attorney."

Nadine was flabbergasted. "How'd you hear that?"

"This is a small town, missy. Bad news travels fast."

"Aunt Velma!"

"So it is true. Keerist A'mighty!" He swiped a big hand over his forehead. "What the hell do ya think you're doin', Nadine?"

"Dad, relax."

The waitress brought them plastic-encased menus, but they ordered without even glancing at the special of the day. "I heard Hayden's already taken over the house on the lake," her father said, once they were alone again. "Probably couldn't wait to get his hands on his old man's money."

"You hear a lot," she said, the muscles in her back tightening defensively.

"It's true, isn't it?"

She lifted a shoulder. "It's true—about him being there. Or at least he was. But I don't think he's interested in the money."

"Everyone's interested in money. You, me, your ma. Everyone. Hayden ain't any different, so don't you be puttin' him up for sainthood."

"Wouldn't dream of it," she said dryly.

"So he's at the house where you're working?"

"He was."

"Keerist!"

"It's a job, Dad," she said, though the lie tripped on her tongue. "Nothing more."

His green eyes, so like hers, sparked with disbelief. He looked about to say something more, thought better of it and played with the cellophane wrapper on a pack of crackers. The waitress brought their lunches—a bowl of soup and a chili burger for her father and a patty-melt with coleslaw for her. She was halfway through her sandwich when he asked, "Heard from your ma lately?"

Nadine's heart squeezed when she noticed the carefully disguised pain on his face. "Not recently."

His gray brows lifted a fraction, but he didn't say a word. They talked about everything and nothing, starting with the weather and ending with a rather heated discussion on how she should raise her boys.

By the time her father had paid the check, a ritual he insisted upon though Nadine paid half the cost of his rent each month, she slipped him the letter from Ben. A smile played upon his features as he read the contents of the letter. "He'll be back soon."

"In time for Christmas."

"Well, that's something to celebrate." He tried to hand the letter back to Nadine, but she slid it into the breast pocket of his wool jacket.

"You keep it, Dad," she insisted.

Outside the restaurant, the weather was cool. A pale sun pierced through the clouds, but the November wind was harsh as it tugged at Nadine's hair and brought color to her father's cheeks. Stiffly, her father slid into the front seat of her Chevy. She drove the few blocks to his apartment and stopped. Before he stepped out of the car, he turned to Nadine. "God gave you more than your share of brains, missy. If you use them you'll know that Hayden Monroe is trouble. Just like his old man."

"Dad." She touched him lightly on the arm to restrain him, and her heart was suddenly in her throat. She hated to ask the question preying upon her mind, but had to know the truth. "Hayden told me that his father paid you money. Five thousand dollars. To make sure that I would drop out of his life." A denial seemed about to form on her father's lips, so she added, "Hayden saw the check years ago and looked into the company books a few days ago."

"That son of a bitch!" Her father swore angrily and stared through the windshield to the rambling retirement complex he'd called home for two years.

"Dad?"

George let out an angry sigh. "Garreth paid me back some of the money I invested with him—a small part. I gave him nearly fifty thousand dollars, all our savings and the equity we had in the house at the time, and all I got back was five grand." He looked down at his feet, suddenly embarrassed. "Your mother called me a fool and she was right. When I finally got the check from Garreth, I handed over the money to her. I figured it was hers. Some of that money went to your education in that boarding school." He blinked suddenly, and his face seemed to age twenty years. "It broke Donna's heart, y'know, and broke us up. That investment with the Monroes was the beginning of the end." He shoved open the car door and eased himself out. "I can't really blame her, I suppose. Stan Farley has a huge farm in Iowa and he could give her everything she wanted." He glanced at his daughter as they walked up the cement path to the front door of his studio apartment. "Is she happy?"

Nadine nodded because she couldn't trust her voice. A searing pain still burned deep in her heart. Donna Powell Farley had found contentment with another man, over three hundred acres and two children who were not much older than her grandchildren. Stan Farley was a stable man, a decent man, a man whose finances were secure.

"Good, good," George muttered. "She deserves happiness." Resting a knotty hand on his daughter's shoulder, he added, "That's why you should keep your distance from Hayden Monroe. He's nothing but trouble and he'll only bring you heartache."

That much was true, she hated to admit. "So how about you, Dad? Are you happy?"

"Can't complain," he said, holding open the glass door for his daughter. "Got everything I need, right here at Rosewood Terrace."

Every muscle in Hayden's body ached from spending five days on the road. He'd logged in fifteen hundred miles and visited seven mills, talking with the employees, watching them at work, noting the condition of the equipment, stores of logs, contracts with logging companies and inventories of raw lumber. His had been a cursory scan at best, each individual sawmill would have to be reevaluated in depth. What he learned by talking to the men was their concerns of losing their jobs as there was less old-growth timber being cut due to dwindling resources, environmental concerns and government restrictions.

Most of the workers had been timber men for generations; their fathers and grandfathers had been part of a working tradition of men who had harvested trees and turned the forests into planed boards. The men knew only one craft.

Hayden climbed out of his Jeep and felt the weight of the world on his shoulders. Bradworth and Thomas Fitzpatrick had been right. People's lives and livelihoods depended upon him and his decision. How many employees, men and women alike, had shaken his hand and smiled at him and mentioned that they were glad the mills were still in Monroe hands? He'd noticed their worries—the knit brows, the eyes that didn't smile, the lips that pinched at the corners and he sensed the unasked questions of the workers: *Will I be laid off? Will you shut the mills down? Will you*

*sell the machinery off, bit by bit? What will I do if there's
no work? How will I feed my family, pay my bills, send my
kids to college?*

Leo bounded into the bushes, scaring up a winter bird
as Hayden trudged to the back porch and wiggled off one
shoe with the toe of his other.

He opened the back door and stopped dead in his tracks.
The house smelled of oil and wax, and every surface
gleamed. The chairs were pushed carefully around the
kitchen table where a crystal vase was filled with several
kinds of fragrant flowers. Brass fixtures sparkled and the
old wood floor shone with a fresh coat of polish.

Nadine. He felt a hard knot tighten his gut as he walked
through the place and saw traces of her work—special
touches such as the rearranging of pictures on the mantle, a
grouping of candles on a table, another vase filled with
flowers.

What was she trying to do? She'd been hired to clean, for
crying out loud, and now it seemed that she had put her
special stamp on the house. Blankets had been folded and
tossed over the arm of the old couch in the den. Dry logs
and split kindling had been set in each fireplace.

He climbed the steps to the second floor and noticed that
each bed was made with clean bedding. In the master bedroom, the king-size bed was freshly made, one window
cracked open to let in clear mountain air, dry kindling
stacked on polished andirons in the fireplace and a large
glass bowl half filled with water and floating blossoms rested
on the bureau.

He smiled despite himself. Maybe she'd forgiven him.
Then he caught his image in the mirror—his dirty jeans,
faded work shirt, sawdust-sprinkled hair and a stupid grin
pinned to his face. Because of her. What a damned fool he
was! Glowering at his reflection, he turned and walked
briskly into the bathroom, intent on cleaning up and for-
getting Nadine. Obviously she was through working here.
The flowers had to be the last touch; so he didn't have to
worry about her again.

That particular thought was disturbing, though he didn't stop to analyze why. Eyeing the tub where he'd found her ring, he noted a bowl of colored soap and matching towels placed carefully on the racks. He twisted on the shower spray, stripped and tried to wash the grime and dirt and aches from the last few days from his body. He'd kept himself so busy that he hadn't had time to think about Nadine and whenever thoughts of her had crept into his mind, he'd stubbornly shoved them into a dark corner.

But now that he was back in Gold Creek, with only the choppy waters of Whitefire Lake separating them, he couldn't easily drive his images of her away. He leaned against the tiles and let the water cascade over his body. The steamy jets felt good; the only thing that would've felt better was Nadine's supple body lying underneath his. He remembered kissing her, touching her face, delving deep into the warmest part of her...

To his consternation, his thoughts had turned a certain part of his anatomy rock hard. Gritting his teeth, he twisted off the hot water spigot and sucked in his breath as the icy spray sent sharp little needles of frigid water against his skin. "Damn you," he muttered, and he didn't know if he was talking to himself or to Nadine.

Nadine checked the kitchen clock again and frowned to herself. Sam had promised to pick up the boys from basketball practice and drop them off. She dusted her hands on her apron, let her sauce simmer and told herself not to worry. They were less than an hour late; maybe Sam had decided the boys needed a little extra time to work on their shots. And yet...a niggle of doubt crawled through her mind. Sam knew that she was cooking dinner for her sons, that they'd both need a shower and they each had to tackle their homework assignments.

She glanced out the window and her eyes strayed to the lake and beyond to the thicket of trees she knew guarded Hayden's house. Her heart nearly stopped when she saw the lights glowing softly through the winter-bare branches.

So he was back. Or if not Hayden, someone close to him. Though she had told herself that she didn't care, that her job with him was nearly finished, that she had scrubbed her last cobweb out of the Monroe house and had composed a list of repairs that needed to be made, she felt her heart turn over. If only she could see him again. Maybe go over to the house for a final touch-up.... But she couldn't. She wouldn't. Instead, she'd spend the time writing down the names of a few local handymen and send the list to Bradworth in San Francisco. The lawyer, or Hayden himself, could oversee the mending of the porch rail and replacement of the gutters and so on. As for Nadine, she was out of there.

She felt a deep loneliness when she thought of Hayden, but she told herself firmly that she was over him. She glanced at the clock again, and lines of worry furrowed her forehead. She turned down the burner where the hot water was boiling, just as she heard the sound of a car in the drive.

"What's for dinner?" John demanded as he burst through the back door. Wrinkling his nose as he eyed the sauce, he sighed theatrically and rolled his eyes. "Stroganoff. Again!"

"I thought you liked Stroganoff."

"Bobby likes it. I hate it. I like goulash."

She could never seem to get this straight. "That's right. Well," she said, touching him fondly on the nose, "next time we'll have goulash. Now go shower. When you get out, dinner will be done. And help your brother—" Glancing worriedly to the back door, she asked, "Where is he?"

Avoiding her gaze, John licked his lips nervously and shifted from one foot to the other. "Bobby fell asleep in the car."

"But the school's only ten minutes away."

"Yeah, but... he was real tired." Without any further explanation, he dashed through the living room. Nadine heard the bathroom door shut as Sam, hauling a dead-to-the-world Bobby, walked into the kitchen.

"What happened to him?" she asked, worried that Bobby was coming down with some virus. Usually after a practice he was so wound up that she had to calm him down. Tonight he was fast asleep.

"I guess practice just did him in."

Nadine touched Bobby's forehead. Her fingers came away cool.

"Yeah, we really worked the boys," Sam said as he carried Bobby into the living room and laid him gently on the couch. Bobby sighed but didn't open his eyes. The smell of smoke mixed with stale beer, a scent Nadine recognized from her years of marriage to Sam, clung to her ex-husband, and she was instantly angry.

"He's not even sweating," she said.

"He was—"

"Somewhere where he shouldn't be." Sick inside, Nadine plucked a kernel of popcorn from Bobby's jacket. "Snacks after the game?" she asked, already knowing and dreading the answer. Anger surged through her blood.

"Well, you know how it is. Phil and Rick wanted to have a beer after the practice, so we stopped at the Buckeye for a quick one."

Nadine's back teeth ground together and silent rage swept through her. "While you were having your 'quick one,' what were the boys doing?"

Sam's face flushed scarlet and a defiant glint shone in his eyes. "I left them in the car. But I could see them through the window and I took them each a cup of popcorn—"

"Sam, how could you!"

"It was only for twenty minutes, Nadine!"

"But they could've been . . . oh, God, who knows what kind of scum lurks in the parking lot of the Buckeye at night. They're just children!"

"And they're fine, aren't they!"

"They could've been kidnapped or hurt or—"

"But they weren't, were they? They're both right as rain."

"I don't care."

"Listen, Nadine, I needed to talk to the guys," Sam nearly shouted. Then, as if hearing himself, he lowered his voice and plowed his fingers through his thinning blond hair. "With all the changes coming down at the mill, who knows what'll happen to our jobs."

"You could've brought them home first," she hissed, her temper still soaring.

Sam was unrepentant. "The Buckeye is only a few blocks from the school. It didn't make sense to come clear up here—"

"Clear up here? What is it—four, maybe five miles? Damn it, Sam, you could've called me. I would have picked them up."

Sam grimaced painfully. "I was busy. Me and the guys, we had things to discuss. Things you probably already know about."

"Things?" she repeated, not following this new twist in the conversation.

"Monroe. The Fourth. I heard he was already here, giving the boys a ride in the boat, making himself at home. With my kids!" Disgust curled his lip. "Jeez, Nadine, don't you ever learn?"

"I don't see what Hayden has to do with this!"

"Don't you? You can't be as blind to him now as you were in high school!"

She started to protest, but Sam was just warming to his subject. "What with 'Junior' owning the mill now, big changes are in the works. It's no secret that he plans to shut us down along with all his mills. Maybe one at a time, maybe all at once, but he'll close mills and consolidate or sell the entire chain of 'em, but believe me, whatever he decides, it won't be good for any of us. Including you. If I'm not working, I won't be able to come up with the support payments, so you'd better hope that 'your friend' keeps the mill open or he sells it to the employees."

"He's not my 'friend.'"

Sam lifted a skeptical thin blond brow and his nostrils flared a little. "Yeah, well, it might be interesting to know exactly what he is to you."

"My employer... or he was."

"Convenient. He pays you to clean his damned mansion."

Nadine squared her shoulders. Sam had never approved of her working, much less cleaning other people's homes, and yet she had to make a living while she took courses to better herself or tried to get her costume jewelry and clothes on the market. "It's a job, Sam, and from the sounds of things I don't think now would be the time to quit, do you?"

His eyes narrowed a fraction, and the smell of flat beer seemed to fill the space between them. "I think I'd better leave."

"Not until you hear me out, Sam Warne." Nadine blocked his path to the back door. "Don't you ever, *ever,* leave my sons alone in a parking lot again. And don't even think about driving them anywhere after you've had a few, okay?"

Sam winced. They both remembered the night while they were married when he'd rolled his pickup. If not for his safety belt, he would have been thrown from the crumpled vehicle and possibly killed. At that time he'd sworn off liquor. His abstinence had lasted all of three months.

"You can't tell me how to handle my sons," he said.

"Oh, yes, I can, Sam. And I will," she proclaimed. "They're my boys, too, and when it comes to their safety—"

"I don't have to listen to this." He hiked his jeans up beneath the sag that was his belly and stormed out. The back door slammed behind him and his truck, as he backed out of the drive, sent a spray of gravel beneath screaming tires.

"Mom?"

Nadine froze. Dread tore at her heart as she turned and found John wrapped in a yellow bath sheet, his skin blue, his hair wet and his eyes round. "You'd better get dressed or you'll catch your death."

"Don't yell at Dad."

"Oh, John." She folded him into her arms and felt his teeth chattering against her shoulder. "I don't mean to argue with him."

"It was okay. Me and Bobby, we were fine in the car."

"He shouldn't have left you."

"I wasn't scared."

"How about Bobby? Wasn't he afraid?" she prodded, knowing about her younger son's vivid imagination.

John shrugged a slim shoulder.

"Tell me."

"Well, just a little, maybe, but then he fell asleep and everything was all right."

She held her oldest son at arm's length and saw the pride in his reddened eyes, felt him square his shoulders. He was just too young to try to be the man of the house. Her heart squeezed painfully and she kissed his damp forehead. "Go on and get your pajamas on and I'll have dinner on the table." She gave him a playful swat on the bottom and he hurried upstairs to the loft.

By the time he came down again, she had a fire roaring in the grate and was trying to awaken a groggy Bobby.

John's appetite was enormous, and Bobby, though he usually liked stroganoff, was glum and too tired to show much interest in food. After dinner, she bathed him, hauled him off to bed and turned out the light after John climbed into the top bunk. They were asleep before she finished the dishes.

Still inwardly seething at Sam, she made herself a cup of coffee, grabbed her sewing kit and glue gun and dragged the nearly finished jacket out of the closet. A few more beads and rhinestones dripping down one sleeve and it would be finished. She felt a small sense of pride. At least this jacket would be sold before Christmas. It was a special order from a bareback rider whom Turner Brooks had known during his days on the rodeo circuit. The woman, buying a horse from Turner, had seen a jacket Nadine had made for Heather and commissioned one for herself on the spot.

"Just make it a little more flashy," she'd said around a long, slim cigarette. "You know, a few more sparkles." Well, the jacket was definitely flashy.

The doorbell rang before she finished. Expecting Sam again, Nadine braced herself for another confrontation, flung open the front door and found Hayden, his hair windblown, his face flushed with the cold. Her stomach slammed hard against her abdomen.

"This is a surprise."

"For both of us," he admitted. "I didn't expect to come back here."

"Did I forget something this time?" she asked, her voice brittle, though her heart was pounding against her ribs.

He shook his head. "I'm the one who forgot."

Her brows drew together. "Forgot? Forgot wha—" Before she'd finished asking the question, he'd grabbed her and clamped his arms around her. His mouth found hers and with anxious, hungry lips, he kissed her.

She couldn't let this happen again! She wouldn't! With all the strength she could muster, she tried to push him away. "Hayden, please...don't..."

Every muscle in his body grew rigid. Slowly he drew his head away from hers and stared into her eyes. What he saw in her gaze, she could only guess, but slowly he released her. "I..." He shoved the hair from his eyes and swore beneath his breath. "Hell, Nadine, I didn't mean to come on like a Neanderthal. But it seems I can't do anything else when I'm around you." He shook his head, disgusted with himself.

"What—what did you mean?" Good Lord, she could barely breathe and her voice sounded so weak and feminine she actually cringed.

A self-deprecating smile touched the corner of his mouth. "Just that I've missed you."

Sweet Lord, now what?

"I left here angry, said things I didn't mean and here I am trying to apologize." Swearing under his breath, he rolled his eyes. "I'm not very good at it."

"Not much practice, I suspect."

"You make me crazy, you know."

She couldn't help but smile. "I've missed you, too," she admitted, though she wanted to lie and tell him that she hadn't lost a moment's sleep over him, that she hadn't tossed and turned every night replaying their lovemaking over and over in her mind, that she didn't sometimes fantasize about loving him and becoming his wife and... Oh, God! Drawing herself up short, she shook her head. "This could never work, Hayden."

"You don't know that."

"We've already had this conversation, remember?" she said, though she wanted nothing more than to drag him into the house with her and throw herself into his arms. She trembled inside but held her ground.

"I just think we should start over. Take one step at a time."

Oh, God, why was he torturing her? "Why?"

"Why?" he repeated, glancing up at the dark sky, as if searching for the reasons. "Because I've gone slowly and steadily out of my mind without you. Because the house seems like a damned morgue without you there. Because...because I've missed you." His gaze settled on hers again, and there was honesty and desperation in his blue eyes.

Inside, she was melting. "I still don't want an affair."

"I'm not asking for one."

"Then what do you want?"

The question hung in the cool air between them, and she waited with her heart in her throat. "What I want is to get to know you, Nadine."

"You may not like me."

One side of his mouth lifted slightly. "I don't think there's much chance of that. Anyway, I'm willing to gamble."

"Damn it all, Hayden, why don't you just go away?" she said, her voice catching. "Leave me alone. Let my life go on as it was."

"I can't," he admitted, and he kissed her again. This time his lips were tender, his tongue undemanding. She sagged against him and realized with a sense of mounting dread that for the rest of her life she'd never be able to say no to Hayden Monroe.

Chapter Ten

Hayden had trouble living up to his promise. Nadine had always exuded an earthiness that he found irresistibly sexy. Her jeans were snug, but not obscene, and yet he couldn't take his eyes off the sway of her rump as she walked. Her mahogany-red hair glinted with gold in the firelight, and her green eyes appeared large and dark above sculpted cheekbones. She served him coffee, then set about finishing work on some glittery jacket she was making for a woman he didn't know.

He settled in on the lumpy antique couch, propping one heel on the arm and watching her work as he sipped the coffee. "Decaf," she'd told him as she'd handed him a wide glazed mug. As if he cared. He wasn't here for the coffee.

She explained about trying to launch her career as a designer of exotic art and clothes or some damned thing—that she'd taken courses at the local junior college in color and art and fabric design, along with more traditional subjects of math and accounting and business law. She wasn't going to clean houses forever. When she finished the jacket, she held it up for his inspection.

"I'm not much of an authority on rodeo wear," he said dryly, and her eyes sparkled with merriment as she sashayed closer, the jacket swinging in front of her.

"Oh, sure. I just bet you want one for yourself."

"Right." A sarcastic smile touched his lips.

"Maybe for Christmas, hmm?" she teased. Her cheeks were rosy, her lips pulled into a thoughtful grin. "Black denim with gold rhinestones. Kind of an Elvis look with—"

He grabbed her quickly, and the jacket slid to the floor as he pulled her down on top of him on the couch.

"Hayden, don't—" she said, but giggled as his arms surrounded her.

"Don't what?" he asked into her open mouth.

"I thought we weren't going to do this—"

"We're not." He kissed her, nibbling on her lower lip and causing shivers to race up her spine. Sighing, she opened her mouth to him and his tongue sought quick entrance. With sure strokes it touched the roof of her mouth and explored the insides of her cheeks before finding its mate.

Closing her eyes, Nadine kissed him back. She didn't protest when his hand cupped her buttocks, drawing her tighter to his hardness.

"You make me do things I've never done in my life," he admitted when he finally broke the kiss and stared up at her. He smoothed the cascade of red curls from her face and let his fingertips press gently against her neck, while his eyes strayed lower, to her breasts as they rose and fell against him. "However, wearing flashy clothes isn't one of them."

"No?" she teased, baiting him on purpose.

"I can think of better things." His gaze locked with hers, and he let his hand slide downward until he felt the weight of one breast in his palm. Nadine moaned softly, and his fingers squeezed. Desire swept through her in a hot torrent as his fingers fondled her through her clothes.

She closed her eyes, arching back, thrusting out her breasts.

"God, you're beautiful," he whispered, drawing her
down and burying his face against her sternum. "I want
you." He closed his eyes as if to clear his head and didn't
open them again as he said, "I've wanted you from the first
time I saw you in your dad's old pickup. I thought years and
time would change that, but I was wrong. The reverse is
true. I want you more now than I did as a kid."

Her throat closed in on itself so she couldn't swallow; she
hardly dared believe him.

Pulling her down to him again, he held her tight and buried his face in the crook of her neck. "This is killing me, but
we'll play it your way, Nadine. I don't know how, but we'll
give it a damned good try."

He slapped her playfully on the butt, then forced them
both into an upright position. Strain showed in the brack-
ets near his mouth. "Do you really believe we can have a
relationship without sex?"

"I don't know," she admitted.

"Well, I guess we'll find out. But let me tell you, it's
gonna be hell!"

Hayden was true to his word. He started showing up at
her house on a regular basis and convinced her to keep
working for him. He wanted her to hire the carpenters and
handymen to oversee the repairs to the summer home while
he spent his days at the mill. He never discussed his plans for
the future of the company, and Nadine had never asked,
though the few times she'd seen Sam, he was convinced that
Hayden was going to do his level best to see that every employee of the company got his walking papers.

Fortunately, the boys hadn't told Sam about the fact that
Hayden visited nearly every night, that sometimes he ate
dinner with them or that he had taken them for speedboat
rides across the lake. He'd promised to take them skiing as
soon as the first storm dumped enough snow onto the
mountains.

And they'd never made love again, though they'd come
close a time or two when the boys were asleep upstairs and
they were alone in front of the fire, but Hayden had always

broken off their embrace and Nadine had been left feeling frustrated and doubting that she would much longer be able to abide by her own moral code.

As Christmas approached, there was more demand for her funky jewelry. She stopped by the Rexall Drugstore in the middle of town to check her inventory. The store, located on the corner of Pine and Main had a turn-of-the-century charm. It seemed more like an old-fashioned mercantile than a modern pharmacy. Paddle fans rotated to the strains of Christmas carols filling the store with soft music. Red and green tinsel was strung over the aisles, which were more crowded than ever with excess merchandise—cards, wrapping paper, gift ideas, decorations, even fruitcakes.

The rack that displayed her jewelry was near the front of the store, and as she approached the counter she realized that more than half of the original inventory had already been sold. There was a "lot of interest" in her pieces, the woman behind the counter confided to her.

Before she left, Nadine decided to buy a cup of cocoa at the back counter. She slid onto a vacant stool and dropped her purse at her feet before she recognized the girl sitting next to her as Carlie Surrett. Their gazes met in the mirror over the soda machine, and Nadine's insides went cold.

"Hello, Nadine," Carlie ventured, and Nadine forced a smile she didn't feel. Carlie was a beautiful girl with long, straight black hair and deep blue eyes. She'd been a model for some years, then turned photographer before she'd returned to Gold Creek only a few months before.

And she'd been the cause of Kevin's death.

This girl—this woman—had broken Nadine's oldest brother's heart, and when he'd discovered his love was unreturned, he'd pulled his car into the garage of his apartment, closed the door and let the engine run until he'd died of carbon monoxide poisoning.

Nadine forced a greeting over her tongue. She told herself she couldn't blame Carlie, but couldn't fight the rage that burned in her heart. If only Carlie had treated Kevin more kindly, he might still be alive today.

Carlie's mother, Thelma, the waitress behind the counter, glanced at Nadine, snapped open her order pad and, without a smile, took her order. The pain between the two families had existed for years, and no one was able, or cared, to bridge the gap.

In a thunder of footsteps, five-year-old Adam Brooks, dressed in full cowboy regalia, scurried to the counter. His mother, Heather, and her sister, Rachelle Moore, were laughing, dragging shopping bags and obviously breathless as they walked down the aisle toward the back of the store. While Heather was petite and blond, and just beginning to show her pregnancy, Rachelle was tall and willowy, with long red-brown hair that fell to her waist.

"Rachelle!" Carlie gasped, then sent Heather a friendly glare. "You *knew* she'd be in town."

"I wasn't sure—" Heather hedged.

"Liar." Rachelle slid onto a stool next to Carlie. "I called her yesterday." She slid her packages under the counter and eyed the fluorescent menu displayed over the back mirror.

Adam scrambled onto a stool next to his aunt and began ordering a banana split, but Heather spied Nadine. "Just the woman I was looking for," she said as Rachelle and Carlie caught up on old times. "I need your help."

"Mine?"

"The studio. It needs all sorts of work and the doctor told me that I had to slow down." She patted her rounding belly. "So, after Christmas sometime I was hoping that you'd help me clean it up, maybe give it a fresh coat of paint—that sort of thing. If you have the time, of course."

"It shouldn't be a problem."

"Good. And I have a list of people for you—oh, where is it?" Heather dug through a voluminous purse, yanked out her wallet and dug through a compartment. "Here you go. All of these people showed an interest in some of your jewelry. That woman there—" she pointed a fingernail at the third name on the list "—owns a chain of boutiques around the bay area. She has a store near Fisherman's Wharf, one in Sausalito and a few sprinkled around Santa Rosa and Sonoma, I think. She displays some of my paintings and was *very* interested in your work. Give her...for that matter, give them all a call.''

Nadine could hardly believe her good luck. She folded the scrap of paper into her purse and said, ''Thanks.''

''No trouble,'' Heather replied with a smile.

''Let me buy you a cup of coffee, at least.''

''You don't have to—'' Heather glanced along the length of the counter where Rachelle, Carlie and Adam were discussing the merits of marshmallow sauce versus pineapple on a sundae.

''I want to.''

''All right.'' Heather eased onto one of the stools, and Nadine wondered how she'd ever been jealous of this woman who seemed to glow in her pregnancy. Her blond hair shimmered in the lights and her eyes sparkled with good humor. Obviously marriage was good for her and Turner Brooks was a good man, a strong man, a passionate man. A man Nadine had come to realize that she'd never really loved.

And what about Hayden? Do you love him?

The thought struck her cold, and she nearly dropped her cup of cocoa, sloshing some of the chocolate onto the counter. *Love?* Why, the notion was ridiculous! She couldn't, wouldn't fall for Hayden.

''Your father says there's talk at the logging company of trouble with the mill. Rumor has it that Garreth's son might sell it or scrap it out,'' Thelma said to Carlie as she slid a glass boat filled with bananas, ice cream and syrup toward Adam. With glee, he plucked the cherry from a bed of whipped cream and plopped it into his mouth.

''I thought you were going to share,'' his aunt Rachelle chided him, and Adam, a smile stretched long on his freckled face, shook his head.

''The mill's closing?'' Carlie repeated.

''It's not for certain yet.''

''But this town will roll up and die,'' Heather observed.

Nadine looked at Carlie's mother. ''Maybe it won't be shut down.''

Thelma regarded Nadine with frosty eyes. "You just watch. Hayden Monroe's always been a pampered rich boy. Never done anyone any good, including that girl he was gonna marry. First he nearly killed her in a boat wreck, then he broke off the engagement." She clucked her tongue. "A real charmer, that one." She plucked a pad from the pocket of her apron and tallied the bill for a couple of men who were sitting at the far end of the counter.

Nadine said goodbye to everyone and thanked Heather again for the list of potential clients. She barely heard the strains of "Silver Bells" as she shoved open the door and walked outside. The cocoa in her stomach seemed to curdle when she thought of Hayden and the power he now had over this town. She'd grown up with the people who worked for him; their children were her own boys' friends. If Hayden did close down the mill, they might as well close down the town. Even Fitzpatrick Logging would be affected.

If Hayden sold the sawmill to a rival firm, there would be changes and the people of Gold Creek, God bless them, weren't all that interested in change. A new owner might bring in his own foremen, his own workers, his own office people and computer system. Jobs could be lost to other men and machinery.

It wasn't hard to see why the citizens of Gold Creek liked things to stay the same. They'd been raised in a timber town as their folks had been. Throughout the generations, logging in northern California had dwindled, but in Gold Creek it was a way of life.

And Hayden Monroe had the power to change it.

"Just take your father's viewpoint into perspective," Thomas Fitzpatrick said, glancing through the window of Hayden's house to the lake. He'd spent the afternoon with his wayward nephew, trying to convince the boy to maintain a status quo. Hayden didn't seem to care what his father wanted nor did he seem all that interested in the fate of Fitzpatrick Logging. In fact, there seemed to be a new bitterness to him, a hardening of his features that Thomas hadn't seen in his previous meeting. As if Hayden knew something he shouldn't.

Thomas was sweating. He and Garreth had worked so well together. They'd built a monopoly here in Gold Creek and enjoyed ruling the town's economy, being Gold Creek's premier citizens. Well, at least Thomas had. Garreth had been more of a legend—what with living in the city and showing up only a few times a week at best.

Thomas cracked his knuckles as Hayden leaned back in the recliner. "What is it you really want?" Hayden asked, eyeing his uncle so intensely that Thomas, always cool, felt the need to squirm in his chair.

"For the time being, until I can come up with more cash, I want you to stay at the helm of Monroe Sawmill."

"And keep buying timber from Fitzpatrick Logging?"

"Of course. We have contracts—"

"You have a lot of things, Thomas. You and Dad." Hayden reached into a drawer and yanked out a stack of yellowed documents that had been forwarded to him, upon request, by Bradworth in San Francisco. He tossed them on the coffee table. "An interest in a soccer team that never got off the ground, a racehorse that couldn't win and oil leases for dry wells, to name just a few. Diversification—isn't that what you called it?"

Thomas tented his hands and nodded slightly, managing to hide his annoyance. "We've had our share of bad investments."

"More than your share, I'd say. In fact, it's my bet that the sawmill and the logging company are the only legitimate, profitable businesses that you're involved with."

"I'm just suggesting that you don't look a gift horse in the mouth."

Hayden's smile was cold. "Gift horse? I think the mills are more of an albatross than anything else."

Thomas's eyes snapped. "You always were too stubborn for your own good. Your father only wanted what was best for you."

"My father didn't give a damn for me, and you know it!" Hayden exploded. "I was just another one of his 'things.'"

Thomas pushed back his chair. "Just don't do anything foolish."

"You'll be one of the first to know it if I do," Hayden replied. "At the board meeting."

"What if I come up with an offer before then?"

Hayden's nostril's flared slightly. "Bring it to me. Then we'll talk."

Thomas left, and Hayden searched the den for a bottle of Scotch or bourbon. He needed a drink. Grabbing a dusty bottle, he poured himself a stiff shot, then, with a growl, dumped the liquor down the bar sink and stared through the window into the coming night. His uncle worried him. The man was slick, oily. For the first time, Hayden wondered about selling out to him and giving him a complete monopoly in town—the owner of the only two industries.

Thomas would have more power than ever over people like Nadine.

He felt a pull on his gut and wondered what Nadine was doing.

Hell, why was it he couldn't stop thinking of her? Whatever his mood—happy, sad, frustrated, elated, worried—he wanted to share it with her. Ever since landing back in this two-bit town and seeing her bending over his bathtub, scrubbing as if her life depended upon it, he'd been fascinated with her.

Leo whined to go outside, and absently Hayden patted the old dog's head. "I know," he said, as he snagged his jacket off the hall tree near the front door. Within minutes he and the dog were driving around the curving road that followed the shoreline of the lake. The night was brisk, stars winked high above the canopy of spruce and redwood branches, but Hayden didn't notice. His concentration was focused on the twin beams of light thrown by his headlights and the single thought that soon he'd be with Nadine again.

"Okay, okay, we'll put up the tree—but just the lights tonight. It's already late," Nadine told her boys. Upset over what she'd learned at the counter of the drugstore, she'd started home, passed the Boy Scout sales lot for Christmas trees and, on impulse, stopped and bought a small tree that she'd lashed to the roof of her car.

She was now holding it up for inspection on the back porch. Hershel growled at the tree, but the boys were delighted. "It's great, Mom," John told her, "but you could've gotten a bigger one. It's a little on the puny side."

"Yeah, like Charlie Brown's," Bobby chimed in, remembering a rerun of a Christmas special they'd seen.

"It's not that bad. With a little trimming, a few lights, and tons of ornaments, it'll be the best tree we've ever had," she insisted. "You'll see. Come on, Bobby, you help me get it inside, and John, look on the top shelf in the garage for the stand."

They wrestled the tree into the dusty stand, though the poor little pine listed to one side.

"It looks like it might fall down," Bobby said.

Nadine, still bent over the stand, shook her head. Pine needles fell into her hair and she had to speak around a protruding branch. "It'll be fine, once it's decorated."

"I don't know," John said, holding up his hand parallel to the wall and closing one eye to measure just how badly the tree leaned. "It could tip over."

"Hogwash. We'll just turn it so that it slants toward the corner. No one will ever know!" Nadine dusted her hands, eyed her handiwork, and had to admit to herself that the tree bordered on pathetic. "Just think Charlie Brown," she told herself as she poured water into the tray.

John was testing the lights, seeing which colorful bulbs still glowed after a year in the garage, by plugging the string into a wall socket, when there was a knock on the door. Hershel, searching the kitchen floor for scraps of food, bolted across the room, growling and snarling and nearly knocking over the tree as he raced by.

Bobby jumped onto the couch and peered out the window. "It's the guy from across the lake!"

"Mr. Monroe?" John asked, and his eyes were suddenly as bright as the string of lights at his feet. "Maybe he wants to take us on a ride in his boat at night! Wouldn't that be great!"

"Hershel, shush!" Nadine commanded. "And I doubt that he wants to take you two boys out on the lake tonight," Nadine added, but her heart seemed to take flight as she opened the door and found Hayden on the front porch. He loomed before her, and his musky male scent wafted on the breeze that crept into the room, billowing the curtains and causing the fire to glow brighter for an instant.

"Hey, did you bring your boat?" Bobby asked, jumping up and down on the couch in his excitement.

Hershel barked loudly.

Nadine snapped her fingers in her youngest son's direction. "Stop that jumping, Bobby, and you—" she whirled on the dog "—Hush! Right now!" She managed a smile for Hayden as she caught Hershel by the collar. "Welcome to my zoo." She swung the door open a little farther with her free hand, and Hayden stepped inside, only to kick the door closed behind him.

Nadine released the dog, and Hayden whispered to her, "This is the nicest damned zoo I've been to in a long time." His gaze found hers again and held. Her breath seemed to stop and time stretched endlessly. In those few seconds Nadine felt as if her future was wrapped up in this man, as if there were some unspoken bond between them.

"Come on, you can help us with the Christmas tree," John said, shattering the moment. "I didn't want to tell Mom that it was crooked, but it really needs some help."

Hayden shook his head. "I didn't mean to interrupt—"

"You didn't. John's right. You can help," Nadine said quickly.

Hayden's forehead creased. "I don't think I'm the right one to ask about this sort of thing."

"Hey, you're the only candidate who walked through the door," she joked, but no trace of humor entered his eyes.

"I've never put up a tree before."

"Oh, sure you have. When you were a kid . . ." Her voice trailed off when she saw the shadows crossing his eyes.

"When I was a kid, my mother hired a decorator to design a tree—actually a look for the house—around a theme,

mind you, and I was never allowed to touch the creation."
He eyed the tiny tree standing in the corner. "One year it
was a Victorian theme, with huge bows and fake candles and
lace, another something very sophisticated and contemporary—that year the tree was flocked pink. One other time it
was sprayed gold and hung with red bells. There were strings
of red bells all over the house—up the stairs, over the mantel, around the front door, in the foyer. Whatever some art-
ist came up with, that was our look—but it was only skin
deep."

"Oh, come on!" John said, sure that Hayden was pulling his leg. "A pink tree? And you didn't get to put it up?"

"Well, there's no time like the present to learn," Nadine
said, despite the tears threatening her eyes. All her life she'd
envied Hayden for his easy existence; she'd never really
bought the "poor little rich boy" scenario, but now she
wished she could ease his pain, tell him that she cared.

For all her family's lack of money, Christmastime had
been a time of celebration. From the tinsel and candles on
the mantel, to Sunday services at the church, where her
mother would sing a solo in the choir, to cups of cocoa and
bowls of popcorn as they decorated the tree with the mea-
ger decorations her mother had collected over the years—the
same decorations that were probably trimming a tree on an
Iowa farm.

Nadine wondered if her mother still made dozens of
Christmas cookies and played her piano after dinner on
Christmas Eve. She'd probably never know. The packages
and cards she received never seemed to tell her much about
Donna's life as a farmer's wife in the Midwest. A huge lump
filled her throat, and she touched Hayden's fingers with her
own.

"It's never too late to learn how to trim a tree," she said,
driving away her own case of melancholy. "John will help
you try to straighten it and Bobby and I will make some
popcorn."

Bobby bounded from the couch and scurried to the
kitchen, and John was all business as he explained what was
wrong with the tree and how he proposed to keep it from

leaning. "... the problem is," John confided to Hayden, "... Mom's a woman."

"I noticed," Hayden replied dryly.

"Well, women don't know nothin' about man things like hatchets and axes and—"

"I heard that, John," Nadine called from the kitchen. Smiling, she added, "Better be careful what you say or you'll be chopping all the firewood yourself...." Winking at Bobby, she plugged in the air popper and couldn't hear the rest of Hayden and John's discussion about the "weaker sex." Usually a conversation in that tone sent her temper skyrocketing, but tonight, with Hayden in the house, she decided not to take offense.

Bobby put a Christmas tape in his boombox, and by the time the popcorn, cranberry juice and cocoa were ready, Hayden and John had revived the little tree. Not only did it stand upright, but the first string of lights was winking between the branches. "How does it look?" John asked proudly.

"Like it was done by professionals."

Hayden shook his head. "Like it was done by amateurs, the way it's supposed to be." They ate the popcorn by the fire, discussed the fact that the boys would be on vacation in less than two weeks and laughed as Hershel tried to steal kernels of popcorn out of Bobby's fingers. "He knows you're a soft touch," Hayden told Bobby. "Be careful of that."

"I'm not!" Bobby said, and to Nadine's surprise, Hayden grabbed the boy and wrestled him onto the floor. Bobby giggled and ended up on top, "pinning" Hayden until John joined in the fun. They rolled across the carpet, three bodies clinging together as one, laughing and muttering and working up a sweat.

Nadine watched in horror and awe. She'd seen the boys wrestle before, just as she'd watched her two brothers lunge and fight with each other when she'd grown up. Once in a while she'd even caught her father rolling around with Kevin and Ben. But Sam had never shown an interest in playing so physically with the boys. At the time she'd thought it a blessing, but now, seeing Bobby's red face and glowing eyes, watching as John leapt onto Hayden's back and unable to pull him down, start to laugh, she wondered if her sons had been missing out on some natural, primeval male bonding.

They crashed into a leg of the coffee table, and Hayden flopped onto his back. "You got me," he told the boys breathlessly, though Nadine suspected he wasn't near as winded as he put on.

"More, more!" Bobby cried.

"Not now, sport. I'm all in."

"No way," John said.

"That's enough, boys. Hayden's right. It's about time for bed," Nadine said.

After the usual protests and the fight over brushing their teeth and scrubbing their faces, both boys climbed into their bunks. Bobby was nearly asleep when Nadine bent over his pillow and kissed him, and John, too, was soon breathing deeply and evenly.

"You're lucky," Hayden told her, as he watched her pick up clothes that had been dropped everywhere on the floor. She tossed the small heap into a hamper.

They walked down the steps together. "Lucky? Because of the boys?" she repeated, then smiled. "I know. I'll never regret marrying Sam if only because he gave me my sons."

"It doesn't take much of a man to conceive a kid. The hard part's the next twenty years." He helped her carry the popcorn bowl and glasses into the kitchen.

"So now you want kids?"

"No," he said quickly, and he might as well have stuck a knife in her heart.

"You might make a wonderful father."

His head jerked up quickly and his gaze sharpened. "You think so?"

"From what I've seen."

"I was just playing with the kids. That's all. It wasn't a big deal!"

"It was just an observation, Hayden." She placed the glasses into the dishwasher before she understood his reaction. As the light dawned, her blood began to boil. "It wasn't a hint, if that's what you're thinking."

"What am I supposed to think?"

"You're the one who showed up on my doorstep." She slammed the dishwasher shut and turned on him. "Was there a reason you came to see me? I mean something more than just to stop by and insult me? If you haven't noticed, I've done all right by myself these past couple of years. I take care of myself and my sons, and I don't need help from you or any other man for that matter, so if you think I'm in the market for a husband, you've got another think coming!" she said with more vehemence than she expected. She started to stride past him, but he hooked the crook of her arm with a hand.

"I'm sorry."

The words hung in the air between them, like icicles that wouldn't melt. She yanked her arm free. "I also don't need your pity, Prince."

"Believe me, you don't have it. I feel a lot of things for you, Nadine—some things I don't even understand myself. I respect you, I care for you, I admire you and sometimes I even envy you—"

She snorted. "You envy me. *That's* a good one."

"It's true. But in all the years I've known you, I've never, ever pitied you," he said firmly. "You know your own mind, take care of yourself, aren't afraid to stand up for what you think's right and I'll bet, if your back's to a corner or someone threatens your kids, you come out fighting like a she-bear. On top of that, you're the sexiest woman I've ever met in my life."

She supposed she should be flattered. She supposed she should take pride in his compliments. But all she felt was an empty void. Wrapping her arms around herself, she rubbed away the goose bumps that had risen on her flesh.

"Why did you come here?" she finally asked.

His jaw worked for a second, and the air between them became thick with emotions. "I came because I couldn't stay away."

"You act as if that's a curse."

He smiled crookedly. "Isn't it?" His eyes searched hers, and for a second she couldn't tear her gaze from his. Rather than answer, she quickly gathered up the empty boxes, which had held the tree ornaments, and carried them to the garage. Hayden followed her and helped her put the containers back on their shelves.

She started for the stairs to the back porch when he reached for her, gently turning her in his arms and tilting her chin up with one of his fingers. The wind touched her hair and moonlight cast the darkness in silver.

"I was wrong," he said.

"About?"

"About not wanting you in my life. I don't understand it and I won't pretend to, but there's something about you that keeps me awake at night, something that I can't resist." Lowering his head, he brushed her lips with his own.

She trembled and let out a soft little cry as he folded his arms around her and his lips became more demanding. Somewhere in the distance a train rattled as it rode the rails of the old trestle bridge near town, and an owl let out a muted string of hoots from the high branches of one of the pine trees. The lake gleamed pearlescent, rippling as it lapped the shore. Nadine closed her eyes, drinking in the scent of Hayden—leather and soap and musk. Her arms circled his neck, and she didn't object when his weight dragged them down onto a gentle cushion of grass.

His tongue pressed against her teeth and she willingly parted her lips to him. She quivered when one of his hands reached below her sweater and long fingers splayed against the bare skin of her back.

Lifting his head for a second, he stared into her eyes and swallowed hard. "This is probably a mistake."

"Not our first," she said, managing a smile.

"Or our last?"

"I hope not."

He kissed her again, more fiercely this time, and his body, hard and wanting, pressed urgently against hers. His hands found her breasts and she arched upward, forcing each rounded swell into the gently kneading fingers that caused her blood to heat and pound in her ears. Deep inside, she began to melt. Like slow-burning oil, a liquid inside her began to simmer with want.

His mouth fastened over hers and she clung to him, holding him closer as he quickly discarded her sweater and bra, and found the anxious hard points that were her nipples. A current of electricity jolted through her as his tongue touched the tip of one breast. She cried out and her back bowed. One of his hands captured her buttock and forced her closer to the rock hardness that was his manhood. He rubbed against her and groaned as he began to suckle. Nadine's thoughts swirled crazily in a whirlpool of starlight and rainbows. She didn't think, only felt, and when the zipper of her skirt opened with a quiet hiss, she was eager for the touch of his bare hands against her skin.

He was quick. He skimmed her of her clothes and guided her hands to help him remove his own shirt and jeans. Without releasing her, he kicked off his running shoes and writhed out of his jeans until at last, beneath the pale disc of the moon, they were naked, their bodies gleaming white, their muscles straining together.

From the bathroom window, still cracked open, the strains of a soft Christmas ballad filtered over the noises of the woods, and the cool air caused a chill that only stoked the fires of their passion hotter still.

Hayden kissed her eyes, her cheeks and lips before lowering himself along the slim arch of her neck and the circle of fragile bones at the base of her throat. She whispered his name and he moved downward, touching the point of each breast with his tongue and licking a hot path down her sternum and over the soft flesh to her navel, where he pressed a hot, insistent kiss.

Moaning, Nadine arched upward and he captured her hips with his hands, kissing her, nibbling at her, caressing her with his tongue as he explored each crease and curve of her body. She clutched fistfuls of his hair as he smoothed his tongue over her so intimately that she thought she might break. The heat within her became lava from a volcano buried deep in her soul. She cried out as the first quake rocked her.

"Hayden!" she screamed, though her voice was only a throaty whisper. "Hayden, please..."

He came to her then. As her body was still in the throes of pleasure, his lips claimed hers and he parted her legs with his knees. "Make love to me, Nadine," he growled into her open, waiting mouth. "Make love to me and never stop."

"Yes, oh, yes—"

He thrust into her then and she welcomed him, sheathing his manhood, becoming one with him, feeling the sweet white-hot heat within her build yet again. Her arms surrounded him and she met each of his thrusts with her own needful movements.

This was so right, so right, she thought as once again she gave herself up to the passion that only he could inspire. Her fingers dug into his shoulders as his rhythm increased and a cry passed her lips. Then his muscles coiled, and he shuddered and fell against her with his own answering call.

"I love you," he said in a rush of breath. "Damn it all, Nadine, I think I love you."

Chapter Eleven

Love? He *loved* her?

Four days later, while driving home from Coleville, Nadine was still trying to absorb this bit of information, but told herself not to believe words whispered in the throes of passion. He'd never said those three magical words again, and she wasn't kidding herself into believing that he'd meant them.

True, she'd been battling her own conflicting emotions for Hayden, but she'd tried to keep herself from fantasizing that love was involved. Attraction, yes. Lust, definitely. But love? She wasn't sure that romantic ideal existed. Her own parents hadn't found happiness, nor had she. Many of her friends had married and divorced; only a handful had stayed together, and they were often unhappy. There were a few exceptions, of course. Turner and Heather seemed blissfully, ecstatically in love and Heather's sister, Rachelle, was madly in love with her husband, Jackson.

But their marriages hadn't stood the test of time—though certainly their love had.

Her fingers tightened over the wheel as she rounded a hairpin curve on the west end of the lake and thought about the long hours after making love to Hayden near the lake. They'd returned to the house, drank wine and had cuddled together on the couch until the fire had died.

He'd come back the next night, eaten dinner with them and helped finish decorating the tree. Hayden had even helped John with his science report on the depletion of the ozone layer. Once the boys had fallen asleep, she and Hayden had walked outside and again given into their passion.

She'd seen Hayden each night and looked forward to greeting him at the front door. Sometimes he smelled of sawdust and oil, and she'd known he'd been at one of the mills. Other times he carried the scent of leather or soap with him, as if he'd just come from the shower.

He'd brought wine for her, soda for the boys and had taken it upon himself to fix the chain on Bobby's bicycle, getting himself greasy in the process and delighting her youngest son. Hayden Monroe certainly knew how to carve his way into her heart.

She couldn't be falling in love with him, she told herself, and wouldn't let it happen. Her runaway emotions were on the loose and it was time to rein them in.

"What a mess," she told herself, and clicked on the radio. She hadn't wanted an affair with any man and certainly not Hayden, yet she was involved with him up to her neck. She thought about him constantly and, as she had throughout her trip from Coleville, she tried to concentrate on her work.

Elizabeth Wheeler, the owner of Beth's Boutique, had been encouraging. She'd ordered three more jackets and two dozen pairs of earrings.

"They're going like hotcakes. Kids as well as adults," Beth had confided in Nadine two hours earlier. "If you can't get them here by Christmas, I'll want them for spring!"

Nadine smiled to herself. It seemed as if her life was turning around, despite everyone's dour predictions about Hayden Monroe and his grim effect upon the town. Even Nadine's father seemed a little happier, and though he wouldn't confide the reason for the spring in his step when they'd gone to lunch this afternoon, Nadine suspected that he was interested in another woman for the first time in years. He'd hardly dated since her mother had walked out on him, but there was definitely something different about him in the past couple of days and she didn't believe his change in mood was just because the spirit of Christmas was in the air or because Ben was on his way home. No, the twinkle in her father's eyes could only be attributed to the attentions of a woman. But whose attentions?

Time would tell, she decided, turning into the drive and spying Hayden's Jeep.

He was waiting for her, legs outstretched, ankles crossed, hips resting on the fender. Her heart skipped a beat and she wondered fleetingly if there was a chance for them. In a millisecond she pictured herself as Hayden's wife, living in the manor across the lake, spending hours with Hayden, making love with him, having more children.... Reality broke the spell. Hayden wasn't going to stay in Gold Creek. He would probably sell his string of sawmills, perhaps even close some of them, and he didn't want a wife and especially not any children; she'd learned that much. Being the product of an unhappy marriage, with unrealistic goals placed upon his young shoulders, Hayden had decided from an early age to depend upon no one but himself. He didn't want a wife and kids.

As her silly bubble of happiness burst, she parked near the garage. With Hayden, she had to live for the moment and forget about a future.

Forcing a smile, she slid out of the car and was rewarded with a crushing embrace and a kiss that sucked the breath from her lungs and made her bones as weak as jelly.

His body fit intimately against hers, and the realization that she loved him hit her like the proverbial ton of bricks. For weeks she'd been denying it, burying her feelings, telling herself her emotions were on the rampage because she'd been without a man for so long. But now, with his arms around her, his lips devouring hers, his hands possessive, she knew she'd lost her heart to him and she doubted she'd ever retrieve it.

He lifted his head to stare into her eyes. "God, I missed you," he said hoarsely as he captured a handful of her hair and twined his fingers through the thick, red curls. Her heart seemed to crack.

"I saw you this morning," she pointed out, thinking of their goodbye kiss on the front porch at one-thirty.

"That was a long time ago."

"Mmm. Too long," she admitted. "I missed you, too," she admitted.

"I could tell." He slapped her on the rump playfully, but let his hand settle over the curve of her hip.

"Could you?" She wound her arms around his neck and licked her lips provocatively. "How?"

He groaned. "You're wicked, woman."

"And you love it."

He laughed and kissed her again. "I have half a mind to carry you into the house, throw you on the bed and ravage you until you beg for mercy."

"The half a mind part, I believe."

His eyes flashed. "Well, I guess I'll just have to prove it to you." Quickly he scooped her up and threw her over his shoulder in a fireman's carry.

"Hayden, no!" she cried, laughing as the blood rushed to her head and her hair nearly swept the ground. Hershel yipped and bounded in excitement, trying to lick Nadine's face. "Please, put me down!"

"You asked for it."

"No, I— Hayden, oh, come on—"

He started packing her up the back steps to the door. "How much time do we have before the boys get home?"

"They'll be here any minute."

"Liar."

"It's . . . it's the truth!"

He set her on her feet, but his arms still surrounded her and he kissed her again. Already breathless, her heart pumping, she kissed him back and playfully darted her tongue between his lips.

"You're asking for trouble."

"Am I gonna get it?" she asked.

He chuckled. "You *are* bad."

"Only with you."

"It better be only with me." His eyes sizzled electric blue just as the sound of shouts and bicycle tires crushing gravel reached her ears.

"See," she taunted.

Hershel gave an expectant bark and streaked down the lane toward the coming noises. With a sigh, she touched a finger to his lips. "I don't think we're alone anymore."

His mouth curved sardonically. "I'm a patient man, Nadine. I'll wait."

John's old bike rounded the corner, and Bobby's smaller two-wheeler was right behind him. Before the bike had stopped, John had leapt off his seat, letting the bicycle fall into the yard.

"What's for dinner?" John demanded as Hershel jumped and barked.

"A surprise."

"Uh-oh." John pulled a face, and Bobby, leaning his bike against the garage, wrinkled his nose.

"Let's go to McDonald's," Bobby suggested.

Nadine shook her head. "No way. I'm not driving back to Coleville tonight. Besides, you like pasta salad—"

"Yuk!" John said. "I *hate* salad."

"This is different. It has chicken and cheese and—"

"And it's still salad," John said.

"We can have Kentucky Fried Chicken," Bobby, ever the fast-food junkie, suggested.

Nadine was starting to fume. "I said we're not going to—"

"I'll take you out."

Nadine turned on Hayden, as if she'd heard him wrong. "But the boys have homework and—"

"You need a night off. Besides, I've bummed more than my share of meals around here."

"Come on, Mom!" Bobby cried.

"Yeah, let's go."

Nadine glared at Hayden. "Why do I have the feeling that I've been conned?" she asked, glancing back to the boys. "I wasn't kidding about the homework."

"We'll do it. Okay? When we get back!" John said.

"Before the TV goes on."

John rolled his eyes before racing after Bobby into the house.

"Lighten up about the homework," Hayden suggested.

"So now you're telling me how to be a parent?" she asked, though she wasn't angry. "What makes you such an expert?"

"I was a kid. A kid who was expected to get straight A's, a kid who was supposed to be the best football player, baseball player, chess player and leader of the debate team. My folks wanted—no, make that *expected*—me to be the smartest kid in my class."

"Were you?" she asked.

His grin turned devilish. "Until about seventh grade. Then I became the biggest hellion."

"I bet your parents were proud," she teased, before she saw the storm clouds gathering in his eyes.

"I doubt that was the word my father would have used to describe anything I did."

Before she could say anything else, the boys had thundered out of the house. They all piled into Hayden's Jeep and he drove into town.

Hayden took them to a small restaurant in the mall near the tricinemas. For the first time in their lives the boys, seated on one side of the booth, were encouraged to order anything off the menu as Hayden insisted this night was his treat. Nadine tried to protest, but he wouldn't hear of it, and in the end, John and Hayden each ordered a steak, Bobby stuck with a hamburger and Nadine chose grilled salmon. The boys were in heaven.

"Why can't we do this all the time?" John asked as he struggled to cut his steak.

"Because it's not practical," Nadine replied.

On the seat of the booth between them, Hayden folded his hand over hers. "Sometimes it's better not to be practical."

His fingers fit into the grooves between her own and she tingled a little.

"Everyone should keep his head," she said. "And think of the consequences of what they're doing."

"We're just eating," John pointed out. "That's no crime."

"But we can't do it all the time because we can't afford it."

"He can!" Bobby said, pointing a fork at Hayden.

"That's right," John chimed in, focusing on Hayden. "Katie Osgood says you're the richest man in Gold Creek. But Mike Katcher thinks it's Mr. Fitzgerald."

Nadine was horrified. "John, it's not polite to—"

Hayden held up a hand. "I don't know about my local status and I really don't care. My father was a very wealthy man. I inherited a lot from him, but it doesn't mean a whole lot to me."

"Well, it should," John said. "Money talks. That's what my dad says."

Nadine wanted to drop through the floorboards of the restaurant.

"He does. Dad is always talking about money," Bobby added as the waitress approached. Luckily the subject was dropped.

Hayden let the boys order dessert and the conversation stayed light as John plowed into apple pie with ice cream and Bobby picked at a huge piece of six-layer chocolate cake.

Upon instruction, both boys thanked Hayden and he made a point of telling them to call him by his first name.

This is going much too fast, Nadine thought, and realized that it wasn't just her heart that would be broken when Hayden left. The boys, too, would miss him. For their own sakes, she had to make sure they didn't get too emotionally attached to a man who would soon return to his life in the city.

Later that night, as she was tucking Bobby into bed, she smoothed his hair from his forehead and gave him a kiss.

"See ya in the morning," she said before turning out the light.

"Mom?"

"Hmm?" She looked over her shoulder at the top of the stairs.

"Are you going to marry Mr. Mon—Hayden?"

She froze, hoping that Hayden, in the living room below, hadn't heard her youngest son's question. John leaned over from the top bunk and stared at his mom, waiting for her answer. Her throat felt like sandpaper, but she shook her head.

"Why not?" Bobby wanted to know.

"He hasn't asked her yet, you dope."

"It's more than that. I . . . Hayden . . . we . . . well, we live in different worlds."

"But you like each other," Bobby pointed out. "He's here a lot."

"Liking each other is not enough."

John propped his head up with his hand. "If he asked you, would you say 'yes'?"

That was a tough one. "I don't think so."

"Aw, Mom!" Bobby said with a sigh. "If you married him we could have everything we wanted. New twenty-one-speed bikes, a big house, a boat that goes real fast like his—"

"And an airplane. Like Mr. Fitzpatrick. Katie Osgood says—"

"I don't care what Katie Osgood says," Nadine snapped at John. "Now, you just close your eyes and go to sleep, and that goes double for you," she added with a smile for Bobby.

Quickly she descended the stairs. "Trouble?" Hayden asked as she reached the first floor.

"Nothing serious," she replied, as he took her into his arms and placed a kiss upon her forehead. She melted willingly against him and wished she could think of a way to protect herself and her children from the great void that would appear in their lives when he locked the doors of the manor across the lake forever.

* * *

Sell out to Thomas Fitzpatrick. The offer was tempting. Uncle Thomas hadn't pulled any punches, which surprised Hayden as he studied the buy-out offer. Thomas wanted all the mills and was offering a decent price, if not top dollar. The deal was neat. All Hayden had to do was sign on the dotted line and make an announcement at the next board meeting. Since he owned controlling interest, no one could raise a stink. So why was he hesitating?

Because of Nadine. If he sold the mills and put the summer house on the market, he would be closing the door to Gold Creek forever and turning his back on Nadine and her children. He smiled as he thought of the boys. The older kid, John, was a handful. Bright and cocky, he was sure to give his mother more than her share of gray hairs, and the younger boy... he was difficult in his own way—a kid who struggled in school and was always at the mercy of his older, stronger brother.

They didn't know how lucky they were, he decided. If only he'd had a brother or a sister in whom he could have shared his problems, confided his darkest secrets and beat the living tar out of when he'd been angry.

The phone rang, and he picked up on the second ring. He nearly slammed the receiver back into its cradle when he recognized Wynona's wheedling voice. "Hayden? Thank God I caught you."

The irony of her words settled like lead on his shoulders. "What do you want, Wynona?" he asked without much interest.

"I want to see you again. We need to talk."

"Talk to Bradworth."

He could almost feel her seething through the wires. "There are things we need to discuss. Important things. Things that I don't want to confide in a lawyer."

"Guilty conscience?" he mocked, and he heard her swift intake of breath. He didn't feel the slightest bit of remorse.

"I'm coming to see you."

"Won't do any good, Wynona. I'm leaving town."

"But—"

"Goodbye," he said, and slammed down the receiver. The phone started ringing again, but he didn't bother answering, just took the stairs two at a time and started planning a weekend away from Gold Creek and the mills and Thomas Fitzpatrick and contracts. Away from the guilt.

But not away from everything. He planned to take Nadine and her boys with him.

Sam clapped his hands and yelled up the stairs to the loft. "Come on, guys. Chop! Chop!"

"Give them a break," Nadine reprimanded. "It was the last day of school today. They're wound up."

"Good. We got lots to do." To the rafters, he called, "Hurry up."

"Coming!" John hollered down.

"So what's the rush?" Nadine asked. She didn't want to sound suspicious, but Sam wasn't usually so anxious to be bothered with the boys. Not that he was a bad father, nor neglectful. He just wasn't usually so attentive.

In a clatter of footsteps the boys hurried down the stairs. After quick kisses to Nadine's cheeks, John and Bobby, their overnight bags slung over their shoulders, were herded out the back door toward Sam's waiting pickup. The passenger door opened with a loud creak just as Hayden's Jeep pulled into the drive.

"What the hell?" Sam said under his breath. "I wonder what *he* wants."

"He's coming to see Mom," Bobby offered and started waving enthusiastically. "He comes all the time."

Sam sent Nadine a sharp glance over his shoulder. "Is that right?"

"Well—"

"And he takes us fishing, and riding in his boat, and to fancy restaurants," Bobby added.

John, sensing the change of atmosphere in the air, didn't add anything to the conversation.

"He said he'd take us skiing, too."

"Bobby, I don't think Dad wants to hear everything that Mr. Monroe has talked about."

"He said we were supposed to call him Hayden," Bobby corrected, and Nadine had to grit her teeth.

Hayden parked next to Sam's Jeep and stretched out. Taller than Sam by nearly three inches, with broader shoulders and harsher features, he looked hard-bodied and tough. "Hayden, you've met Sam, I think."

"At the mill," Sam supplied, his eyes narrowing a fraction. "And a long time ago. Company picnic, or something."

Hayden extended his hand, but Sam ignored it.

"Is there something you want?"

Hayden offered a practiced smile. "I just came to see Nadine and the kids."

Sam bristled a little, and Nadine wondered again where his sudden sense of fatherhood had come from. "Well, you'd better say 'hello' now because the boys are leaving with me. For the weekend."

Hayden's lips stretched into a wide grin, as if he harbored a secret he wouldn't share. "Have a great time."

"We always do," Sam said stiffly as he climbed into the cab of his truck and roared off.

"What was that all about?" Hayden asked.

"You know perfectly well, Hayden Monroe. I think it's called marking his territory. The boys were going on and on about you and all the things you've done for them and Sam got his fatherly hackles up." She glanced at the disappearing truck. "About time."

"So," Hayden asked, placing his hands on her waist, "does that mean you're free for the weekend?"

"It means I'm alone."

His grin turned positively evil. "Not anymore. I'm taking you out—"

"Where?"

"It's a surprise."

"I don't like surprises."

"You'll like this one," he guaranteed.

"Hayden, I don't think—"

"Humor me. Believe me, you won't be disappointed."

* * *

He was right. Three hours later, as the Jeep rounded a final curve through the pine trees in the mountains, Nadine held her breath. Lights glowed through the windows of a rambling, three-storied lodge. Built of cedar and pine, with a wide porch, the building was settled in a thicket of pine trees and nearly twenty miles from the nearest small town.

Inside, the walls were raw wood, aged dark without the hint of varnish and covered with paraphernalia of the Wild West—saws, wagon yokes, axes and picks, even a full-size canoe. Wagon-wheel chandeliers offered flickering light. "I was afraid you were going to take me somewhere stuffy."

"Me?" he laughed. "Never."

They were seated near a bay window decorated with a cedar garland and sprigs of pine and mistletoe. Soon a waiter poured the wine Hayden had chosen, then took their orders. A hurricane lantern flickered on the cloth-covered table and reflected in the glass. Nadine sipped her wine and talked with Hayden before noticing, through the window, snow beginning to fall in thick, heavy flakes.

"If this keeps up, we could be trapped here all night," Hayden teased.

"I don't think so."

"Would it be so horrible?" he asked, the light from the lantern reflecting in his warm blue eyes.

"I'm a mother. I have responsibilities."

"The kids are with their dad. And your answering machine's on. If there's a problem, you'll know about it."

"Why Mr. Monroe, I think you're trying to seduce me," she teased, and her pulse jumped.

"Count on it." Her throat went dry as he touched his glass to hers with a soft clink, then finished his wine in one swallow.

They talked through courses of Caesar salad, French onion soup, stuffed trout and raspberry mousse. Hayden told her he'd found a buyer for the sawmills and that he was considering the offer. Her heart felt as if it had been pierced by a sharp needle as she considered the fact that he might soon be gone, perhaps before the first of the year. A coldness settled in her stomach and seeped through her limbs.

All along she'd known that he would leave, of course, but she'd never let herself think about the date; it had seemed a long way into the future, some indefinable time that she would worry about come spring . . . or maybe summer. But now? She managed to pretend that his talk of selling the sawmill didn't bother her, that she was sophisticated enough to deal with the inevitable fact that they would soon be separated by time and distance, but the small puncture wound in her heart seemed to rip a little more with each of her breaths.

She didn't notice the time passing, nor did she observe the snow that had accumulated on the ground around the lodge. She concentrated totally on Hayden, the inflexible line of his jaw, the angles of his cheekbones, the way his lips barely moved as he spoke.

By the time they'd finished coffee, two inches of snow had fallen. "Looks like we're here for the night," Hayden observed as he paid the bill and glanced outside.

"Doesn't your Jeep have four-wheel drive?"

His grin crept from one side of his mouth to the other. "Yes, but it would be a waste not to take advantage of the room I've already paid for, don't you think?"

"What I think," she said, standing as they left the table, "is that you should have asked me first."

He pulled her into a shadowy corner near the lobby. "All right. I'm asking." His eyes held hers. "Will you spend the night with me?"

She swallowed hard and considered all the reasons she should tell him to take her home. Staying would only prolong the heartache and keep the pain alive, and yet she couldn't resist. "Of course I'll stay with you," she whispered, knowing that he didn't realize she meant for the rest of her life.

The room sprawled across most of the top floor. Lustrous hardwood peeked out from beneath thick Oriental carpets and the furnishings of the suite were crafted to look antique. A hurricane lamp sat on the corner of the mantel in the bedroom occupied by a queen-size canopy bed.

A bottle of champagne stood chilling in a stand, and through the French doors leading to a private deck, Nadine noticed steam rising from an outdoor hot tub in a thick cloud, reminding her of the morning fog on Whitefire Lake.

"This is quite a place," she observed, running her hand over the curve of the bed frame.

"It's nice." He struck a match to the fire and lit the lantern before turning down the lights.

"You've been here before?" Why it mattered, she didn't know, but she didn't want to be just one in a long line of the women he'd brought here.

He nodded, watching her reaction in the beveled glass mirror over the bureau. She felt a jab of pain, but hoped he didn't notice. In the firelight, his features seemed harsher, more male, and the thought of him with another woman... Oh, God, she loved him too much. "With whom?" she asked, her voice sounding oddly strangled.

While icicles formed in her heart, he had the audacity to smile. "A woman."

Oh, God.

She fought the urge to walk straight out the door, and when he stood behind her and placed his hands on her shoulders, she wished she could find the strength to shake them off. But her willpower seemed to vanish at his touch and her skin heated beneath his fingertips. "Do I know her?"

"You've met, I think. A long time ago."

Wynona. She felt like such a fool and her shoulders drooped a little. He pulled her closer and whispered into her ear. "I was here with my mother. I was ten or eleven at the time, I think."

Relief flooded through her, and when she met his gaze in the mirror again, she saw the hint of laughter in his crystal-blue eyes. "You are a rotten, mean, miserable—"

"Prince," he supplied, and she couldn't help but grin as he twirled her in his arms.

"You're the king now, you know."

He shook his head. "Not me. Just a regular Joe."

"Regular Joes don't do this—" She motioned to the room and deck.

"They should," he said, as he lowered his lips over hers and dragged her onto the bed with him. She quit arguing and gave herself body and soul to him. The doubts and fears in her mind were stripped away as surely as were her clothes. The old bed creaked as he removed her jacket, sweater and slacks and, while she was dressed only in her bra and panties, he tore off his own clothes. His shoes clunked as they hit the floor and were followed quickly by his slacks and shirt. In the firelight, his chest seemed bronze, the swirling black hairs darker than ever. His body was taut and strong, and she was reminded of a Native American warrior, so sinewy were his thighs and shoulders. But his eyes were blue, a tribute to his Anglo ancestors.

"This is the way it should be," he whispered, as his arms folded around her and he nibbled at the skin of her neck. Her pulse jumped and her blood flowed like liquid fire through her veins. His chest hair was stiff and curly against her skin and he seemed all hard and angular where she was soft and supple. His mouth found hers, and he kissed her long and hard, his tongue exploring, his hands moving sensually along her rib cage.

He shoved her bra away from her breast, kissing the nipple with feather-light strokes that caused her to writhe and arch against him.

"Slow down," he said, his lips brushing her breasts, his breath caressing her nipple. "We've got all night."

It sounded so good. She cradled his head against her breast as he removed the rest of her clothes. She reveled in his touch and her heart pounded as his fingers grazed her nipple before he lowered his mouth and teased her with his lips and tongue. His hands sculpted her back, holding her firmly to him, making her feel the length of his hardness pressed deep against her abdomen.

His hands worked magic as they explored her, touching her in intimate places, causing her heart to beat as rapidly as the wings of a hummingbird. Lovingly he caressed her, moving with a slow steady hand that only increased when her body requested a faster tempo.

The room seemed to spin, the heat within her coiled, whirling so quickly that she closed her eyes. But still the candlelight was there, in bright vibrant colors that exploded behind her eyelids and caused her body to quake in violent convulsions that ripped a primeval sound from her throat. "Hayden," she cried in that foreign voice.

"I'm right here," he assured her as she clung to him. He let her body slow, and only when her breathing was even and her eyelids fluttered open, did he kiss her again. "Okay, love, now it's my turn," he said.

She reached for him, but he picked her up and carried her outside where the cold air brought goose bumps to her flesh. "Are you crazy? What're you doing?" she cried as he set her into the hot tub and followed after her. "It's freezing out here."

"Not in the water."

"But—"

He kissed her and cut off further protests, and there in the steamy water, with snowflakes sticking to their hair, he gently prodded her knees apart and claimed her for his own.

Later, wrapped only in a bath sheet, she dialed her home, accessed her answering machine code and discovered no messages, so she hung up feeling less irresponsible. Hayden came up behind her, stripped away the bath towel and forced her back to the bed.

The night passed quickly in a haze of lovemaking and glasses of champagne. They fell asleep sometime before dawn and when she finally awoke, the sun was high in the sky, glistening off six inches of fresh snow. Hayden stood by the window, dressed only in his shorts, staring at the trees. When he heard her stir, he turned and spying her sprawled upon the bed, grinned mischievously.

"This is the way I'd like to wake up every morning."

Her traitorous heart skipped a beat, but she ignored it and stretched lazily.

Hayden's gaze moved to her breasts, covered only by the sheets, and he stifled a groan. "We'll never get out of here if you don't quit that."

"Quit what?" she taunted, and he swore under his breath.

"You little tease."

"Me?" she asked innocently, and he crossed the few feet and threw himself over the bed.

"Yes, you."

She laughed as he pinned her beneath the covers and kissed her.

"You are the most exciting, impulsive and impossible woman ever to set foot on this earth."

"May I take that as a compliment?"

"Take it any way you like." He kissed her gently, then propped his head up with one hand. "If you don't get up, you're in for serious trouble, lady."

She knew that. But she didn't want this bliss to end. She stroked his beard-roughened cheek with her hand and touched the tiny scar that sliced through one of his brows. "What's this from?" she asked, and watched as his smile faded.

"Compliments of my old man."

"But how?"

"We had a disagreement. He couldn't get through to me with words, so he used his fist. Not here . . . but he hit me so hard I fell and cut myself on the stair rail. I think I was fifteen."

Her stomach squeezed in pain. "What was the fight about?"

He snorted. "I can't even remember." He was stretched out on the top of the sheet and she saw the other scars on his body, neatly stitched gashes on his legs.

"And these?"

He glanced down when her finger touched one of the bluish marks. "From the accident," he said coldly.

"The what?"

"In the boat. With Wynona."

"Oh." She drew back her hand, but he threaded his fingers through hers and sighed.

"It's okay. That all happened a long time ago. Now, you'd better get up. I'd love to spend the rest of the weekend here, but unfortunately duty calls."

"The mill?"

"The mill," he replied grimly, as he reached for his slacks. "But before we go back, we should eat breakfast. Steak, eggs, pancakes—the works."

She shook her head. "How about coffee and a piece of toast?"

"Whatever your heart desires," he said, kissing her lightly on the forehead before throwing back the covers and exposing her naked form. With a sardonic smile, he kicked off his slacks again. "On second thought . . ."

By the time they returned to Gold Creek, the sun was low in the sky. Nadine thought about the work stretched out before her; she had promised Elizabeth new merchandise. Two of the jackets were complete, the third was almost done, but she only had about a dozen pairs of earrings finished. Then there was some Christmas shopping and planning the traditional meal for her father, the boys and Ben. *And Hayden?* Was that possible?

Hayden folded his hand over hers. "You could come spend the rest of the weekend at my house."

The offer was tempting. "I don't think so. I've got a lot of work to do—"

He placed his hand on her knee, and his gaze slid in her direction. "Won't it keep overnight? I'll build a fire and we'll have eggnog and you can help me with my tree. Remember, I'm still an amateur at this."

"You're twisting my arm."

"I'll bring you back early in the morning, I promise."

"I've heard that one before," she said with a chuckle. "This time I'm going to hold you to it."

They stopped by Nadine's place, where she gave Hershel fresh food and water, checked the mail and the phone messages, grabbed a small suitcase with a change of clothes and her makeup, and then they were on their way. In Gold Creek they purchased a Christmas tree, a stand and some decorations along with a few supplies and groceries.

Darkness had settled on the lake as they pulled into the drive of Hayden's house. Through the tall trees, the lights of the house winked brightly.

"That's odd," Hayden said, his hands tightening over the wheel as they rounded the final bend and the headlights of his rig washed over the shiny finish of a white Jaguar. "Damn it all to hell," he ground out as he stood on the brakes and the Jeep slid to a stop.

"Who's here?" Nadine asked, uneasiness tightening into a hard ball in the pit of her stomach.

"Wynona," he ground out, stepping down from the Jeep.

Nadine froze. *Wynona Galveston was here? Through the locked gates and inside the locked house? As if she had her own key?*

Hayden was striding furiously up the front walk when the door burst open, and Wynona, her supple body framed by interior lights, appeared.

"Thank God you're here," she said, smiling brightly. Her blond hair caught in the moonlight as she ran from the front door and threw herself into Hayden's arms.

Nadine held back a small cry. Her insides shriveled and she felt the urge to run, to get as far away from Hayden as possible. But she kept her wits about her and took a deep breath. His relationship with Wynona might not be what it seemed.

Gathering her courage, Nadine found the door handle of the Jeep and slowly let herself out. The air was cold, blowing off the lake in wintry gusts. A thin layer of clouds partially obscured the moon, but she could see clearly as Hayden slowly peeled Wynona's arms from around his neck.

"...but you have to help me," Wynona was saying, tears frozen in her eyes.

"I don't have to do a damned thing."

"You *owe* me."

"I told you before I owe you nothing." His voice was harsh and callous. Nadine felt bitter and betrayed.

"How can you be so cruel?" Wynona demanded, sobbing openly. "If it weren't for you—"

"Don't start this."

"You nearly killed me," she cried, tears running freely from her eyes.

Nadine's stomach turned sour. She shouldn't listen to this. Yet she couldn't turn away.

"I didn't—"

Wynona's fury unleashed. "The accident was your fault, Hayden. It was your fault I nearly died, and damn it all to hell, it was your fault I lost the baby!"

Chapter Twelve

A baby?

Nadine's knees nearly gave out. Hayden and Wynona had created an unborn baby who had died in the boating accident? Oh, God, what was she doing here? Pain seared her soul. She'd believed him, she'd loved him, she'd given herself to him; and Hayden hadn't even thought enough of her to tell her the truth. "How can you be so cruel?" Wynona broke into hysterical sobs, and Nadine felt as if she'd been hit in the stomach by an iron fist. She leaned against a tall pine for support and wished she'd never become involved with him again, never heard Wynona's pathetic pleas. Her stomach roiled to think she'd imagined she'd loved him—a man who had— Oh, God, little by little she was dying inside.

Hayden swore loudly. "Damn it, Wynona, don't you think you've got your facts twisted a bit?"

"You were there, Hayden. And you abandoned me. For some cheap little small-town whore—ouch!"

Stricken, Nadine glanced up and saw Hayden grab Wynona by the shoulders and give her an angry shake. "Don't you ever talk about her—"

"Oh, Christ, don't tell me you're still in love with her!" Wynona's eyes narrowed, and the tears seemed to melt away. As Nadine drew closer, Wynona's gaze collided with hers and she sucked in her breath. "Well, I'll be," she whispered, shaking her head. "You still have your little red-headed piece of—"

"Stop it!" He shook her again.

Wynona's eyes were frigid and her lip curled. "Just like your old man, aren't you, Hayden? One woman was never enough for him and it looks like you're just the same."

He dropped her as if touching her skin had scorched his fingers. "Get out, Wynona."

Rubbing her arms, she said, "You haven't seen the last of me. You and your father *owe* me. Big-time. Promises were made. Nothing's changed just because he died."

"Like hell. I'm in charge now."

"And you're trying to cut me off!"

"Take it up with Bradworth. Maybe you can strike a private deal with him."

She tried to slap him, but he was too quick. He caught her wrist in his hand and shoved her back. "Don't be stupid, Wynona."

"You bastard! You sick, filthy bastard!"

"Flattery will get you nowhere," he said, and she yanked her hand away. Throwing a scathing glance at Nadine, she strode into the house, grabbed her purse and fur coat, and with the mink waving behind her like a sleek banner, she stormed to her car.

She threw the Jaguar into reverse, backed into a tree and smashed her taillight. Metal crunched and glass splintered. Wynona shoved the car into Drive and roared away, tires spitting gravel, one red taillight winking brightly through the trees.

Nadine was shaking so badly, she could barely move. She thought she might throw up as the pieces of Hayden's past fit together into an ugly, painful puzzle.

"What do they say about a woman scorned?" Hayden asked.

Nadine couldn't answer. Her mouth was dry as cotton, her guts twisted and the pain in her bruised heart wouldn't go away. "I think I should leave," she said, tears threatening her eyes.

"Because of what Wynona said?"

She nodded, and the first drops of rain started to fall from the sky, touching her cheeks and splashing on the ground. "There was a baby?" she whispered, her fists clenched so tightly, her fingernails dug into her palms. She prayed that she misunderstood, but the hardening of Hayden's jaw, the tightening of his mouth at its corners only confirmed the worst of her fears. The bottom of Nadine's world seemed to fall out from under her.

"Yes, there was a baby, but it wasn't mine."

"Hayden, don't lie—"

"I'm not, damn it!" He grabbed her and dragged her wooden body close to his. "You have to believe me."

"But you never said a word," she cried, her trust in him unraveling as quickly as an old seam in an antique dress. How could she have trusted him, made love to him, given her heart to him when she knew so little about him?

"There are reasons."

"Reasons? What reasons? You didn't want me to know because then I wouldn't be so easily seduced, is that it? Or were you trying to make yourself look better in my eyes?" Icy rain was falling heavily now, trickling in the gutters and pooling on the walks. Frigid drops drizzled down Nadine's face and throat.

"Of course not!"

"Then why?"

His jaw worked and he closed his eyes. "The baby was my father's."

Nadine gasped, and her insides churned as wildly as the storm-tossed lake. "Your father's?" She couldn't believe it. Wouldn't. "But you were engaged to her. Come on, Hayden, you don't really expect me to believe that—"

"That my father would seduce a woman half his age? That she would be flattered by his attention since she couldn't have mine? That Wynona Galveston was more interested in Monroe money than she was in me or my dad?" he asked, shoving his wet hair from his face. "Which part is so unbelievable?"

"It never came out that she was pregnant. In all the press about the accident. Never once—"

"Her father is a doctor. He hushed it up. It was part of the deal he made with my dad... Oh, hell, it's complicated. Come inside before we're both soaked. You may as well know the whole sordid story."

"I don't think I should—"

He held her hand in his and looked into her eyes with such pain and torment, she couldn't say no. "I must be crazy. I should just walk away from all this."

"No, you shouldn't." His thumb rubbed gently across the back of her hand. "Just hear me out."

Telling herself she was a fool of the highest order, Nadine helped him unpack the car. Her insides were knotted, and she told herself she was only prolonging the agony by watching him start a fire. "We'll eat first," he said, and she didn't argue. She wasn't sure that she wanted to hear all of the details of his affair—or his father's—with another woman, but knew that if there was any chance of a future for them, she had to.

She heated clam chowder and warmed the bread. They ate in the den, in front of the crackling flames, sipping wine and trying to ignore the tension that seemed to mount with each slow tick of the grandfather clock.

"I never loved her," Hayden admitted, setting his empty bowl on the coffee table.

"You don't have to—"

"She was handpicked by my mother. From the right family. Her father was a doctor and her mother had inherited 'old money.' She was pretty and smart and my mother thought she'd make the perfect match. Her parents, too, were thrilled at the prospect. Even Wynona bought into the plan. But I wasn't about to be bullied into marrying someone I didn't really care about. Oh, I liked her. A lot. What was there not to like?

"What I didn't know, and my parents didn't realize, was that most of Wynona's inheritance didn't exist. Her father had sizable debts that he'd incurred while going to school and he had a little problem at the racetrack. He liked to bet on the ponies. The family still had money, of course, but not the kind of wealth my mother expected. Most of what was left of the Galveston fortune would be passed on to their son, Wynona's brother, Gerard. So, I was the perfect catch.

"Remember the Mercedes I left in the sawmill lot the day I met you?" She nodded and he said, "Well, it was an engagement present from my father. To Wynona and me. Only, there was no engagement. So I didn't accept the gift and my old man was furious."

Nadine remembered the day as vividly as if it had occurred just last week. Meeting Hayden had changed her life forever. She stared at him now, his features solemn in the firelight, his eyes lifeless. "When I wasn't interested in her, Wynona was desperate and then . . . my father stepped in. I don't really know when they started their affair. I've told myself that it had to have happened *after* I'd told her I wouldn't marry her, but I'm not so sure. She was pregnant. Oh, hell!" He stood and walked to the fireplace, adding a small log and watching the flames devour the mossy oak.

"I didn't know about their affair at first, nor did my mom. Dad had always had a thing for women, younger beautiful women, and Mom had always turned her head. She would rather suffer his infidelity than divorce him and admit that she couldn't hold her man. How she put up with him, I'll never know. Remember I told you that my mom and I stayed at the lodge in the mountains? Well, she took me there once when she walked out on dad after learning that he was involved with his secretary. But, as always, she went back to him."

Nadine felt as if she'd been led down a private stairway and into a dark room where she didn't belong. "I don't think I want to know the rest—"

"I want you to. While my mom was trying to patch things up with Wynona and me, my dad was already taking her to his bed."

"And she got pregnant."

"Right. Then all hell broke loose." He stared at Nadine, saw the doubts in her eyes and took her hand between his two larger palms. "Believe me, Nadine, I never slept with her. The baby couldn't have been mine."

"There was no mention of a baby in the paper."

"Lots of things were left out," he said flatly. "As I said, her old man was a doctor and made sure that no one learned that she was pregnant. Oh, a few medical people knew, but they kept their mouths shut."

"Oh, God, Hayden. This is too much," she said, shaking her head. "Even if the baby wasn't yours—"

"It wasn't," he said firmly, his nostrils flaring.

"It died. *Died* in the accident. Your half brother or sister."

He took her into his arms and held her close. She felt near tears, for a baby who had never had the chance to live, for Hayden who had endured the hardship of being fathered by a man who had never known the meaning of the word *love* and for herself. She loved him. With all her stupid heart, she loved him and yet there was so much she didn't know about him. He'd been raised in a different world from hers and there was so much pain between their families.

"You may as well know it all," Hayden said, holding her close.

"There's more?"

"I wasn't driving the boat."

"But the accident report—"

"Shh." His breath ruffled her hair. "Wynona blamed me because we had a fight. Because of the baby, she begged me to marry her and I wouldn't. She was out of her mind and told me she was going to kill herself. I didn't really believe her but she ran out of the house and down the dock. I chased after her, and managed to get into the boat before she took off, but she was already at the helm. She tore away from the dock as fast as she could and I let her drive. I figured it would do her good to let off steam. So I didn't try to wrestle the helm from her. She tried to scare me, driving recklessly, but I didn't stop her. I saw the other boat before she did and yelled at her, but it was too late. The other guy bailed out and we struck the fishing boat broadside.''

''But everyone thinks . . . the police reports . . .''

''They said I was the driver. For insurance purposes. No one was supposed to drive the boat but members of the family. There was some restriction because the boat was so powerful. Lots of other people did, but when the accident occurred, everyone thought I was behind the wheel. I was unconscious for a couple of days and by the time I came around and the police talked to me, my dad had told me what to say. I didn't want to, of course, but he convinced me it would look best for everyone. Especially Wynona. She was already blaming me for the accident because I was the reason she took the boat in the first place. And I felt guilty about the baby. For once I believed my old man and rather than cause more of a scandal, I went along with the story.'' He sighed. ''For keeping my mouth shut so long, my dad finally paid me off.'' He motioned to the room around him. ''With this.''

She wanted to believe him, to trust him, but needed time to sort through his story, decide for herself what was fact and what was fiction. Slowly she pulled herself out of his embrace and asked a question that had been on her mind for years. ''There were rumors, Hayden. Lots of them. You had a reputation.'' She eyed him thoughtfully. ''A girl named Trish London.''

''Hell.''

Again a sick feeling. ''You were involved with her?''

''Yes.''

''And she was sent to stay in Portland with her sister to have your baby?''

''What?'' His head snapped up and his eyes focused hard on Nadine. ''There wasn't a baby. Dad gave her family money, true, but she left because her mother was unfit to care for her. Her older sister offered to give her a place to live and help her with college. Trish really didn't have a choice. She'd already been branded in this town, so she took off. Wrote me one letter. Trish and I had an affair, I won't deny it, but we were careful.'' He looked at her long and hard. "In fact, the only woman I haven't been careful with has been you. Until the past couple of weeks I never wanted children and I was damned careful to make sure that I didn't sire any.''

His world was so different from hers. Money was and always would be the answer. He grew up learning that money could solve any problem. She heard his change of heart toward a family, but she wasn't sure she believed him. There was just so much to learn.... "What does Wynona want from you now?''

His lips curled in disgust. "What do you think?''

"Money.''

"Right. The old man didn't leave her much and she wants more, plans on suing his estate for what she considers her share.''

So it all came down to money. And it always would. As long as Hayden was the rich boy, money would always rule his life.

She stood quickly. He reached for her but she drew away. Why was she prolonging this agony? Why didn't she just leave him now, break it off, save herself and her children any further heartache?

He drew her into his arms, but she resisted. "I think I should leave,'' she said again, her heart breaking into a thousand pieces.

"You don't believe me.''

Fighting tears, she placed her hand along his jaw, felt the beard stubble in her palms and nearly broke down. "That's the problem. I do believe you. I believe that you're right. For the rest of your life you'll live in a world I can't begin to understand, a world run by money. You said you didn't want a wife and children and I said I didn't want a husband. However, there's no future for us. There's no reason to prolong this any further.''

He touched her and she fell back a step. "Don't.''

"Nadine, listen, I—''

"Shh." Placing a finger against his lips, she shook her head. "It's over, Hayden. It really never did exist. We can be happy now, knowing we fulfilled our childhood fantasies, but we can't expect this to go on indefinitely. You're planning to sell the mill, and what then?"

He didn't say a word, and she suddenly felt as cold as the bottom of the ocean. "Believe me, this is for the best." Turning quickly, she headed for the door, hoping to feel his hand on the crook of her elbow, silently praying that he'd grab her and tell her he couldn't live without her, dying with each step as she approached the door.

Finally she heard him move, heard his footsteps behind her. Her heart leapt unexpectedly when she thought he would crush her to him and tell her that he wouldn't let her go.

Instead he said, "I think you'll need a ride."

Hayden kicked himself for being such a damned fool. She'd only been gone eighteen hours and he was going out of his mind. Like an idiot, he'd decorated the house by himself and now he sneered at his attempts at Christmas spirit. The house with lights and tinsel and a tree near the fire was as cold as the feeling in the middle of his heart. All the decorations and lights and gifts in the world wouldn't make up for the emptiness he felt without her and the boys. He'd even bought gifts, wrapped them and placed them under the tree. For Nadine and her kids. Not that she'd want them.

He'd learned long ago that everything came with a price, and her price was his loss of freedom and a life in Gold Creek. The freedom part he could handle. The family part he surprisingly decided he would embrace. But Gold Creek and his father's sawmills? He could still sell them, of course, but that thought was beginning to sour his stomach and he didn't want to be a part of the "idle rich." No way. Selling out to Thomas Fitzpatrick or some other rich timber baron was the coward's way out.

He climbed into the Jeep and drove into town. Snow had been predicted, and the first flakes were starting to collect on the ground. Good. It didn't matter if the whole damned lake froze over. Hayden couldn't get any colder.

The Silver Horseshoe wasn't very crowded on the twenty-third of December. A few of the regulars hung out at the bar, several younger guys played pool and Hayden recognized a few faces. Erik Patton, who worked at the mill, was huddled over a mug of beer, a cigarette burning in the ashtray beside him. Ed Foster, who had recently retired from the coaching staff at Tyler High, was nursing a tall one, and Patty Osgood Smythe gave him the once-over as he approached the bar. There were other people there, as well, men who seemed to bristle when he slid onto his stool. In the mirror behind the bar, he caught a few hard glances cast his way and knew that some of these men and women were dependent upon him for their livelihoods.

He ordered an ale, nibbled at peanuts and wondered what life would be like if he settled down in Gold Creek for good. What if he buried the past, made peace with his father and took over the helm of the sawmills? He could go through the company books, make restitution where it was necessary. If other people had been swindled by his father, maybe there was something that could be done. Better late than never.

He could run the mills. He had the education and the experience. What he didn't have was the employees behind him. That would take time. No one really trusted him.

A gust of cold wind followed a newcomer into the bar. Hayden glanced over his shoulder and spied Ben Powell, Nadine's older brother, as he sauntered in. His dark hair cut military-short, Ben surveyed the room in one glance, caught sight of Hayden and froze. "I figured you were back," he said, his features hard, his hazel eyes cold. "I heard that your father had died."

"That's right."

"Running things, are you, now?"

Hayden nodded. "Let me buy you a beer."

Ben's mouth twisted into a mirthless grin. He reached into his pocket and threw a couple of bucks onto the polished counter. "I don't want any of your money, Monroe." To the bartender, "Give me a draft—anything you've got on tap."

Leaning closer to Hayden, Ben said, "Well, I'm back, too. For good. So just stay out of my way."

"Might be hard."

Ben's eyes narrowed.

"Why's that?"

"Because I'm going to ask your sister to marry me."

"You're what?" Ben asked, paling a little.

"You heard me."

Ben's reactions were quick. With skill learned in the army, he hauled back and landed a right cross to Hayden's face. Hayden's head snapped back, but he heard the rip of cartilage and felt blood gush from his nostrils as he stumbled against the bar.

A woman screamed as all eyes in the bar turned toward the two men squaring off.

Quickly he was on the balls of his feet, spoiling for the fight. It would do him good to hit something, and Ben's angular face seemed a ready target. "Come on," he taunted, "brother."

"You bloody son of a bitch!" Ben came at him again, and Hayden sidestepped the blow.

The bartender vaulted over the bar. "Enough. You're outta here, mister," he said to Ben, but Hayden waved and found a cocktail napkin to staunch the flow of his blood. "Don't you two know anything about the Christmas spirit?"

"Outside!" Ben demanded, but Hayden only laughed.

"It's over," he said to the bartender. "Let me buy this man a drink. Hell, I'll buy a round for everyone."

The bartender hesitated, but the small crowd in the bar cheered, and Hayden felt that for the first time since he'd returned to Gold Creek, he was beginning to belong. Still eyeing Ben, the bartender started pouring drinks.

Ben's expression was thunderous; his eyes narrowed in fury. He grabbed his bottle of beer and poured it slowly onto the floor. Without bothering to pick up his change, he turned on his heel and left.

"Who was that guy?" the bartender asked.

"Someone with a grudge," Hayden said. "And it's only going to get worse." Just wait until Ben found out that he and Nadine had been sleeping together. All hell was bound to break loose. Hayden grinned. Ben wouldn't make such a bad brother-in-law.

"You did what?" Ben roared, his face florid, his hands balled into tight fists of rage.

Standing at the dining room table, Nadine smoothed the foil wrap around a game that she'd bought for John. Christmas cookies were baking in the oven, and the exterior lights glowed in the falling snow. If not for Ben's bad mood and her heartache over Hayden, this Christmas could be the best one in a long, long while. "I said I went out with Hayden last night," she repeated, unnerved by the fire in Ben's eye. She'd been happy to find him in the house, waiting for her, his duffle bag stuffed in a corner of the living room. But he'd come at her like a tiger.

"You've been seeing him again? Damn, what do you think you're doing?" Ben strode in front of the fireplace, his back stiff, his eyes flashing with anger. "Does Dad know?"

"Yes," she replied sweetly. "And he's given me his blessing, just like you."

"But Monroe—"

"Stop it, Ben! You can't walk back into my life and start big-brothering me all over again. I'm a grown woman, for God's sake. I take care of myself and my children, and you have no right, no right whatsoever, to tell me what to do or start second-guessing my judgment. Besides—" she taped the package and worked on the bow, avoiding his eyes "—I think it's over. I left his place tonight and it was pretty much understood that we wouldn't see each other again."

He opened his mouth to say something, thought better of it and leaned a shoulder against the mantel. "Good—just remember what that bastard and his father did to this family."

Her head snapped up and she pinned him with a glare meant to cut steel. "I haven't forgotten, Ben, but it's time to bury the past, don't you think?"

"Never."

"It's Christmas."

"So I've heard," he said cryptically.

"Well, I've at least come to terms with what happened. You'd better, too."

"Why? So you can marry the bum?"

Her spine stiffened. "No. It's over with Hayden."

"You wouldn't do anything as stupid as marry him, right?"

"Marry him?" she repeated, her heart tugging. "I don't think you've got to worry about that."

He rubbed the back of his neck uneasily. "He hasn't asked you?"

Her heart thudded painfully. "It won't happen, Ben. Don't worry about it." The bell on the stove rang softly, indicating that the cookies she was baking were done. She left the package to take out one sheet of apple squares and shove in another of pumpkin bars.

The house smelled of warm cinnamon and nutmeg, fragrant pine and bayberry candles. A fire blazed in the hearth; the Christmas tree glowed warmly in the corner, its lights reflecting in the windows. Everything was perfect, except the house seemed empty. Even with Ben here. The boys were still with Sam, and Hayden...God only knew where he was and what he was doing. She glanced out the window, past the snow falling upon the dark waters of the lake to the pinpoints of light she knew were burning from the Monroe home.

She didn't hear Ben approach. His voice startled her. "More snow's been predicted. Looks like we might have a white Christmas."

A lonely white Christmas, she thought, burning herself on the hot cookie sheet as she brushed up against it. "Hmm."

Ben found a knife and cut himself a gooey apple square.

"Help yourself," she said, teasing, as she handed him a napkin. "Milk's in the fridge. Or I can make coffee—"

He waved away her offer. "Don't bother." When she glanced through the window again, he said, "You're really hung up on that bastard, aren't you?"

"I told you I'm not seeing him again. I told him so tonight." Glancing back at him, she saw the ghost of a smile touch his thin lips. "But if I change my mind, I expect you to keep your mouth shut about it."

Ben smiled coldly. "You always did have a way with words."

"So did you. Now, come on, make yourself useful. I bought new bikes for the boys, and you can put them together. I'll even make you something to eat. Something more than cookies."

"I'm not all that hungry. I'll just have another one of these—" he said, and winced as he grabbed the knife. For the first time she noticed that the knuckles on his right hand were swollen. "What happened to you?" she asked, and he cut another bar from the pan.

"I, um, had a little altercation down at the Silver Horseshoe."

"A fight? You've been in town less that twenty-four hours and you've already been in a fistfight? Didn't you learn anything while you were in the army?"

"The guy had it coming."

"Oh. Okay, sure," she said sarcastically as she peered into the oven. "Who was the guy and what did he do?"

Ben didn't say a word, just looked at her and she knew. Her heart sank. Her brother had rolled into town, run into Hayden and promptly tried to punch out his lights.

"You already saw Hayden? That's how you found out about us?" she said, sick at heart. "What happened?"

"He tried to buy me a drink."

"And you hit him. Nice, Ben. Real nice."

"He had it coming," he said, rubbing his wounded hand with his fingers. "Has had for years."

Nadine shook her head. One part of her wanted to run to Hayden, to see that he was all right. The other wanted to slap her older brother across his self-righteous chin. "So you took it upon yourself to defend my honor."

Ben rubbed his jaw and for the first time seemed slightly contrite. "I couldn't help it, Nadine. The bastard said something about marrying you."

* * *

Ben's words had stuck with her. *Marriage? Hayden was talking about marriage?*

She couldn't still the beat of her heart, and expected him to show up on her doorstep. But he didn't. Nor did he call. Nadine was beginning to think that Ben hadn't heard Hayden correctly or that Hayden had been teasing Ben, just to get a rise out of him.

She considered calling Hayden, but didn't. Nothing had really changed. Though Hayden had mellowed a little on his stance about children, he still didn't want to be tied down. Never had, never would. He'd said as much.

Nadine slept restlessly, thinking of Hayden, and Ben left early the next morning to spend the day looking for an apartment he could rent, as well as visit their father.

Nadine kept herself busy cooking and cleaning, wrapping a few presents and putting the finishing touches on the house. By the time the boys arrived home, she wanted everything to be perfect. She glanced across the lake more times than she could count and found herself listening for the whine of Hayden's Jeep's engine.

The phone rang and she nearly jumped out of her skin. She answered with a breathless hello and was disappointed when Sam told her he was running a little late; he and the kids were at a Christmas party and he'd bring the boys home a little later.

"When?" Nadine asked.

"Does it matter? There's no school tomorrow."

"I know, but—"

"Don't worry, Nadine. They'll be home in a little while."

A few hours later, Sam was true to his word. He brought the boys into the house and dropped their overnight bags in the middle of the living room. His face was red and his eyes a little glazed from too much partying. Snow melted off his boots and clung to his collar.

"Hey, Mom, there's already presents under the tree!" Bobby said, his eyes as round as saucers.

"A few from me."

"Any from Monroe?" Sam asked, his eyes as cold as the December storm.

Bobby was already checking the brightly colored packages. "Santa's still gonna come, isn't he?"

"You bet. I baked some cookies today and you and I will make a special batch tomorrow."

"Aw, Mom, there's no such thing as—" John started to protest, but Nadine cast him a sharp look that shut him up.

Sam lingered, taking in the cozy room and frowning. "The boys say you're pretty thick with Monroe."

"We've seen a little of each other."

He lifted his hat and rubbed his head. "You might as well know that I don't approve."

"I figured that," she said, bristling.

"And don't tell me it's none of my business."

"What I do with my life—"

"I'm talkin' about the kids, damn it. They're seeing entirely too much of the guy." Sam was getting angry, and the drinks he'd obviously consumed had begun to affect his speech. He waved one arm wildly to make his point. "That son of a bitch is gonna close the mills—"

"He wouldn't do that, Dad," John said.

"What would you know about it?"

"I like him. He's a good guy."

"What he is," Sam said, weaving a little, "is a no-good, pampered rich bastard, and I don't like him buying fancy things for my boys."

"It's not like that, Dad," John argued.

"You back-talkin' me?" Sam asked, lunging a little as he caught John by the collar.

"Let go of him!" Nadine stepped in front of her son as if to use her body as a barrier. "Don't you dare lay a hand on him," she warned.

But Sam was suddenly mad at the world. "You're too easy on the kids. Git out of my way." He tried to push Nadine aside, but she held her ground.

"You'd better leave."

"Why?" He rolled back on his heels and smiled sickly. "So you can entertain your rich boyfriend?"

"That's enough!"

Sam's glazed eyes narrowed in hatred. "So have you given it to him yet? You always wanted to. Don't think I didn't know it. Every time we were in bed, you were thinking about him, imagining that I—"

"Stop it!" she cried, marching to the door and opening it. Cold wind crept in and the fire stoked higher. "Go on, Sam. Go sleep it off."

"I think I'll stay here. Too dangerous for me to drive."

"I'll call someone."

"Come on, Nadine. Let me stay. For old times." His grin turned into a leer and he started for her, but tripped on the edge of the rug. "Goddamn it," he said, reaching for anything to keep his balance. He stumbled over the coffee table, caught hold of the branch of the tree and grabbed on, but the little Christmas tree was no match for his weight. It toppled to the floor and one branch fell into the fireplace. With a rush of air, the dry needles ignited and flames consumed them.

"Oh, God! Sam, watch out! Boys, get out quick!" Nadine cried, and when her sons stood immobile, she screamed. "Now! Outside, run over to the Thornton's, have them call the fire department!"

Trying to get free of the tree, Sam was screaming. Both boys took off through the front door and Hershel gave chase. Nadine ran to the kitchen, grabbed the fire extinguisher and started spraying, but it was too late, the fire had caught on the rug and curtains. Flames leapt high in the tree and though Sam was free, his clothes were on fire. He was screaming horribly.

She didn't hear him arrive, but suddenly Hayden was there, shouting orders, yelling at her to go outside to the lake, kicking at the tree with his boots and dragging a writhing Sam from the conflagration.

Adrenaline pumped through Nadine's bloodstream, she grabbed a photo album and her purse from a table, and then she, in horror, helped Hayden drag Sam outside, down the rise in the ground, toward the lake. They yanked off his clothes, leaving him in his underwear. His screams filled the night and snow melted on his skin.

Nadine glanced frantically around for her boys in the darkness, but they and the dog had disappeared and her little cottage, her pride and joy, the only possession she held dear had become an inferno and reflected in bloodred shadows on the snow.

"You're gonna be all right," Hayden said to Sam.

"Help me. God Almighty, help me."

"Help's coming." Hayden took Nadine's hand. "Stay with him but give me your keys."

"My what—?" But she was already digging through her purse. In the distance, she heard the first wail of a siren.

Hayden stripped the keys from her shaking hands and ran toward the house. She screamed at him until she saw him climb into her little Nova, back the car as far from the conflagration as possible and park.

"Oh, God," she whispered, still searching the night for her children. "John? Bobby? Please, please—" They wouldn't have run back into the house, would they? Searching for her, the boys wouldn't have gone into the kitchen through the back door?

Terror squeezed her heart and she heard Sam moan. Dropping to her knees she tried to hold his hand and comfort him, keeping snow against his skin as she searched the darkness.

Hayden jogged back to her as the first window exploded.

"Oh, God—the boys?" she cried.

"They'll be fine," he said, wrapping her in his arms and kissing her forehead. "Thank God. Just hang in here. Be strong." In a second he released her and was bending over Sam. "Help will be here soon." And for the first time Nadine realized how close Sam had come to death. She heard her children running along the shoreline with the neighbors, and thankfully Jane Thornton, a nurse who worked at the county hospital and lived on the south shore of the lake was with them. She immediately tended to Sam as Nadine gathered her boys close.

Flames shot through the dry roof of the house, flickering red fingers reaching hellishly toward the black night sky, and tears began to fall from Nadine's eyes. Everything was gone. Everything she'd worked for, every possession she'd held dear.

"You're safe now," Hayden whispered into her ear.

"But the cabin—"

"It can be rebuilt."

"No, I—everything's in there—"

"Not everything," he said, his voice rough, tears glistening in his eyes. "You've got me. And the boys. Forever."

She glanced up at him, hardly daring to believe him.

Sirens wailed closer. Firelight shone in his eyes. The stench of smoke filled the air. Trucks with firemen rolled into the yard. An ambulance slid to a stop and paramedics quickly took over, helping Sam. Within minutes they'd taken him to County Hospital after assuring Nadine that he would survive.

She watched for over an hour as the firemen doused the flames and her cabin was reduced to a dripping, blackened skeleton.

When the firemen finally left, tears drizzled from her eyes. "It's gone," she whispered. "It's all gone."

Hayden held her tighter. "I came here to ask you to be my wife, Nadine, and when I saw you in the fire, that there was a chance I could lose you, I . . . I knew I'd never live without you. Marry me." He kissed her on the lips. "Please. Tell me you'll be my wife."

"I—"

"I love you," he said, and his face was serious with emotions that burned deep in his soul. "Make this Christmas our first as a family."

She laughed and cried at the same time. Relief mingled with happiness as snow settled on the remains of a cottage where she'd brought her children into the world, suffered through her divorce and made love to Hayden.

Her gaze drifted over his shoulder, past the dark depths of Whitefire Lake to the lights glowing in the distance. Her new home. With Hayden.

Her throat so thick she could barely speak, she gathered her boys close. "I guess we get to start over," she said, her eyes shining as she stared into Hayden's eyes. "Of course I'll marry you."

Epilogue

From the landing on the stairs of her new home, Nadine tossed her bridal bouquet to the crowd gathered in her foyer. A scream of delight went up when Carlie Surrett caught the flowers.

Half the town had been invited to the hastily planned wedding, including the Surretts, in an attempt to mend all the old rifts. A pianist was playing love songs on the baby grand in the living room and guests mingled and danced, talked and laughed and sipped champagne.

As she descended toward the crowd, Nadine spied Hayden, dressed in a black tuxedo, his eyes as blue as a summer morning. "It seems to be some pagan tradition that we dance," he whispered into her ear.

Nadine smiled up at him. In the living room, they started the dance, with a crowd of onlookers watching. Tiny white lights were strewn in the potted plants and twelve-foot Christmas tree in the corner. Eventually, one by one, other couples followed their lead. Heather Brooks, draped in shimmery pale blue, danced with Turner, who, dressed in a

Western-cut black suit, his blond-streaked hair unruly as ever, winked broadly at Nadine. "I get the next dance," he said, and Hayden grinned. "Not on your life."

Rachelle and her husband, Jackson Moore, took a turn about the floor and Rachelle's hazel eyes were full of a secret only a few people knew. In the spring, she and Jackson would become parents. She laughed up at her husband and he held her with a possession that bordered upon fierce.

"Everyone's happy," Hayden said.

"Mmm." Even her father, sitting in the corner chair, was talking and laughing with Ellen Little, Heather and Rachelle's mother, and Nadine's heart warmed.

Only Ben seemed out of place. Grudgingly, he'd accepted Hayden as his brother-in-law. Since Hayden had decided to stay in Gold Creek and run the sawmills he'd inherited, not as his father had from a distance, but here, as a citizen of the town, Ben had decided he might turn out all right.

The fact that Hayden approved of his new wife's career and was willing to help her get started with her wearable art had convinced Ben that Hayden wasn't all bad.

Even John and Bobby were having a good time, though John spent entirely too much time at the punch bowl with Katie Osgood.

The music changed, and Hayden drew his wife through the French doors to the back deck. "Hey... what?" she asked, as he led her, running through the snow and dark night, down a lighted path to the shores of the lake. "Are you crazy?" she cried, as he pulled her to the ground and her dress was suddenly wet from the snow.

With a devilish grin, he scooped up a handful of the icy water and held it to his bride's lips. "Drink," he ordered, "and let the God of the Sun or whatever bless us."

"I think he already has." She sipped the water from his hands and looked deep into his eyes. "You're going to be a father."

"I'm what—?"

"John and Bobby won't be the only children," she said, and watched as he blinked rapidly.

"Oh, God."

"Happy?"

In answer, he drew her into his arms and kissed her long and hard, but she pulled away, and giggling, offered him a scoop of lake water.

"Don't be greedy," she said, as he touched his lips to her palm and the water dripped through her fingers.

"Me?" His blue eyes sparked with an inner fire and his fingers twined in her hair, dragging her face to bare inches from his own. "There's only one thing on this earth I can never get enough of, lady," he vowed, his voice growing gruff with conviction, "and you may as well know that one thing is you."

His lips found hers, and as an owl hooted softly in the trees, Nadine was certain she heard the ghosts of the lake whisper their blessing on the rich boy of Gold Creek.

* * * * *

Author's Note

The Native American legend of Whitefire Lake was whispered to the white men who came from the east in search of gold in the mountains. Even in the missions, there was talk of the legend, though men of the Christian God professed to disbelieve any pagan myths.

None was less believing than Kelvin Fitzpatrick, a brawny Irish man who was rumored to have killed a man before he first thrust his pickax into the hills surrounding the lake. No body was ever found, and the claim jumper vanished, so a murder couldn't be proved. But the rumors around Fitzpatrick didn't disappear.

He found the first gold in the hills on a morning when the lake was still shrouded in the white mist that was as beautiful as it was deceptive. Fitzpatrick staked his claim and drank lustily from the water. He'd found his home and his fortune in these hills.

He named the creek near his claim Gold Creek and decided to become the first founding father of a town by the same name. He took his pebbles southwest to the city of San Francisco, where he transformed gold to money and a scrubby forty-niner into what appeared to be a wealthy gentleman. With his money and looks, Kelvin wooed and married a socialite from the city, Marian Dubois.

News of Fitzpatrick's gold strike traveled fast, and soon Gold Creek had grown into a small shantytown. With the prospectors came the merchants, the gamblers, the saloon keepers, the clergy and the whores. The Silver Horseshoe Saloon stood on the west end of town and the Presbyterian church was built on the east, and Gold Creek soon earned a reputation for fistfights, barroom brawls and hangings.

Kelvin's wealth increased and he fathered four children—all girls. Two were from Marian, the third from a town whore and the fourth by a Native American woman. All children were disappointments as Kelvin Fitzpatrick needed an heir for his empire.

The community was growing from a boisterous mining camp to a full-fledged town, with Kelvin Fitzpatrick as Gold Creek's first mayor and most prominent citizen. The persecuted Native Americans with their legends and pagan ways were soon forced into servitude or thrown from their land. They made their way into the hills, away from the white man's town and the white man's troubles.

In 1860, when Kelvin was forty-three, his wife finally bore him a son, Rodwell Kelvin Fitzpatrick. Roddy, handsome and precocious, became the apple of his father's eye. Though considered "bad seed" and a hellion by most of the churchgoing citizens of Gold Creek, Roddy Fitzpatrick was the crown prince to the Fitzpatrick fortune, and when his father could no longer mine gold from the earth's crust, he discovered a new mode of wealth and, perhaps, more sacred: the forest.

Roddy Fitzpatrick started the first logging operation and opened the first sawmill. All competitors were quickly bought or forced out of business. But other men, bankers and smiths, carpenters and doctors, settled down to stay and hopefully smooth out the rough edges of the town. Men with names of Kendrick, Monroe and Powell made Gold Creek their home and brought their wives in homespun and woolens, women who baked pies, planned fairs and corralled their wayward Saturday night drinking men into church each Sunday morning.

Roddy Fitzpatrick, who grew into a handsome but cruel man, ran the family businesses when the older Fitzpatrick retired. In a few short years, Roddy had gambled or squandered most of the family fortune. Competitors had finally gotten a toehold in the lumber-rich mountains surrounding Gold Creek and new businesses were sprouting along the muddy streets of the town.

The railroad arrived, bringing with its coal-spewing engines much wealth and commerce. The railway station was situated on the west end of town, not too far from the Silver Horseshoe Saloon and a skeletal trestle bridged the gorge of the creek. Ranchers and farmers brought their produce into town for the market and more people stayed on, settling in the growing community, though Gold Creek was still known for the bullet holes above the bar in the saloon.

And still there was the rumor of some Indian curse that occasionally was whispered by the older people of the town.

Roddy Fitzpatrick married a woman of breeding, a woman who was as quick with a gun as she was to quote a verse. Belinda Surrett became his wife and bore him three sons.

Roddy, always a hothead and frustrated at his shrinking empire, was involved in more than his share of brawls. Knives flashed, guns smoked and threats and curses were spat around a wad of tobacco and a shot of whiskey.

When a man tried to cheat him at cards, Roddy plunged a knife into the blackguard's heart and killed him before a packed house of gamblers, drinkers, barkeeps and whores. After a night in jail, Roddy was set free with no charges leveled agaianst him by the sheriff, who was a fast friend of the elder Fitzpatrick.

But Roddy's life was not to be the same. One night he didn't return home to his wife. She located Kelvin and they formed a search party. Two days later, Roddy's body was washed up on the shore of Whitefire Lake. There was a bullet hole in his chest and his wallet was empty.

Some people thought he was killed by a thief; still others decided Roddy had been shot by a jealous husband, but some, those who still believed in the legend, knew that the God of the Sun had taken Roddy's life to punish Kelvin Fitzpatrick by not only taking away his wealth but the only thing Kelvin had loved: his son.

The older Fitzpatrick, hovering on the brink of bankruptcy, took his own life after learning that his son was dead. Kelvin's daughters, those legitimate, and those who were born out of wedlock, each began their own lives.

The town survived the dwindling empire of the Fitzpatricks and new people arrived at the turn of the century. New names were added to the town records. Industry and commerce brought the flagging community into the twentieth century, though the great earthquake of 1906 did much damage. Many buildings toppled, but the Silver Horseshoe Saloon and the Presbyterian church and the railroad trestle survived.

Monore Sawmill, a new company owned and operated by Hayden Garreth Monroe, bought some of the dwindling Fitzpatrick forests and mills and during the twenties, thirties and forties, Gold Creek became a company town. The people were spared destitution during the depression as the company kept the workers employed, even when they were forced to pay in company cash that could only be spent on goods at the company store. But no family employed by Monroe Sawmill went hungry; therefore, the community, who had hated Fitzpatrick's empire, paid homage to Hayden Garreth Monroe, even when the forests dwindled, logging prices dropped and the mills were shut down.

In the early 1960s, the largest sawmill burned to the ground. The police suspected arson. As the night sky turned orange by the flames licking toward the black heavens, and the volunteer firemen fought the blaze, the townspeople stood and watched. Some thought the fire was a random act of violence, others believed that Hayden Garreth Monroe

III, grandson of the well-loved old man, had lost favor and developed more than his share of enemies when the company cash became worthless and the townspeople, other than those who were already wealthy, began to go bankrupt. They thought the fire was personal revenge. Names of those he'd harmed were murmured. Fitzpatrick came to mind, though by now, the families had been bonded by marriage and the timber empire of the Fitzpatricks had experienced another boom.

Some of the townspeople, the very old with long memories, thought of the legend that had nearly been forgotten. Hayden Garreth Monore III had drunk like a glutton from Whitefire Lake and he, too, would lose all that he held dear—first his wealth and eventually his wife.

As time passed, other firms found toeholds in Gold Creek, and in the seventies and eighties, technology crept over the hills. From the ashes of Kelvin Fitzpatrick's gold and timber empire rose the new wealth of other families.

The Fitzpatricks still rule the town, and Thomas Fitzpatrick, patriarch of the family, intends one day to turn to state politics. However, scandal has tarnished his name and as his political aspiration turns to ashes and his once-envied life crumbles, he will have to give way to new rulers—young men who are willing to fight for what they want. Men like Jackson Moore and Turner Brooks and Hayden Garreth Monroe IV.

Old names mingle and marry with new, but the town and its legend continue to exist. To this day, the people of Gold Creek cannot shake the gold dust of those California hills from their feet. Though they walk many paths away from the shores of the lake, the men and women of Gold Creek— the boys and girls—can never forget their hometown. Nor can they forget the legend and curse of Whitefire Lake.

Take 4 bestselling love stories FREE

Plus get a FREE surprise gift!

Special Limited-time Offer

Mail to Harlequin Reader Service®

3010 Walden Avenue
P.O. Box 1867
Buffalo, N.Y. 14269-1867

YES! Please send me 4 free Silhouette Special Edition® novels and my free surprise gift. Then send me 6 brand-new novels every month, which I will receive months before they appear in bookstores. Bill me at the low price of $2.71* each plus 25¢ delivery and applicable sales tax, if any.* I understand that accepting the books and gift places me under no obligation ever to buy any books. I can always return a shipment and cancel at any time. Even if I never buy another book from Silhouette, the 4 free books and the surprise gift are mine to keep forever.

235 BPA AJCH

Name	(PLEASE PRINT)	
Address	Apt. No.	
City	State	Zip

This offer is limited to one order per household and not valid to present Silhouette Special Edition® subscribers. *Terms and prices are subject to change without notice. Sales tax applicable in N.Y.

USPED-93

©1990 Harlequin Enterprises Limited